The Scarlet Rose

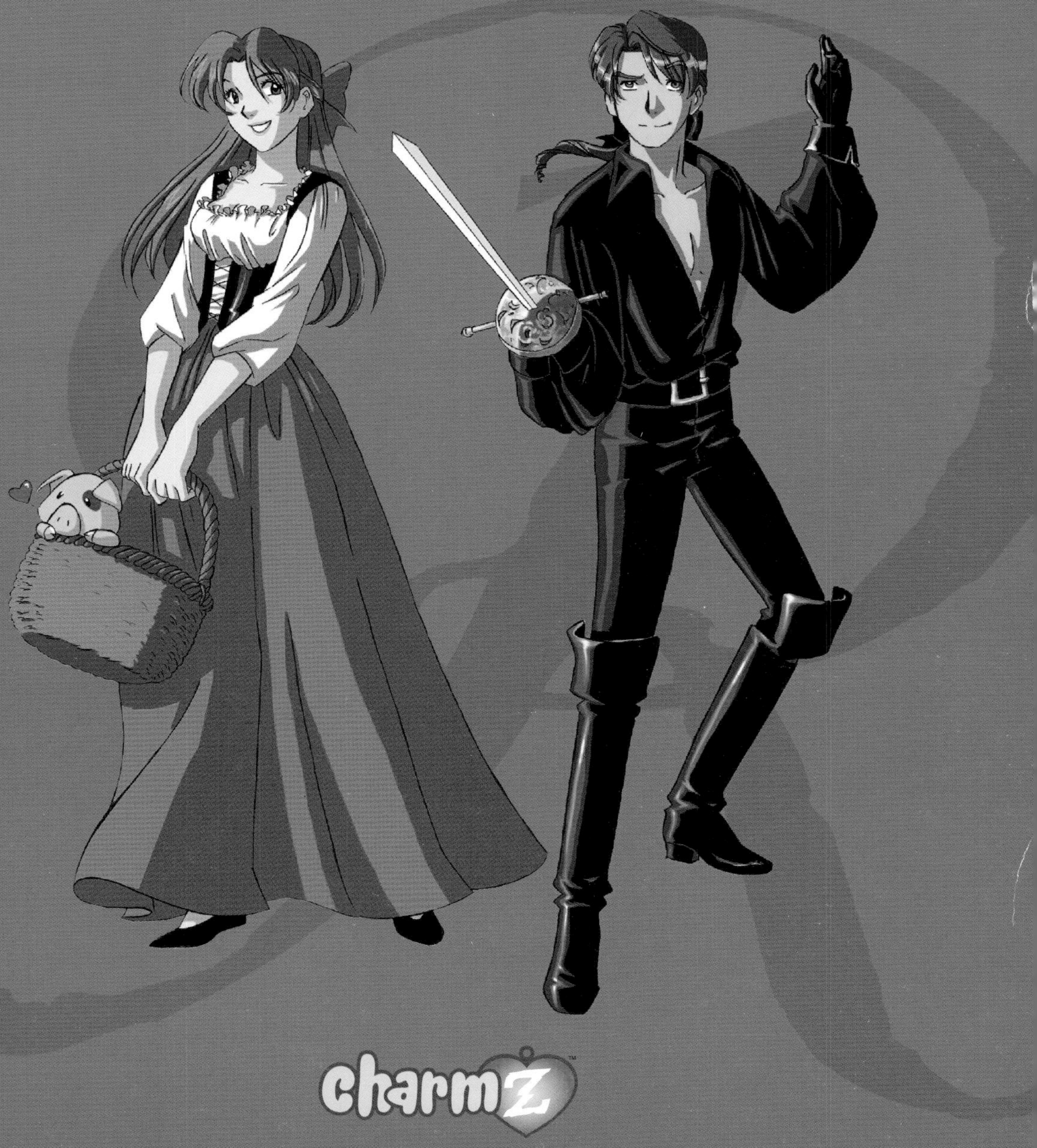

charmz

MORE GRAPHIC NOVELS AVAILABLE from Charmz™

COMING SOON!

STITCHED
MARIAH McCOURT
AARON ALEXOVICH
The First Day of the Rest of her Life
charmz

STITCHED
MARIAH McCOURT • AARON ALEXOVICH
Love in the Time of Assumption
charmz

PATRICIA LYFOUNG
The Scarlet Rose
charmz

PATRICIA LYFOUNG
The Scarlet Rose
I'll Go Where You Go
charmz

STITCHED #1 "THE FIRST DAY OF THE REST OF HER LIFE"

STITCHED #2 "LOVE IN THE TIME OF ASSUMPTION"

SCARLET ROSE #1 "I KNEW I'D MEET YOU"

SCARLET ROSE #2 "I'LL GO WHERE YOU GO"

Greg Tessier and Amandine
Chloe
The New Girl
charmz

Greg Tessier and Amandine
Chloe
The Queen of High School
charmz

ALL-NEW Graphic Novel by Greg Tessier & Amandine
Chloe
Frenemies
charmz

Sweeties
CHERRY SKYE
charmz

CHLOE #1 "THE NEW GIRL"

CHLOE #2 "THE QUEEN OF HIGH SCHOOL"

CHLOE #3 "FRENEMIES"

SWEETIES #1 "CHERRY SKYE"

GFFs
GHOST FRIENDS FOREVER
charmz

Ana and the COSMIC RACE
THE RACE BEGINS
charmz

G.F.F.s #1 "I LEFT MY HEART IN THE 90s"

ANA AND THE COSMIC RACE #1 "THE RACE BEGINS"

Charmz graphic novels are available for $9.99 in paperback, and $14.99 in hardcover. Available from booksellers everywhere. You can also order online from www.papercutz.com. Or call 1-800-886-1223, Monday through Friday, 9–5 EST. MC, Visa, and AmEx accepted. To order by mail, please add $5.00 for postage and handling for first book ordered, $1.00 for each additional book and make check payable to NBM Publishing.
Send to: Charmz, 160 Broadway, Suite 700, East Wing, New York, NY 10038.

Charmz graphic novels are also available wherever e-books are sold.

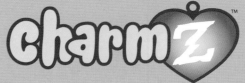

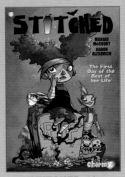

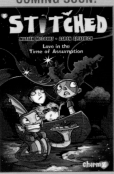

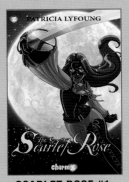

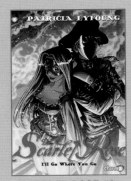

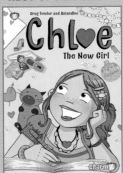

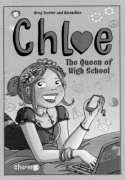

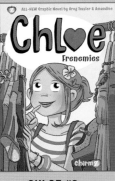

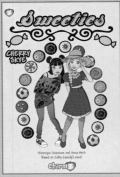

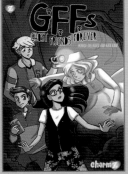

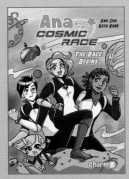

The Scarlet Rose

"I'll Go Where You Go"

STORY & ART BY

PATRICIA LYFOUNG

COLOR BY

PHILIPPE OGAKI

NEW YORK

To Pelote, I love you, you little scamp.
To Joëlle.

Thanks to Hulya and Françoise for "loaning" Fanelli to me,
Thanks to Sevda for "loaning" Medusa to me.
Thanks to the readers of THE SCARLET ROSE.
Every day, your enthusiasm helps me continue this adventure.
To Pepito, the living room prince.
And finally, to Philippe, mi amor, I totally dig you!
–Patricia Lyfoung

PREVIOUSLY IN *Scarlet Rose* ...

After witnessing the murder of her blacksmith father, Jean-Baptiste de Laroche, eighteen year-old Maud moves to a country estate outside of Paris to live with her disapproving grandfather. Along the way she encounters The Fox, a masked Robin Hood–like rogue—a dashing figure she falls for. Her grandfather struggles to tame her wild spirit and introduce her to Society. He arranges for Guilhem de Landrey to be her fencing instructor hoping that might rein her in. Still seeking to avenge the murder of her father, with her new fencing skills, and inspired by the Fox, Maud becomes the masked avenger, The Scarlet Rose, much to the dismay of Count de Landrey. Fearing for Maud's safety, Guilhelm reveals his secret to her, that he is actually The Fox!

Scarlet Rose

By Patricia Lyfoung
La Rose Écarlate, volumes 3 and 4
Lyfoung © Éditions Delcourt–2007/2008
Originally Published in French as "J'irai où tu iras"
and "J'irai voir Venis."

English translation and all other editorial
material © 2018 by Papercutz.
All rights reserved.

THE SCARLET ROSE #2
"I'll Go Where You Go"

Story, art, and cover by Patricia Lyfoung
Color by Philippe Ogaki
Translation by Joe Johnson
Lettering by Bryan Senka

Spenser Nellis—Editorial Intern
Jeff Whitman – Assistant Managing Edtior
Jim Salicrup
Editor-in-Chief

PB ISBN: 978-1-62991-874-7
HC ISBN: 978-1-62991-875-4

Charmz is an imprint of Papercutz.

Chamz books may be purchased for business or promotional use.
For information on bulk purchases please contact Macmillan
Corporate and Premium Sales Department at
(800) 221-7945 x5442

Printed in India
April 2018

Distributed by Macmillan
First Charmz Printing

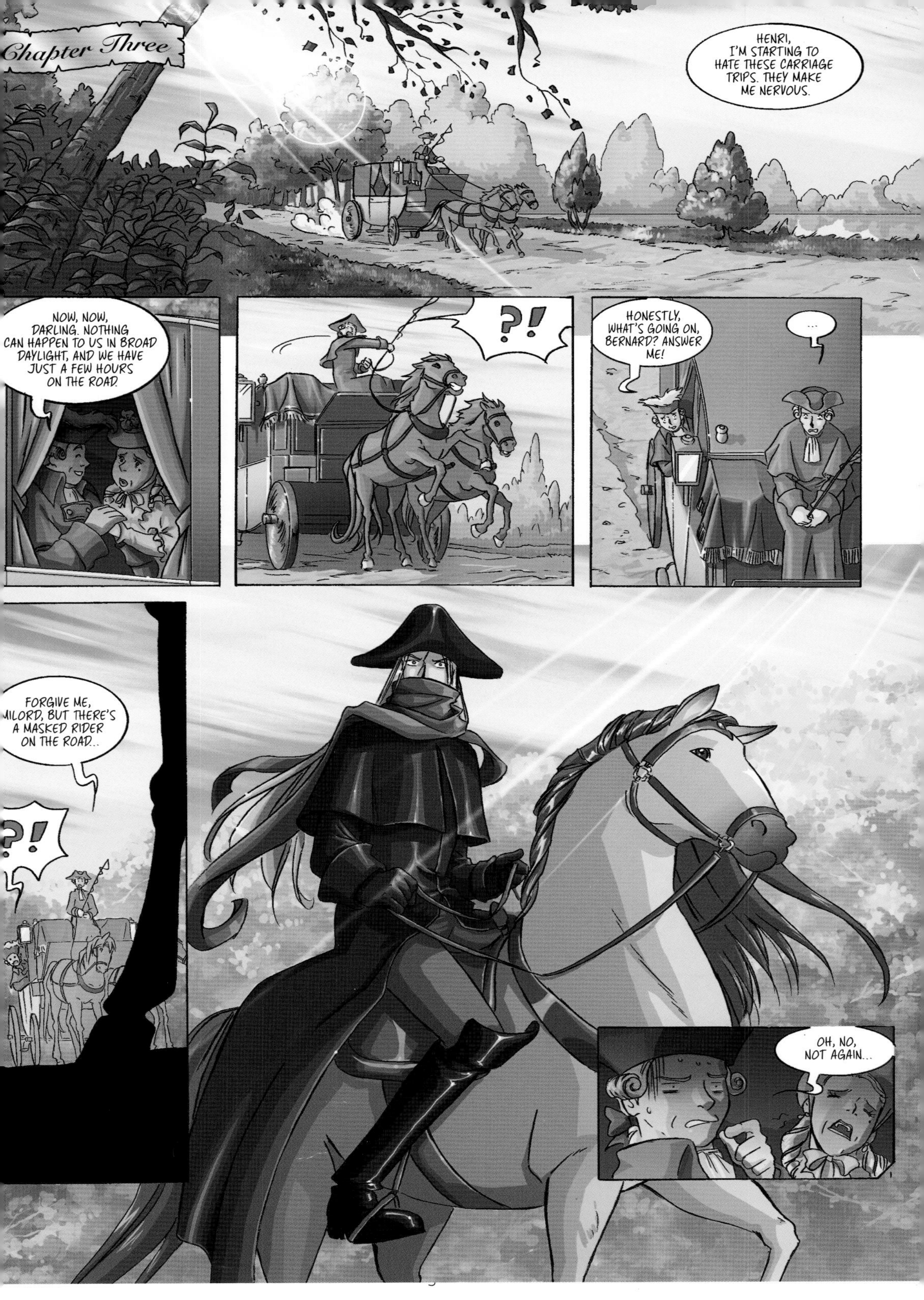
Chapter Three
HENRI, I'M STARTING TO HATE THESE CARRIAGE TRIPS. THEY MAKE ME NERVOUS.
NOW, NOW, DARLING. NOTHING CAN HAPPEN TO US IN BROAD DAYLIGHT, AND WE HAVE JUST A FEW HOURS ON THE ROAD.
?!
HONESTLY, WHAT'S GOING ON, BERNARD? ANSWER ME!
...
FORGIVE ME, MILORD, BUT THERE'S A MASKED RIDER ON THE ROAD...
?!
OH, NO, NOT AGAIN...

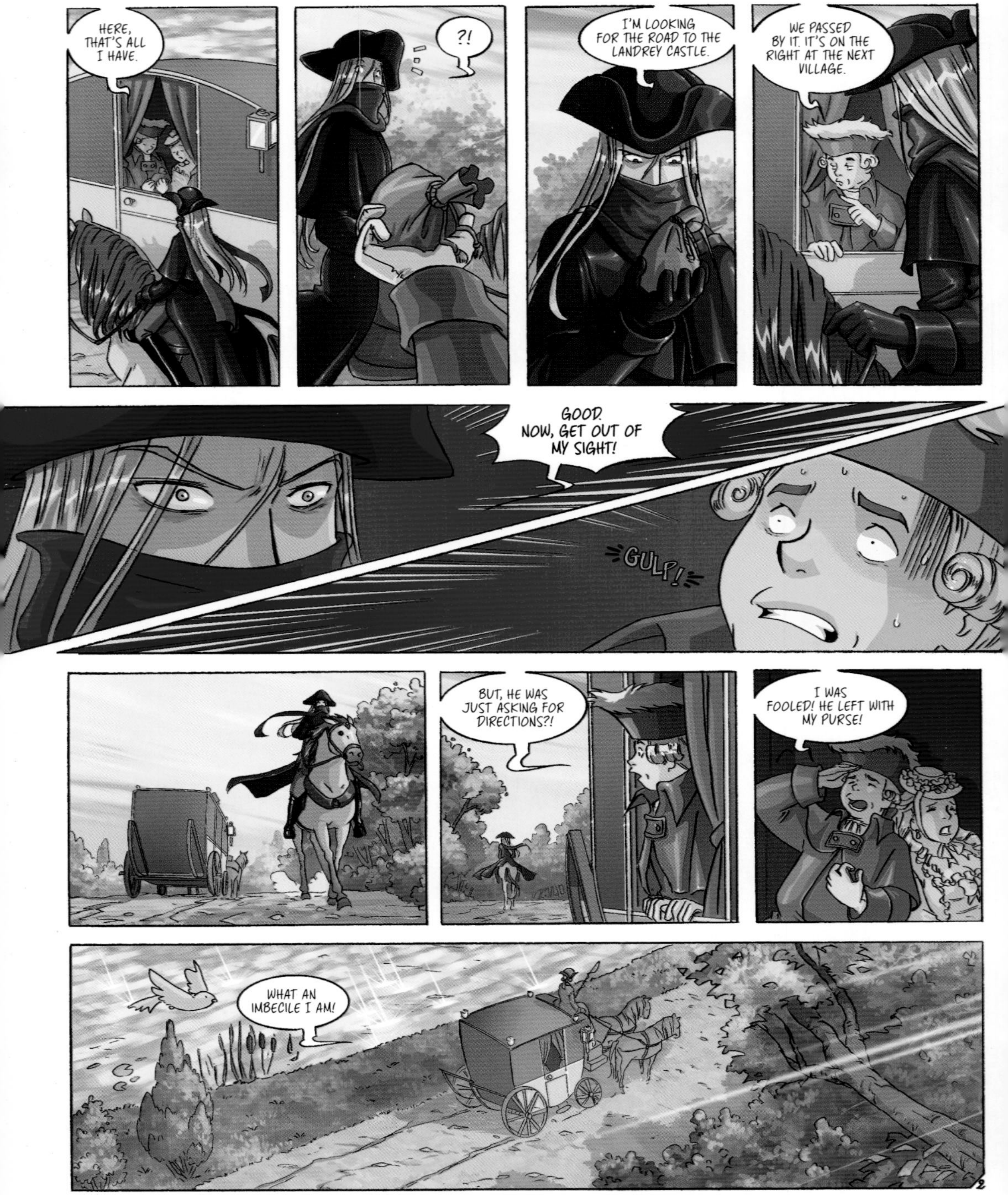
HERE, THAT'S ALL I HAVE.
?!
I'M LOOKING FOR THE ROAD TO THE LANDREY CASTLE.
WE PASSED BY IT. IT'S ON THE RIGHT AT THE NEXT VILLAGE.
GOOD. NOW, GET OUT OF MY SIGHT!
GULP!
BUT, HE WAS JUST ASKING FOR DIRECTIONS?!
I WAS FOOLED! HE LEFT WITH MY PURSE!
WHAT AN IMBECILE I AM!
2

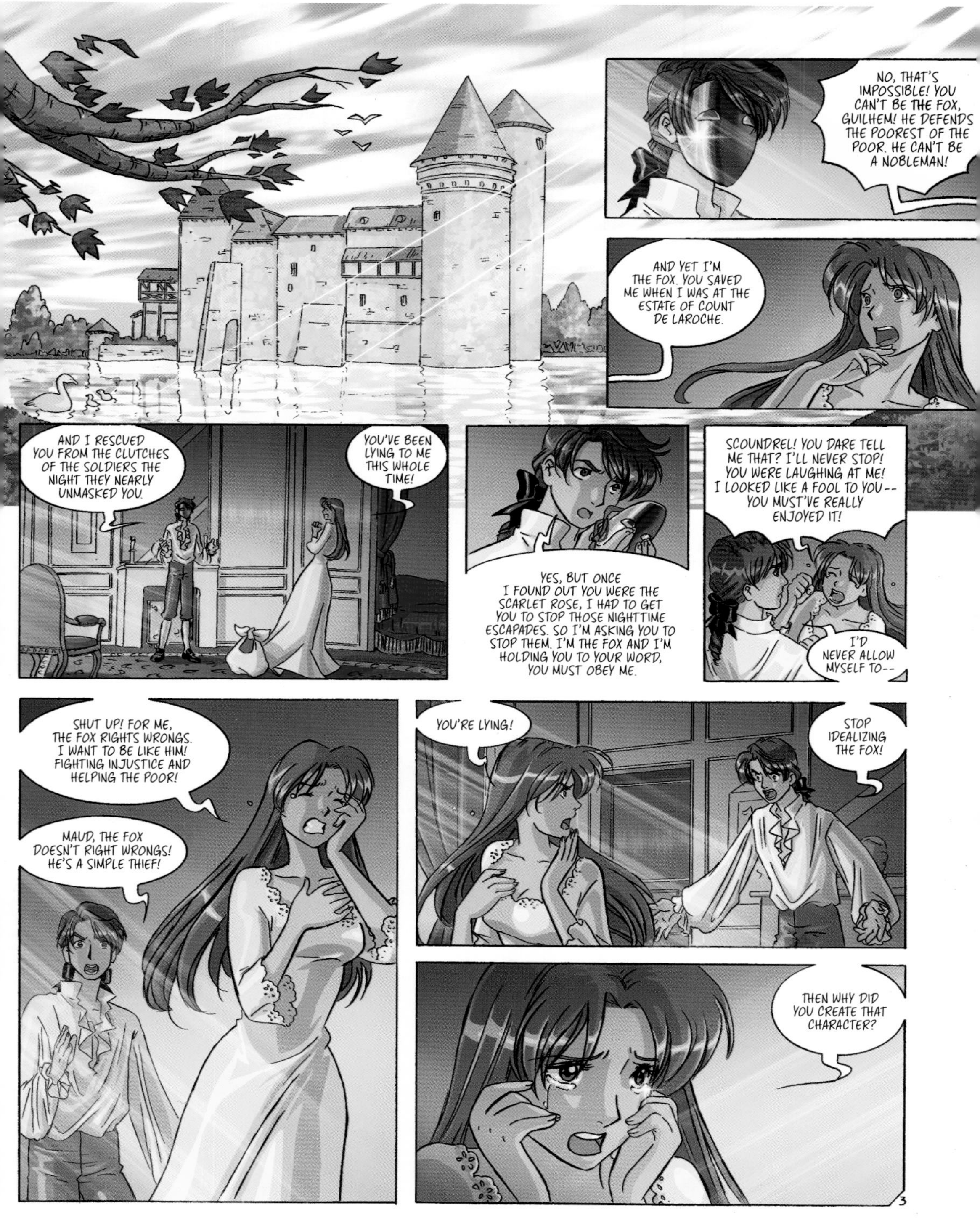
NO, THAT'S IMPOSSIBLE! YOU CAN'T BE THE FOX, GUILHEM! HE DEFENDS THE POOREST OF THE POOR. HE CAN'T BE A NOBLEMAN!
AND YET I'M THE FOX. YOU SAVED ME WHEN I WAS AT THE ESTATE OF COUNT DE LAROCHE.
AND I RESCUED YOU FROM THE CLUTCHES OF THE SOLDIERS THE NIGHT THEY NEARLY UNMASKED YOU.
YOU'VE BEEN LYING TO ME THIS WHOLE TIME!
YES, BUT ONCE I FOUND OUT YOU WERE THE SCARLET ROSE, I HAD TO GET YOU TO STOP THOSE NIGHTTIME ESCAPADES. SO I'M ASKING YOU TO STOP THEM. I'M THE FOX AND I'M HOLDING YOU TO YOUR WORD, YOU MUST OBEY ME.
SCOUNDREL! YOU DARE TELL ME THAT? I'LL NEVER STOP! YOU WERE LAUGHING AT ME! I LOOKED LIKE A FOOL TO YOU-- YOU MUST'VE REALLY ENJOYED IT!
I'D NEVER ALLOW MYSELF TO--
SHUT UP! FOR ME, THE FOX RIGHTS WRONGS. I WANT TO BE LIKE HIM! FIGHTING INJUSTICE AND HELPING THE POOR!
MAUD, THE FOX DOESN'T RIGHT WRONGS! HE'S A SIMPLE THIEF!
YOU'RE LYING!
STOP IDEALIZING THE FOX!
THEN WHY DID YOU CREATE THAT CHARACTER?
3

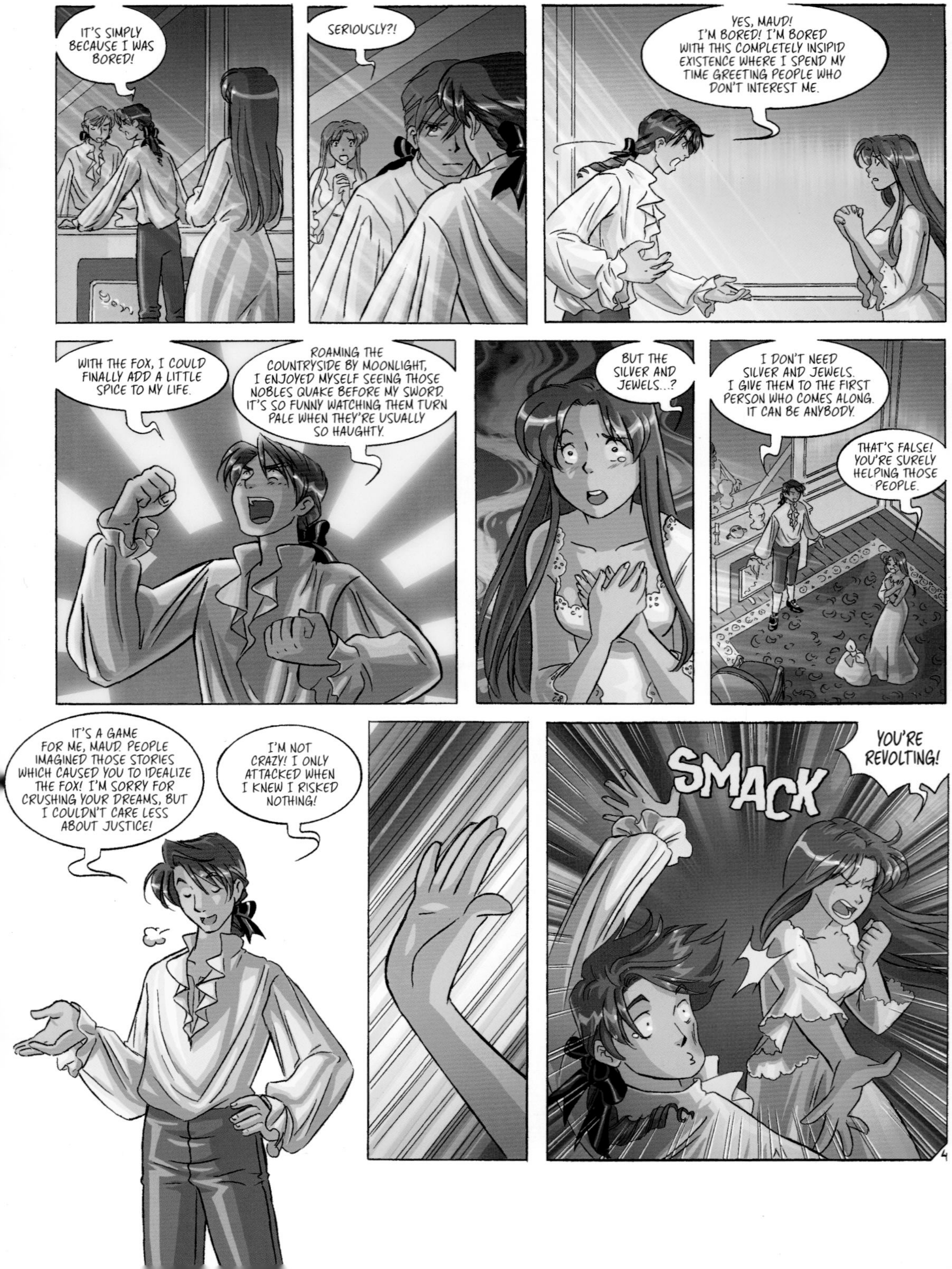
IT'S SIMPLY BECAUSE I WAS BORED!
SERIOUSLY?!
YES, MAUD! I'M BORED! I'M BORED WITH THIS COMPLETELY INSIPID EXISTENCE WHERE I SPEND MY TIME GREETING PEOPLE WHO DON'T INTEREST ME.
WITH THE FOX, I COULD FINALLY ADD A LITTLE SPICE TO MY LIFE.
ROAMING THE COUNTRYSIDE BY MOONLIGHT, I ENJOYED MYSELF SEEING THOSE NOBLES QUAKE BEFORE MY SWORD. IT'S SO FUNNY WATCHING THEM TURN PALE WHEN THEY'RE USUALLY SO HAUGHTY.
BUT THE SILVER AND JEWELS...?
I DON'T NEED SILVER AND JEWELS. I GIVE THEM TO THE FIRST PERSON WHO COMES ALONG. IT CAN BE ANYBODY.
THAT'S FALSE! YOU'RE SURELY HELPING THOSE PEOPLE.
IT'S A GAME FOR ME, MAUD. PEOPLE IMAGINED THOSE STORIES WHICH CAUSED YOU TO IDEALIZE THE FOX! I'M SORRY FOR CRUSHING YOUR DREAMS, BUT I COULDN'T CARE LESS ABOUT JUSTICE!
I'M NOT CRAZY! I ONLY ATTACKED WHEN I KNEW I RISKED NOTHING!
SMACK
YOU'RE REVOLTING!

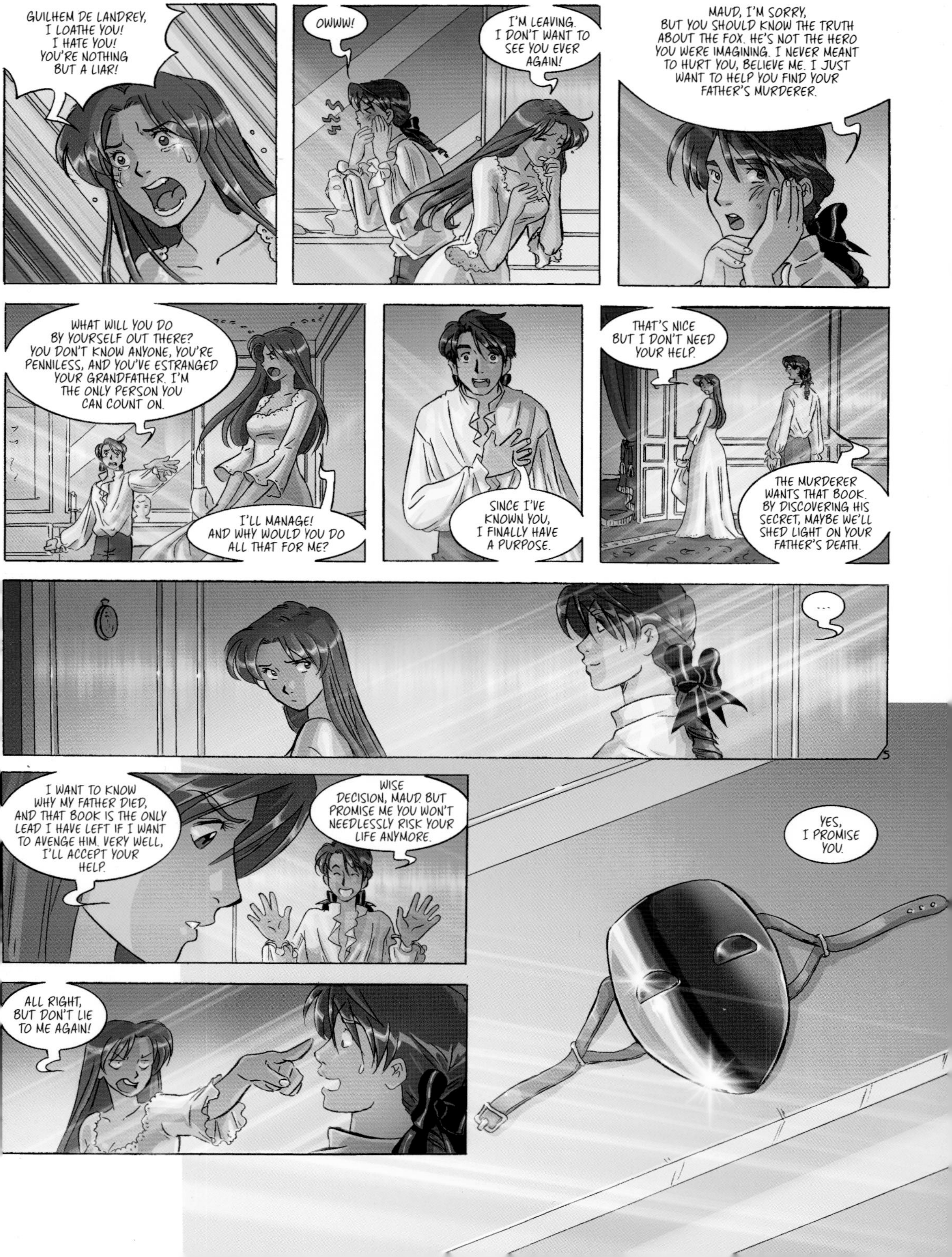
GUILHEM DE LANDREY, I LOATHE YOU! I HATE YOU! YOU'RE NOTHING BUT A LIAR!
OWWW!
I'M LEAVING. I DON'T WANT TO SEE YOU EVER AGAIN!
MAUD, I'M SORRY, BUT YOU SHOULD KNOW THE TRUTH ABOUT THE FOX. HE'S NOT THE HERO YOU WERE IMAGINING. I NEVER MEANT TO HURT YOU, BELIEVE ME. I JUST WANT TO HELP YOU FIND YOUR FATHER'S MURDERER.
WHAT WILL YOU DO BY YOURSELF OUT THERE? YOU DON'T KNOW ANYONE, YOU'RE PENNILESS, AND YOU'VE ESTRANGED YOUR GRANDFATHER. I'M THE ONLY PERSON YOU CAN COUNT ON.
I'LL MANAGE! AND WHY WOULD YOU DO ALL THAT FOR ME?
SINCE I'VE KNOWN YOU, I FINALLY HAVE A PURPOSE.
THAT'S NICE BUT I DON'T NEED YOUR HELP.
THE MURDERER WANTS THAT BOOK. BY DISCOVERING HIS SECRET, MAYBE WE'LL SHED LIGHT ON YOUR FATHER'S DEATH.
...
I WANT TO KNOW WHY MY FATHER DIED, AND THAT BOOK IS THE ONLY LEAD I HAVE LEFT IF I WANT TO AVENGE HIM. VERY WELL, I'LL ACCEPT YOUR HELP.
WISE DECISION, MAUD BUT PROMISE ME YOU WON'T NEEDLESSLY RISK YOUR LIFE ANYMORE.
YES, I PROMISE YOU.
ALL RIGHT, BUT DON'T LIE TO ME AGAIN!

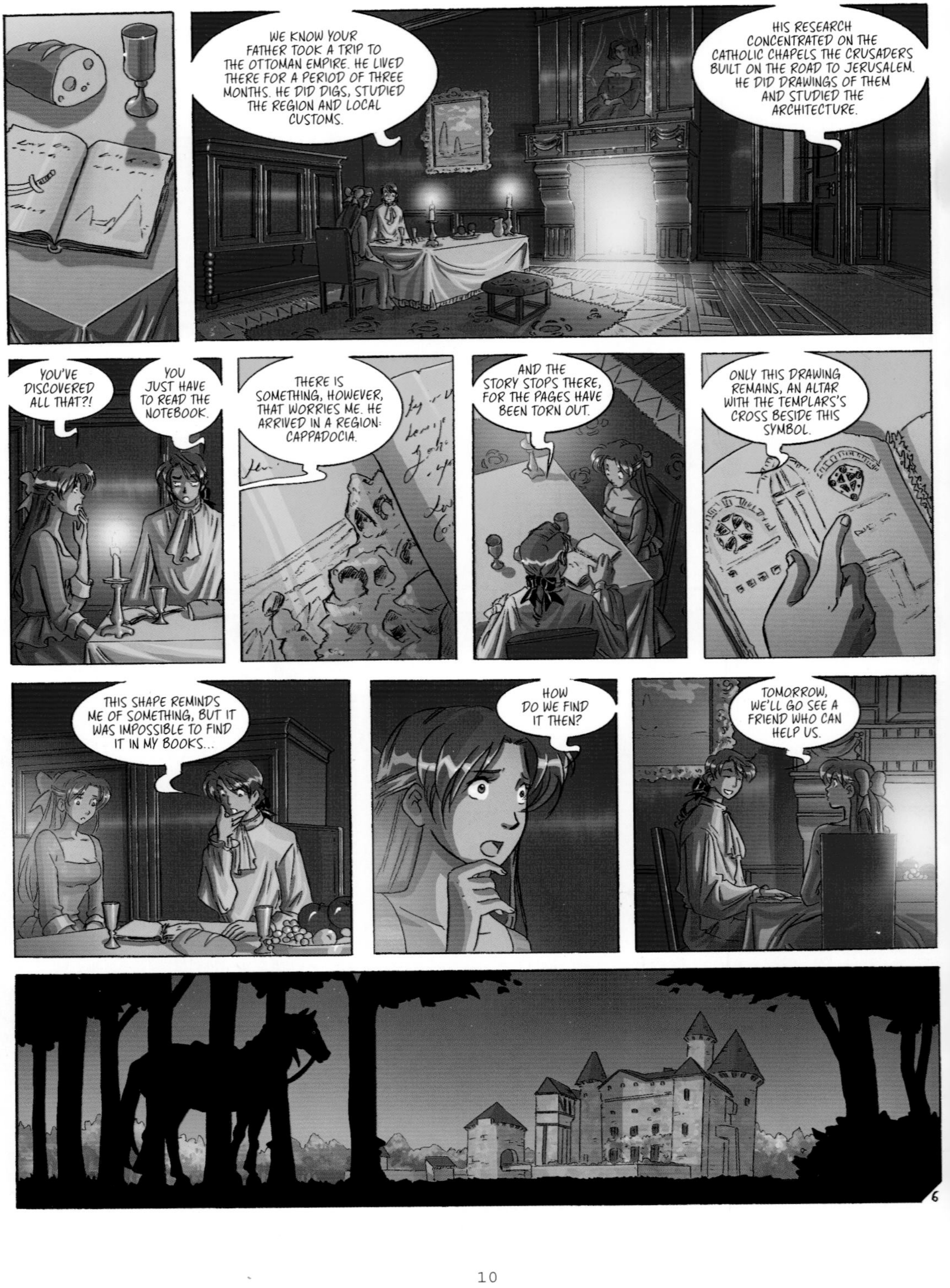
WE KNOW YOUR FATHER TOOK A TRIP TO THE OTTOMAN EMPIRE. HE LIVED THERE FOR A PERIOD OF THREE MONTHS. HE DID DIGS, STUDIED THE REGION AND LOCAL CUSTOMS.
HIS RESEARCH CONCENTRATED ON THE CATHOLIC CHAPELS THE CRUSADERS BUILT ON THE ROAD TO JERUSALEM. HE DID DRAWINGS OF THEM AND STUDIED THE ARCHITECTURE.
YOU'VE DISCOVERED ALL THAT?!
YOU JUST HAVE TO READ THE NOTEBOOK.
THERE IS SOMETHING, HOWEVER, THAT WORRIES ME. HE ARRIVED IN A REGION: CAPPADOCIA.
AND THE STORY STOPS THERE, FOR THE PAGES HAVE BEEN TORN OUT.
ONLY THIS DRAWING REMAINS, AN ALTAR WITH THE TEMPLARS'S CROSS BESIDE THIS SYMBOL.
THIS SHAPE REMINDS ME OF SOMETHING, BUT IT WAS IMPOSSIBLE TO FIND IT IN MY BOOKS...
HOW DO WE FIND IT THEN?
TOMORROW, WE'LL GO SEE A FRIEND WHO CAN HELP US.
6

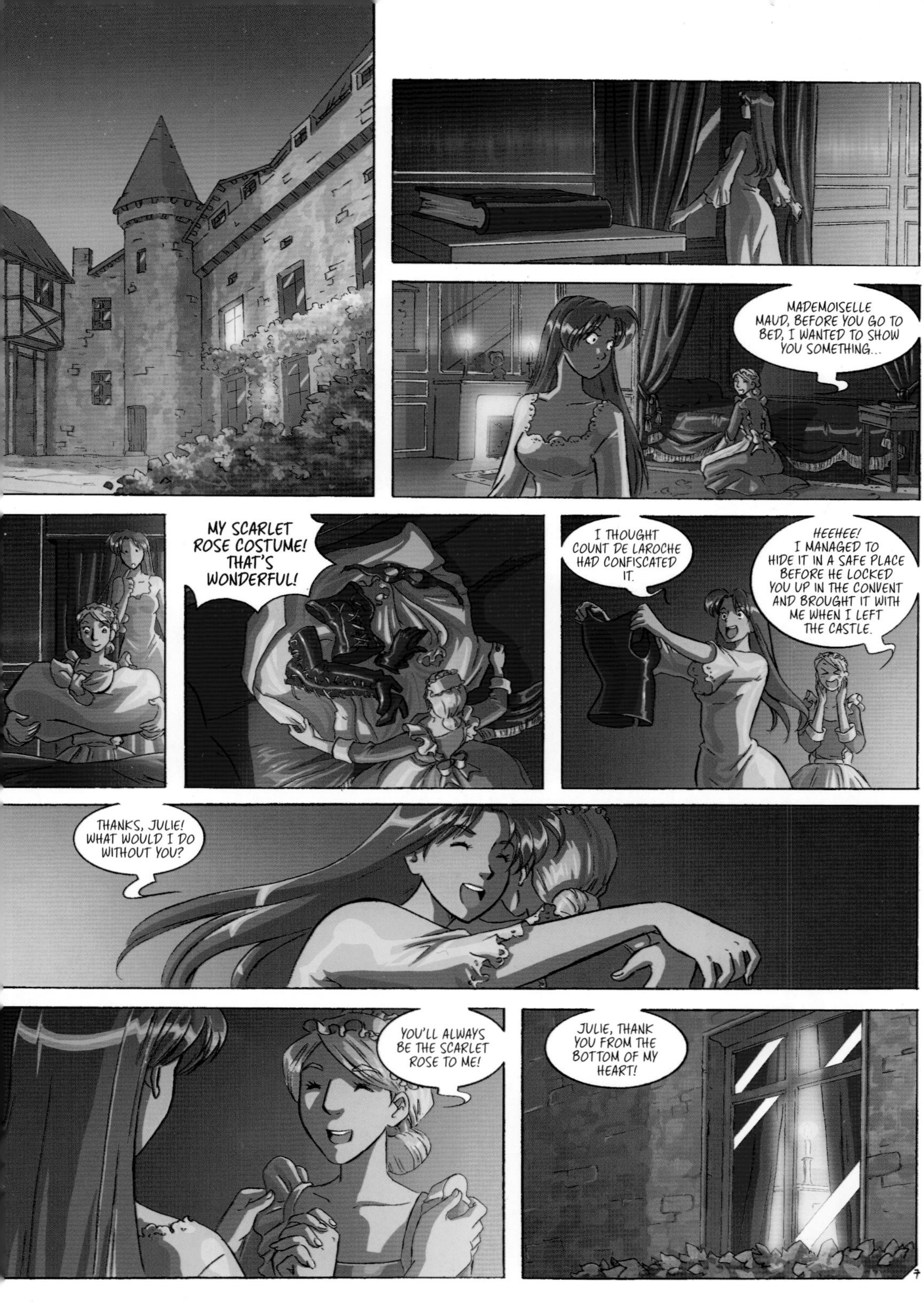
MADEMOISELLE MAUD, BEFORE YOU GO TO BED, I WANTED TO SHOW YOU SOMETHING...
MY SCARLET ROSE COSTUME! THAT'S WONDERFUL!
I THOUGHT COUNT DE LAROCHE HAD CONFISCATED IT.
HEEHEE! I MANAGED TO HIDE IT IN A SAFE PLACE BEFORE HE LOCKED YOU UP IN THE CONVENT AND BROUGHT IT WITH ME WHEN I LEFT THE CASTLE.
THANKS, JULIE! WHAT WOULD I DO WITHOUT YOU?
YOU'LL ALWAYS BE THE SCARLET ROSE TO ME!
JULIE, THANK YOU FROM THE BOTTOM OF MY HEART!
7

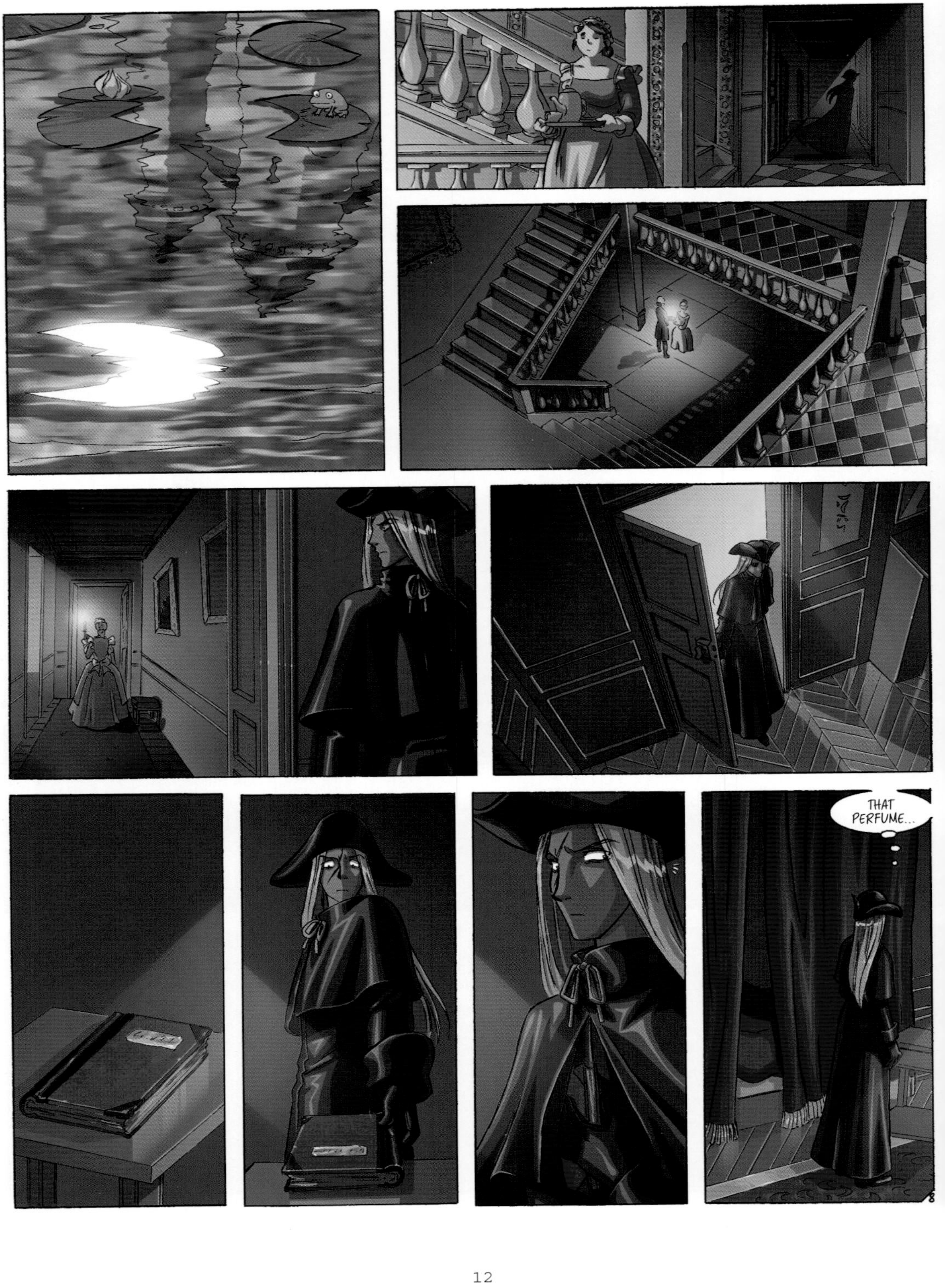
THAT PERFUME...

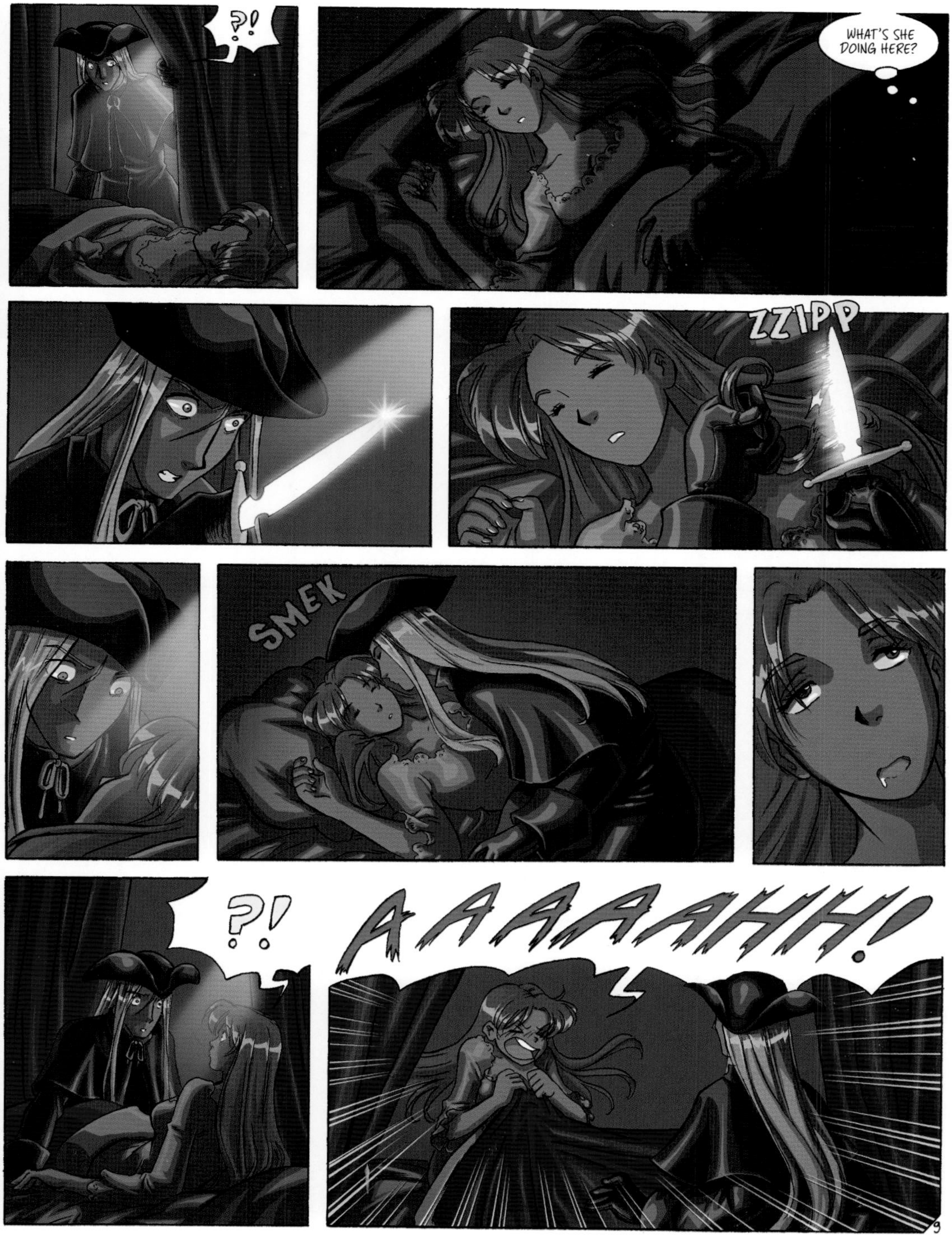
?!
WHAT'S SHE DOING HERE?
ZZIPP
SMEK
?!
AAAAAHH!
9

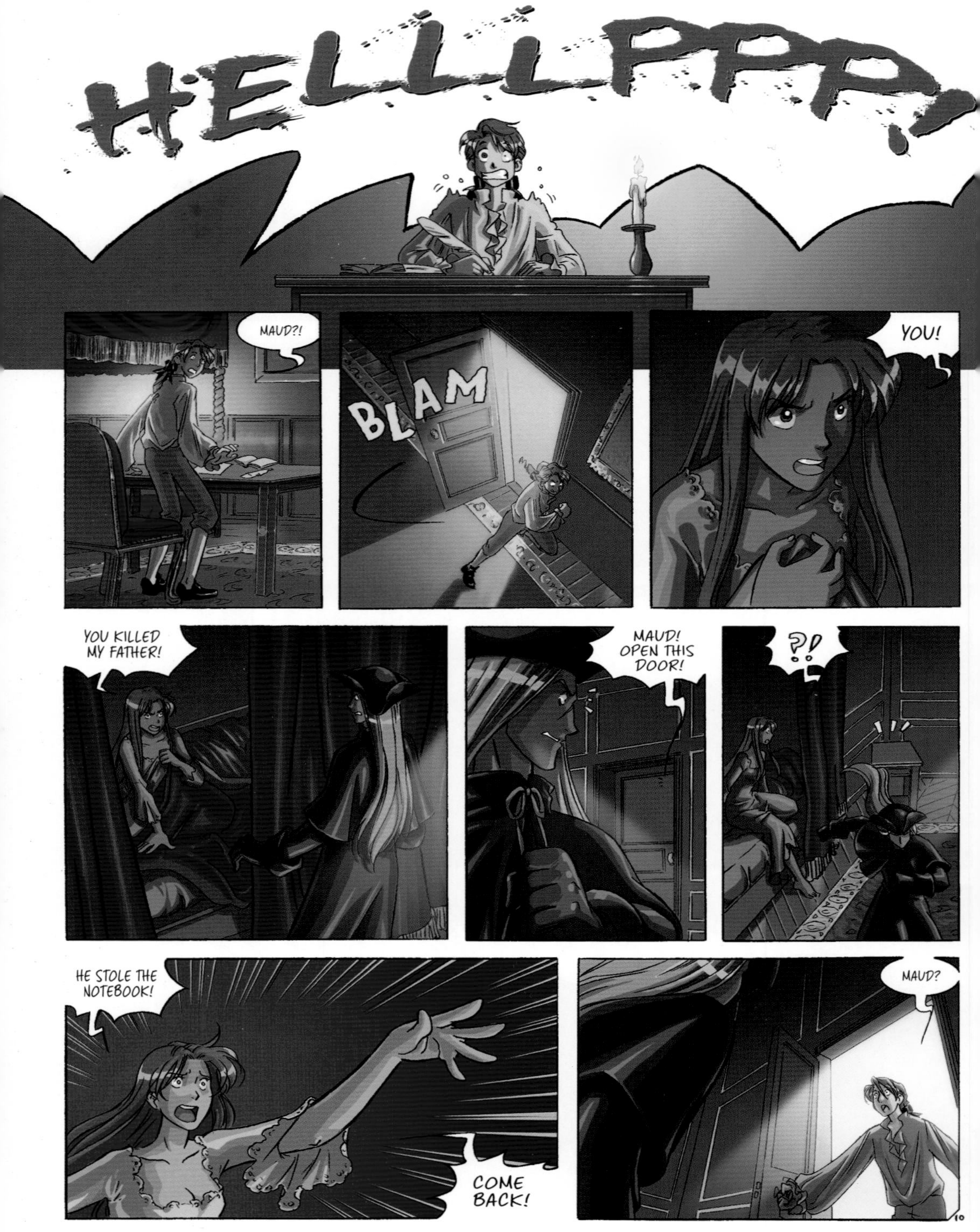
HELLLPPP!
MAUD?!
BLAM
YOU!
YOU KILLED MY FATHER!
MAUD! OPEN THIS DOOR!
?!
HE STOLE THE NOTEBOOK!
COME BACK!
MAUD?

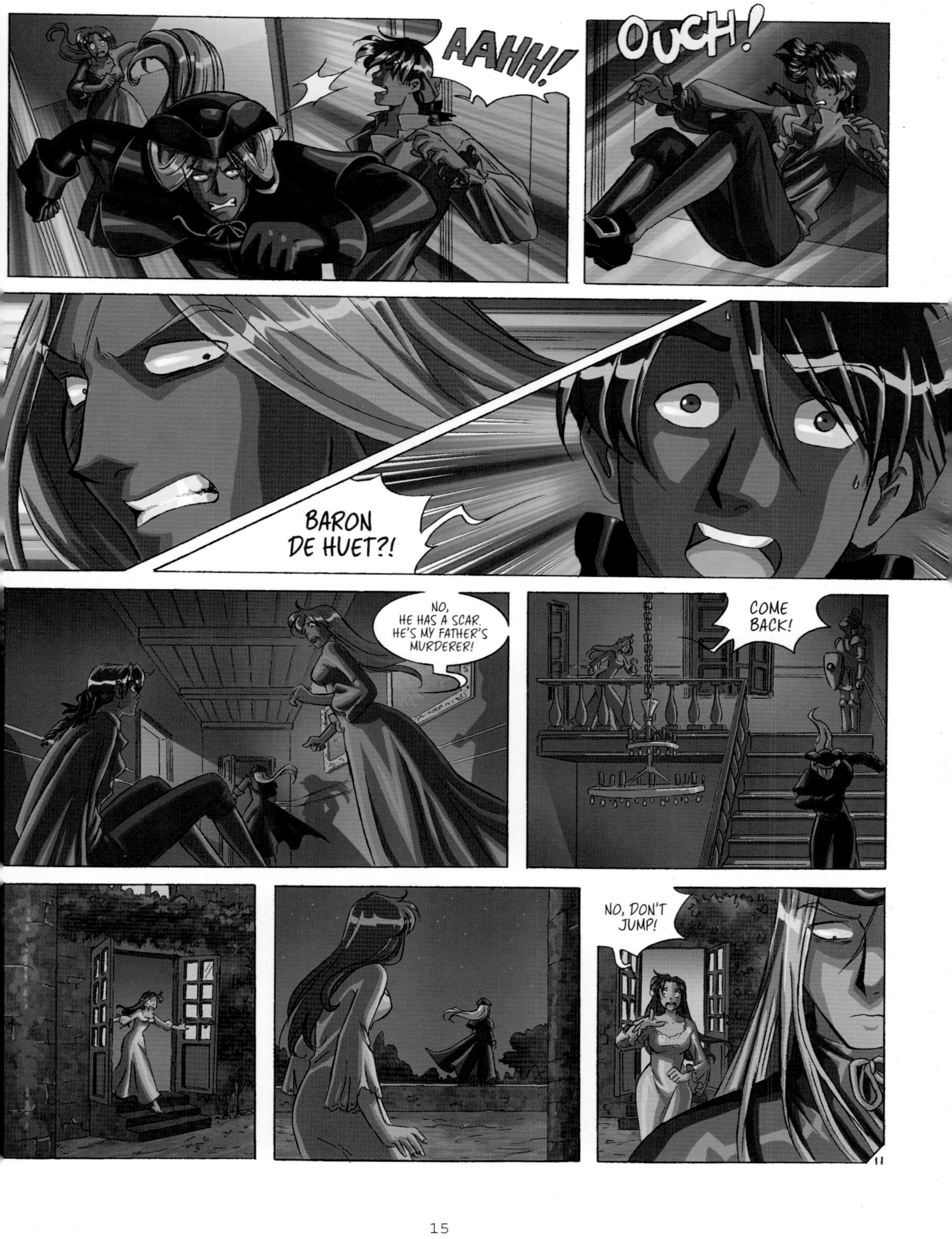
AAHH!
OUCH!
BARON DE HUET?!
NO, HE HAS A SCAR. HE'S MY FATHER'S MURDERER!
COME BACK!
NO, DON'T JUMP!
11

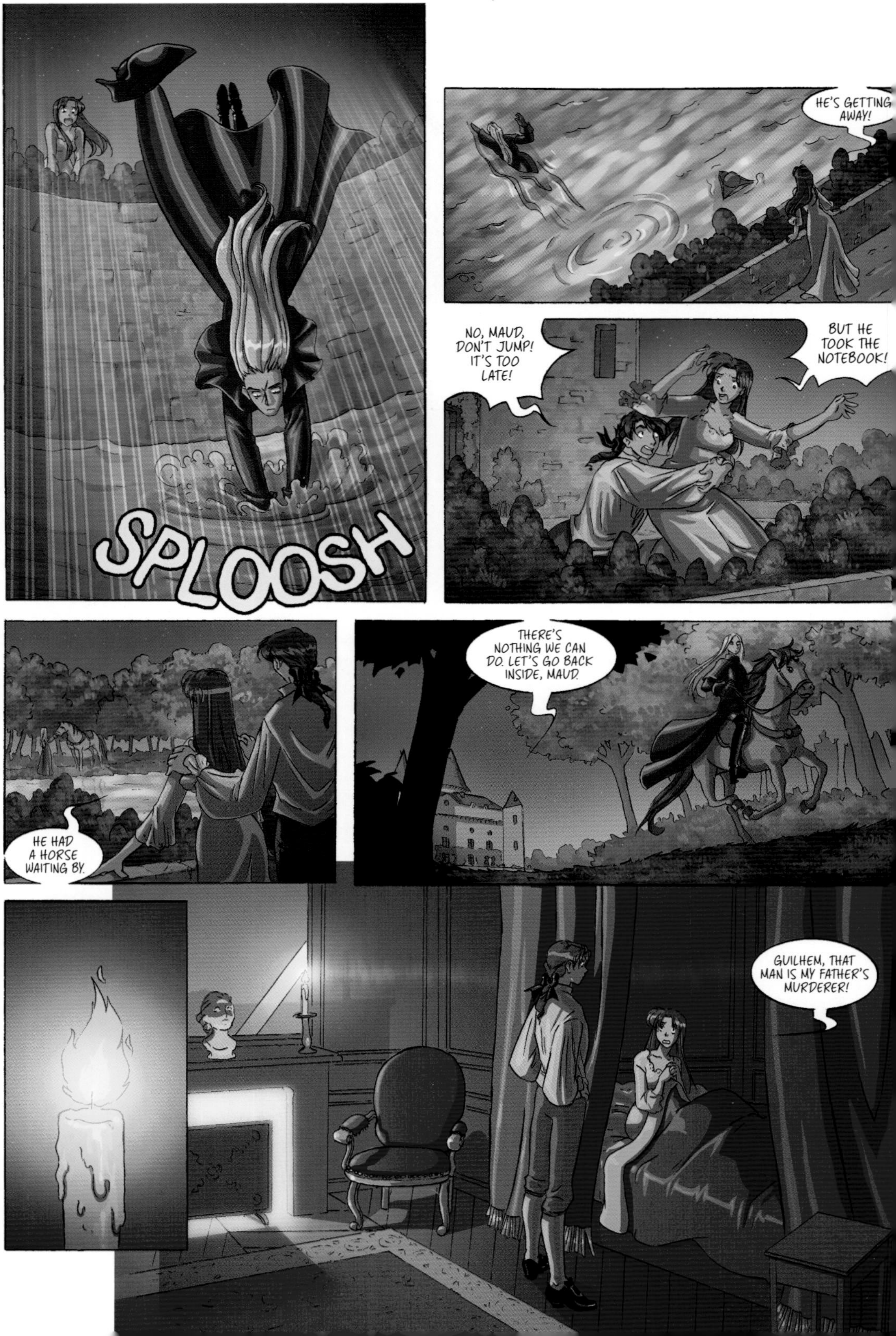
SPLOOSH
HE'S GETTING AWAY!
NO, MAUD, DON'T JUMP! IT'S TOO LATE!
BUT HE TOOK THE NOTEBOOK!
HE HAD A HORSE WAITING BY.
THERE'S NOTHING WE CAN DO. LET'S GO BACK INSIDE, MAUD.
GUILHEM, THAT MAN IS MY FATHER'S MURDERER!

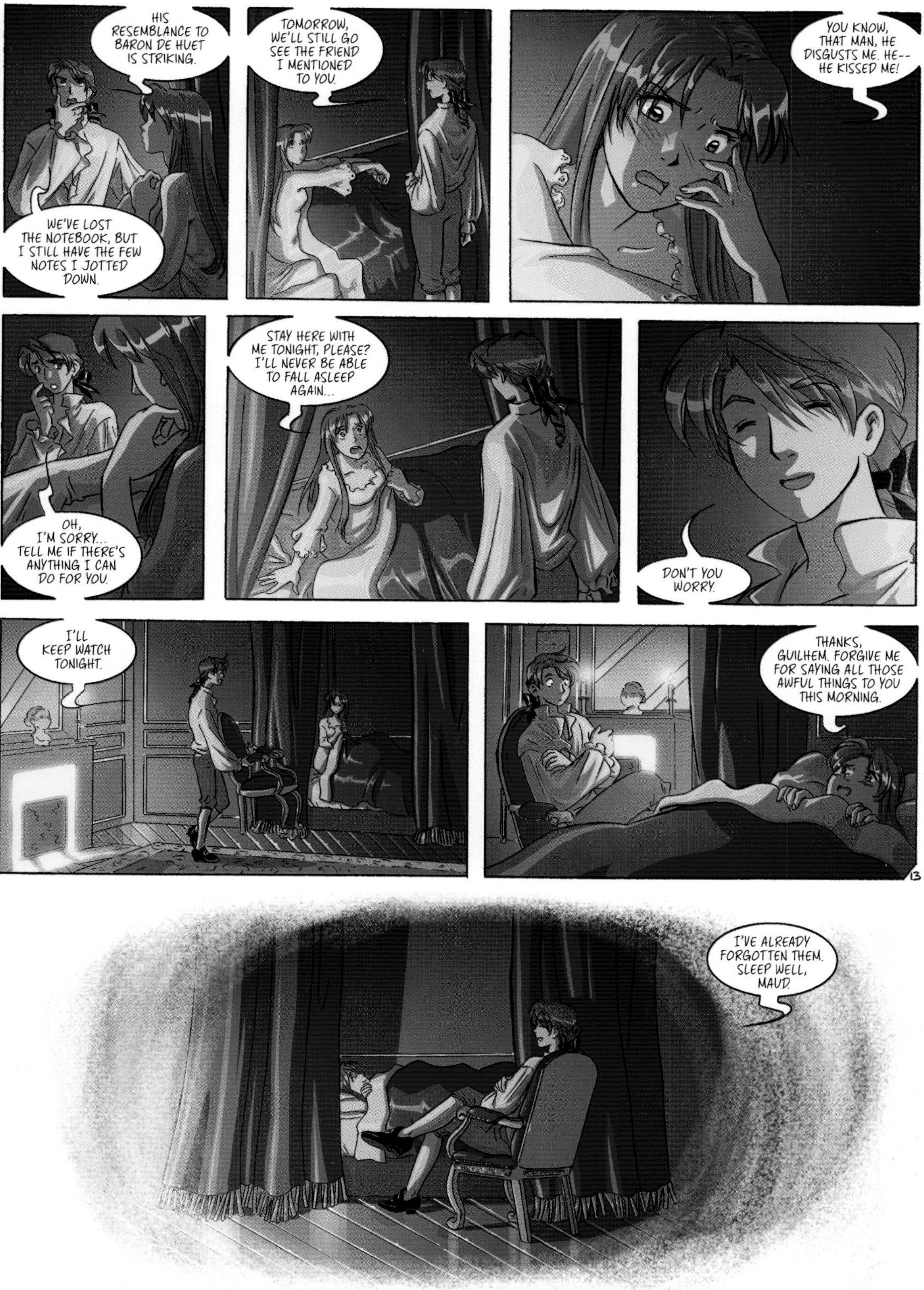
HIS RESEMBLANCE TO BARON DE HUET IS STRIKING.
WE'VE LOST THE NOTEBOOK, BUT I STILL HAVE THE FEW NOTES I JOTTED DOWN.
TOMORROW, WE'LL STILL GO SEE THE FRIEND I MENTIONED TO YOU.
YOU KNOW, THAT MAN, HE DISGUSTS ME. HE-- HE KISSED ME!
OH, I'M SORRY... TELL ME IF THERE'S ANYTHING I CAN DO FOR YOU.
STAY HERE WITH ME TONIGHT, PLEASE? I'LL NEVER BE ABLE TO FALL ASLEEP AGAIN...
DON'T YOU WORRY.
I'LL KEEP WATCH TONIGHT.
THANKS, GUILHEM. FORGIVE ME FOR SAYING ALL THOSE AWFUL THINGS TO YOU THIS MORNING.
I'VE ALREADY FORGOTTEN THEM. SLEEP WELL, MAUD.

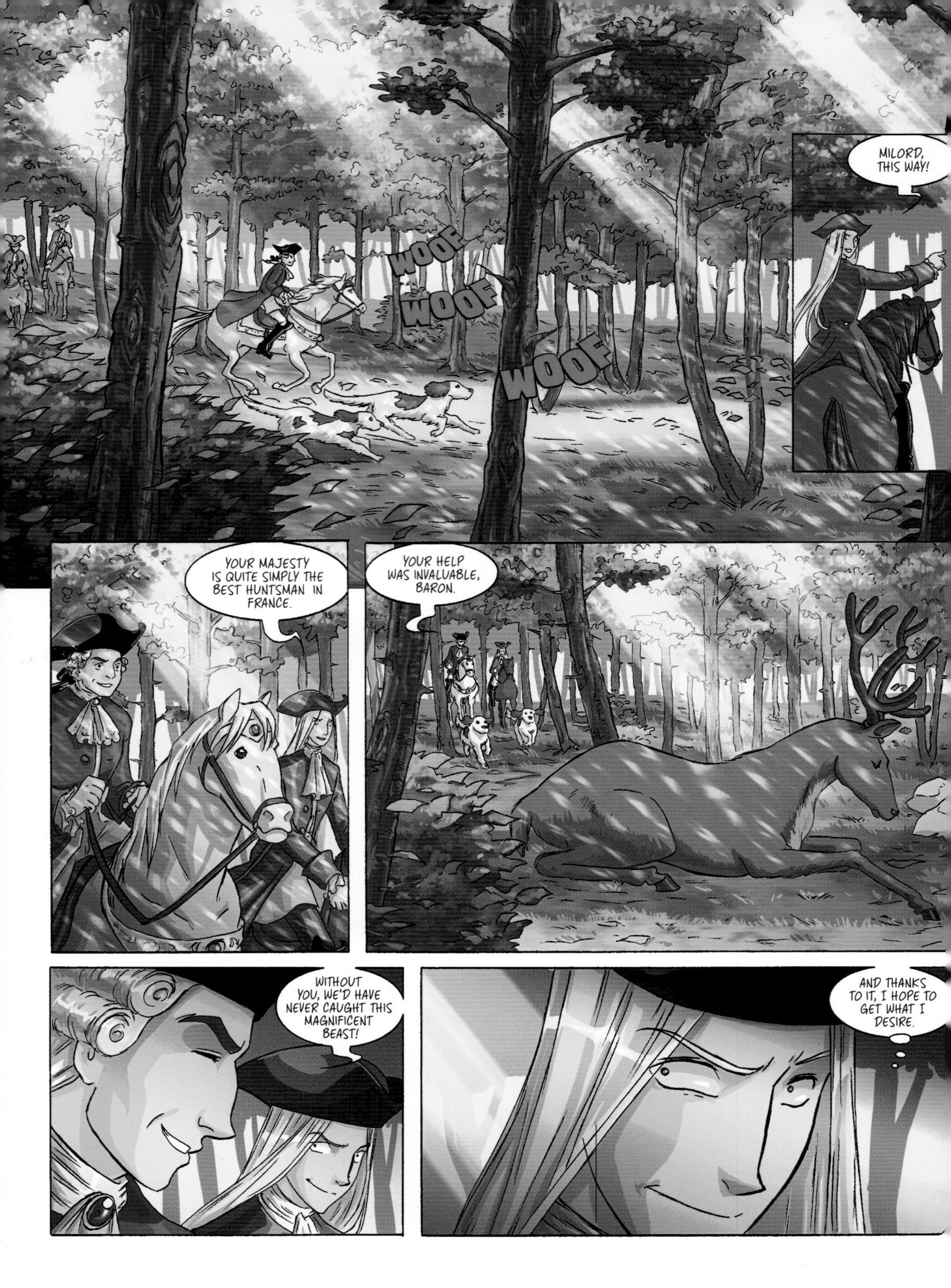
WOOF
WOOF
WOOF
MILORD, THIS WAY!
YOUR MAJESTY IS QUITE SIMPLY THE BEST HUNTSMAN IN FRANCE.
YOUR HELP WAS INVALUABLE, BARON.
WITHOUT YOU, WE'D HAVE NEVER CAUGHT THIS MAGNIFICENT BEAST!
AND THANKS TO IT, I HOPE TO GET WHAT I DESIRE.

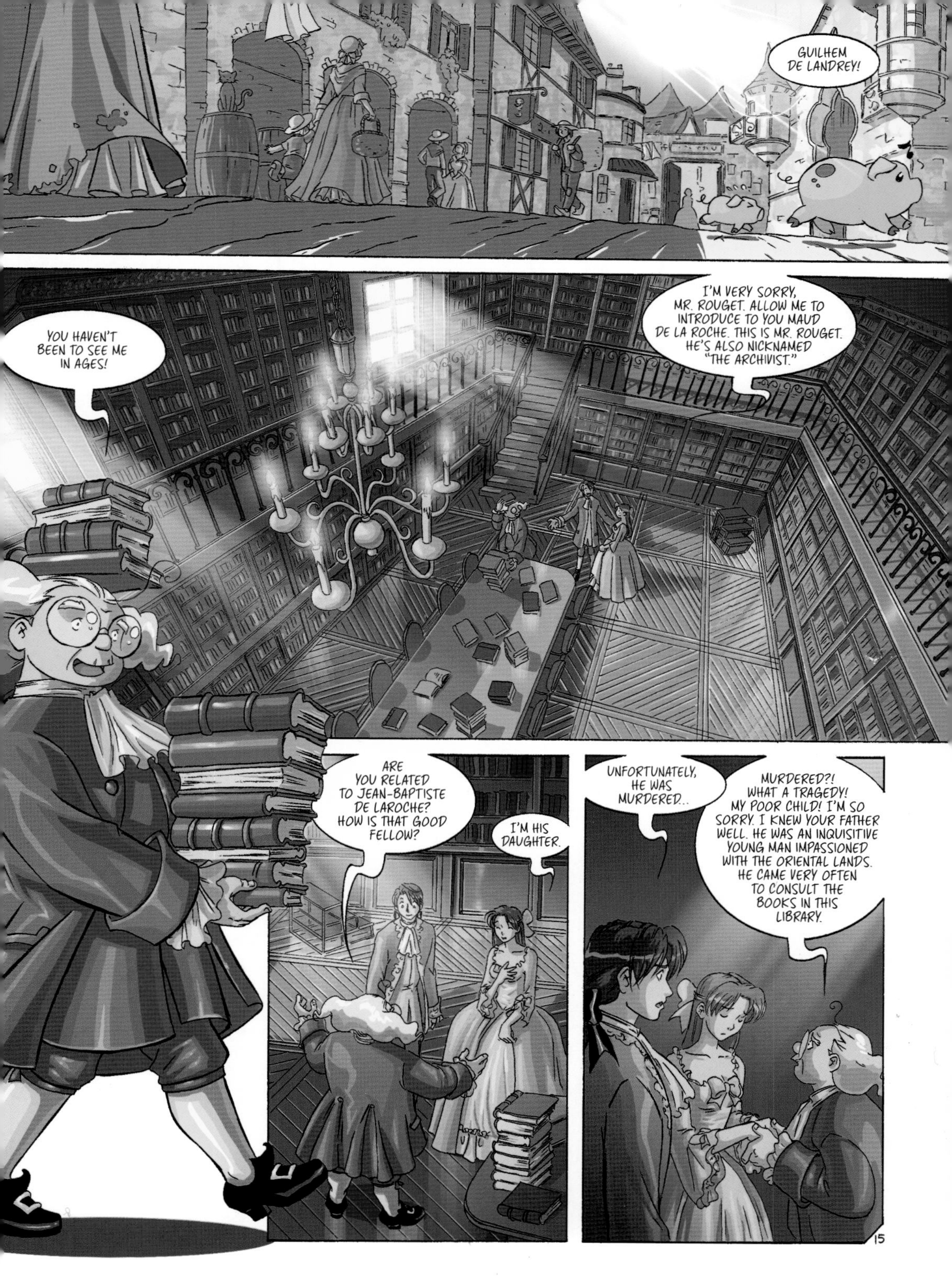
GUILHEM DE LANDREY!
YOU HAVEN'T BEEN TO SEE ME IN AGES!
I'M VERY SORRY, MR. ROUGET. ALLOW ME TO INTRODUCE TO YOU MAUD DE LA ROCHE. THIS IS MR. ROUGET. HE'S ALSO NICKNAMED "THE ARCHIVIST."
ARE YOU RELATED TO JEAN-BAPTISTE DE LAROCHE? HOW IS THAT GOOD FELLOW?
I'M HIS DAUGHTER.
UNFORTUNATELY, HE WAS MURDERED...
MURDERED?! WHAT A TRAGEDY! MY POOR CHILD! I'M SO SORRY. I KNEW YOUR FATHER WELL. HE WAS AN INQUISITIVE YOUNG MAN IMPASSIONED WITH THE ORIENTAL LANDS. HE CAME VERY OFTEN TO CONSULT THE BOOKS IN THIS LIBRARY.
15

HIS MURDERER WAS TRYING TO GAIN POSSESSION OF ONE OF HIS NOTEBOOKS. APPARENTLY, DURING HIS VOYAGE IN THE OTTOMAN EMPIRE, MAUD'S FATHER DISCOVERED A SECRET PLACE.

WE THINK THAT SECRET MIGHT HAVE A CONNECTION WITH THE TEMPLARS. MAUD WANTS TO FIND HIS MURDERER, AND THIS IS OUR ONLY LEAD

MY CHILDREN, I'LL HELP YOU IN YOUR RESEARCH. I OWE IT TO POOR JEAN-BAPTISTE.

THANK YOU, MR. ROUGET.

HAVE YOU SEEN THIS SYMBOL ANYWHERE?

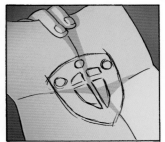

LET'S SEE... YES, IT'S LIKE A SEAL... MAYBE EVEN A JEWEL.

LET'S LOOK IN THESE BOOKS.

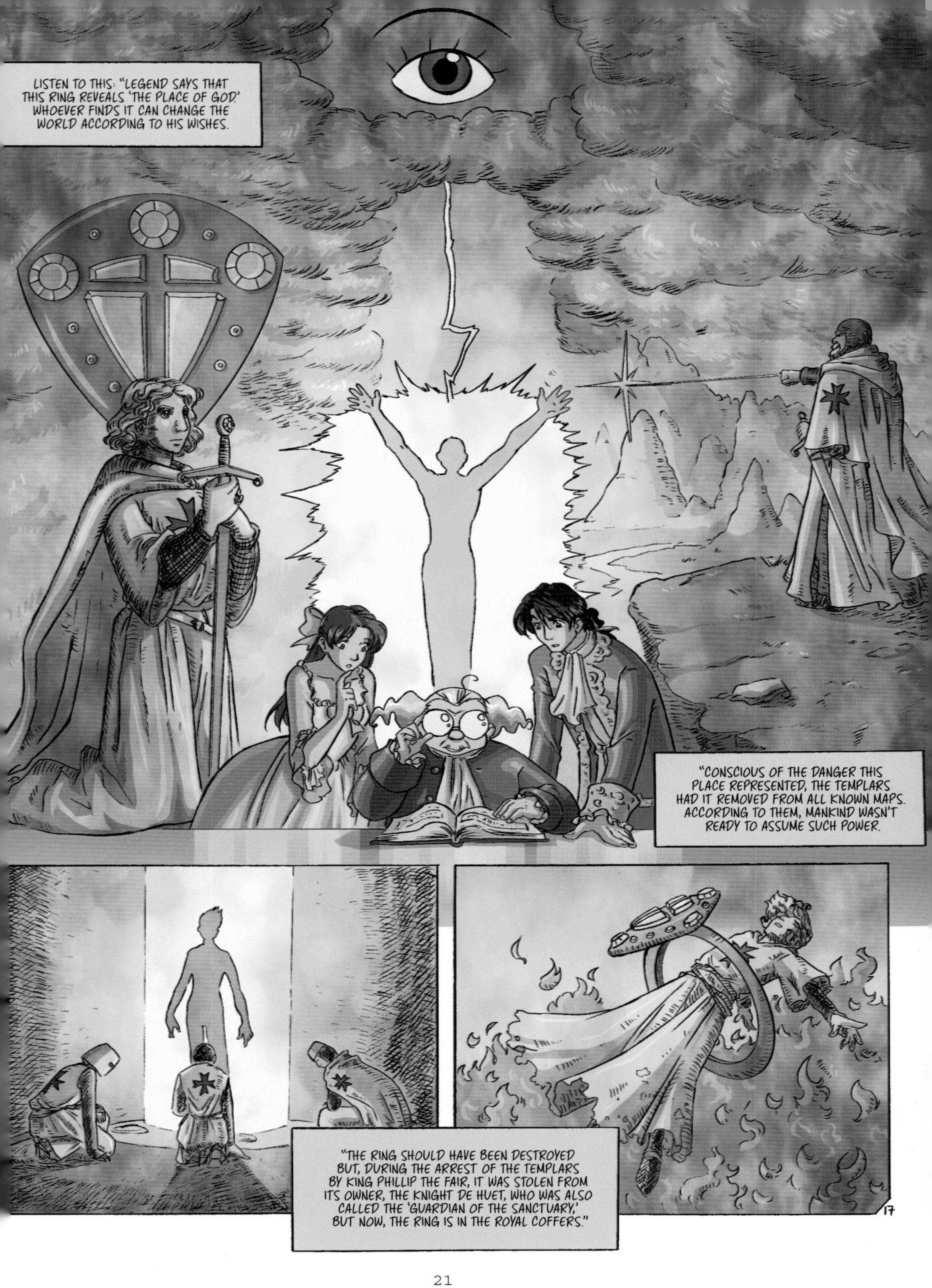
LISTEN TO THIS: "LEGEND SAYS THAT THIS RING REVEALS 'THE PLACE OF GOD.' WHOEVER FINDS IT CAN CHANGE THE WORLD ACCORDING TO HIS WISHES.
"CONSCIOUS OF THE DANGER THIS PLACE REPRESENTED, THE TEMPLARS HAD IT REMOVED FROM ALL KNOWN MAPS. ACCORDING TO THEM, MANKIND WASN'T READY TO ASSUME SUCH POWER.
"THE RING SHOULD HAVE BEEN DESTROYED BUT, DURING THE ARREST OF THE TEMPLARS BY KING PHILLIP THE FAIR, IT WAS STOLEN FROM ITS OWNER, THE KNIGHT DE HUET, WHO WAS ALSO CALLED THE 'GUARDIAN OF THE SANCTUARY,' BUT NOW, THE RING IS IN THE ROYAL COFFERS."
17

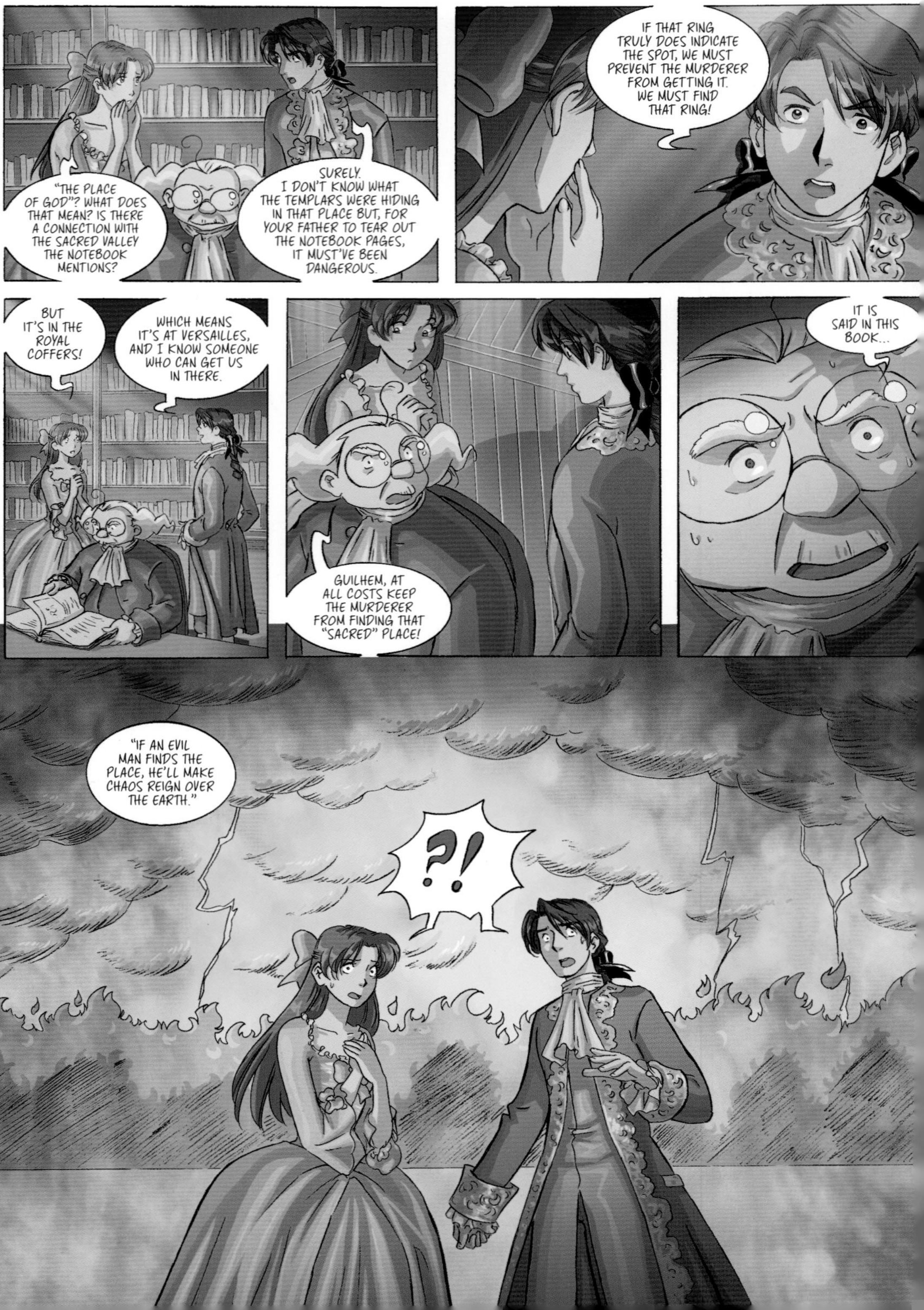
"THE PLACE OF GOD"? WHAT DOES THAT MEAN? IS THERE A CONNECTION WITH THE SACRED VALLEY THE NOTEBOOK MENTIONS?
SURELY. I DON'T KNOW WHAT THE TEMPLARS WERE HIDING IN THAT PLACE BUT, FOR YOUR FATHER TO TEAR OUT THE NOTEBOOK PAGES, IT MUST'VE BEEN DANGEROUS.
IF THAT RING TRULY DOES INDICATE THE SPOT, WE MUST PREVENT THE MURDERER FROM GETTING IT. WE MUST FIND THAT RING!
BUT IT'S IN THE ROYAL COFFERS!
WHICH MEANS IT'S AT VERSAILLES, AND I KNOW SOMEONE WHO CAN GET US IN THERE.
GUILHEM, AT ALL COSTS KEEP THE MURDERER FROM FINDING THAT "SACRED" PLACE!
IT IS SAID IN THIS BOOK...
"IF AN EVIL MAN FINDS THE PLACE, HE'LL MAKE CHAOS REIGN OVER THE EARTH."
?!

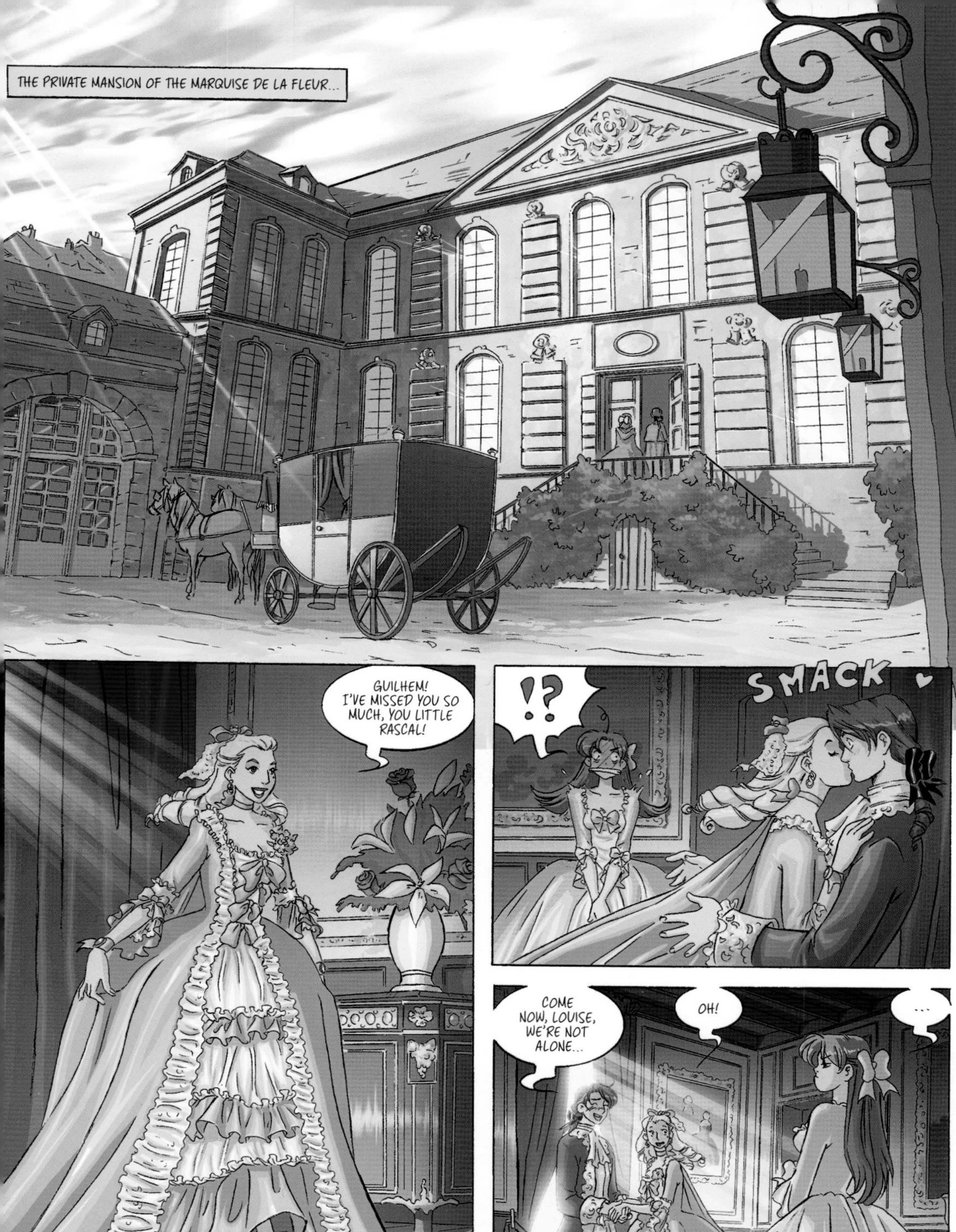
THE PRIVATE MANSION OF THE MARQUISE DE LA FLEUR...
GUILHEM! I'VE MISSED YOU SO MUCH, YOU LITTLE RASCAL!
!?
SMACK
COME NOW, LOUISE, WE'RE NOT ALONE...
OH!
...
19

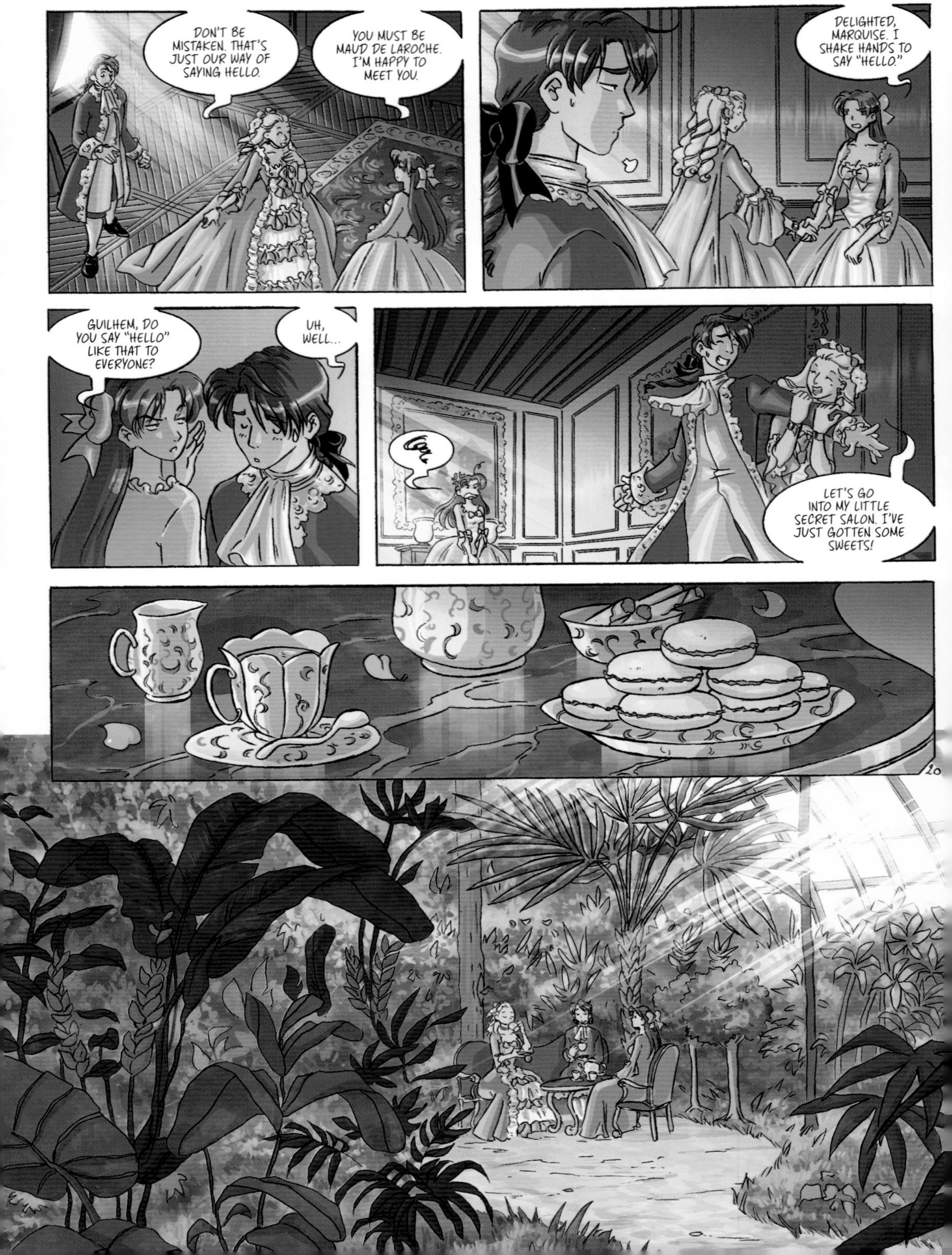
DON'T BE MISTAKEN. THAT'S JUST OUR WAY OF SAYING HELLO.
YOU MUST BE MAUD DE LAROCHE. I'M HAPPY TO MEET YOU.
DELIGHTED, MARQUISE. I SHAKE HANDS TO SAY "HELLO."
GUILHEM, DO YOU SAY "HELLO" LIKE THAT TO EVERYONE?
UH, WELL...
LET'S GO INTO MY LITTLE SECRET SALON. I'VE JUST GOTTEN SOME SWEETS!

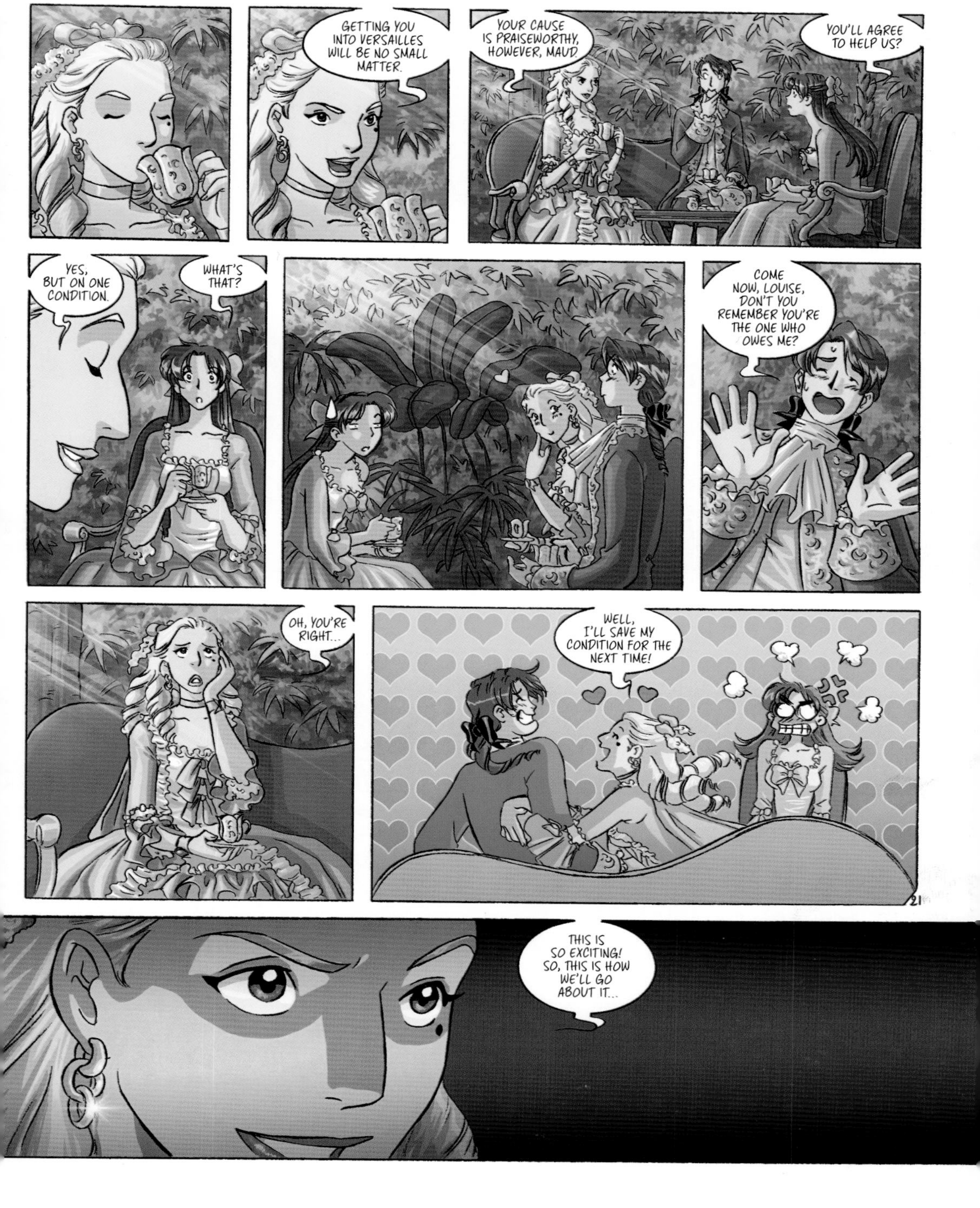
GETTING YOU INTO VERSAILLES WILL BE NO SMALL MATTER.
YOUR CAUSE IS PRAISEWORTHY, HOWEVER, MAUD.
YOU'LL AGREE TO HELP US?
YES, BUT ON ONE CONDITION.
WHAT'S THAT?
COME NOW, LOUISE, DON'T YOU REMEMBER YOU'RE THE ONE WHO OWES ME?
OH, YOU'RE RIGHT...
WELL, I'LL SAVE MY CONDITION FOR THE NEXT TIME!
21
THIS IS SO EXCITING! SO, THIS IS HOW WE'LL GO ABOUT IT...

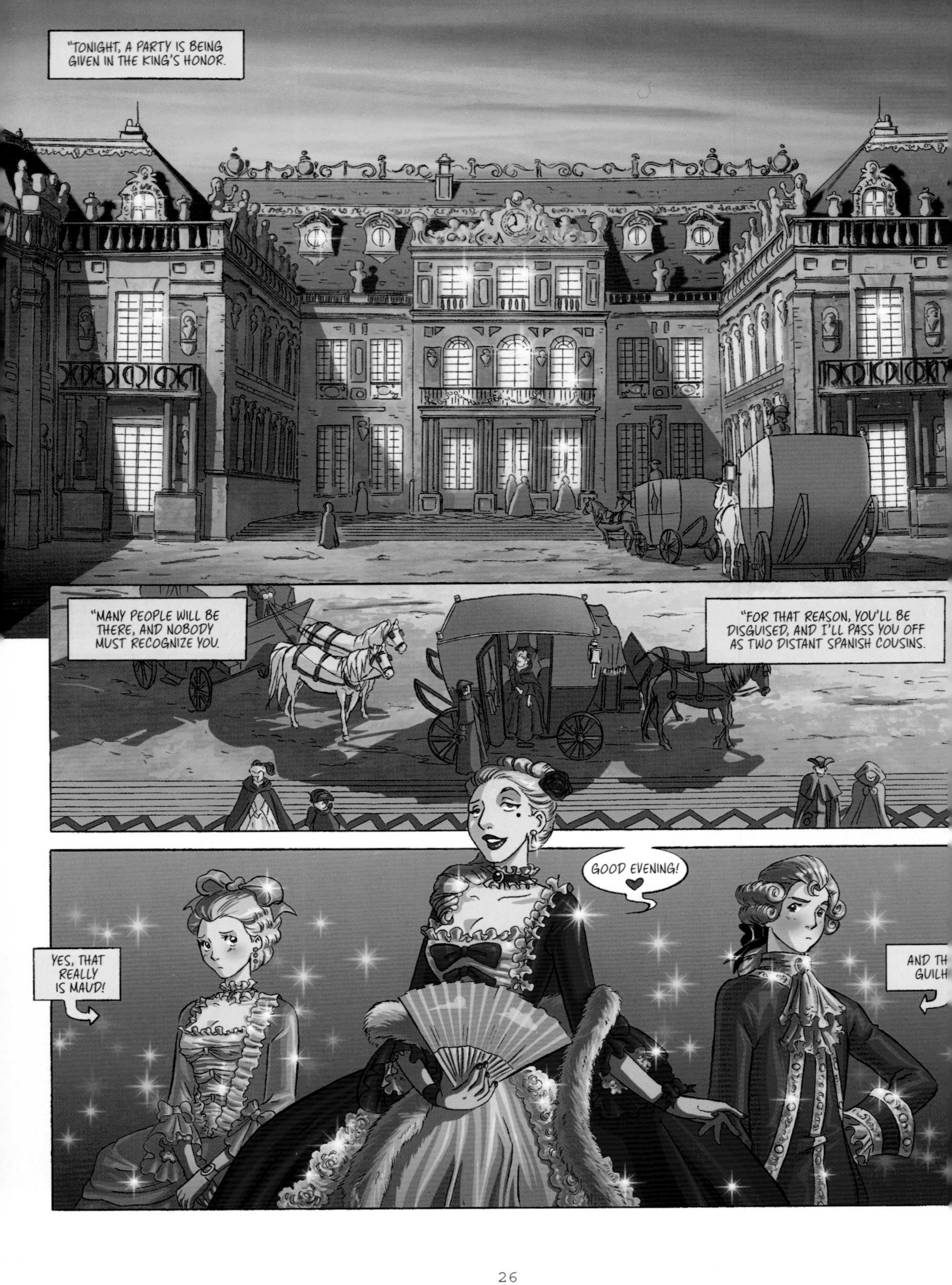
"TONIGHT, A PARTY IS BEING GIVEN IN THE KING'S HONOR.
"MANY PEOPLE WILL BE THERE, AND NOBODY MUST RECOGNIZE YOU.
"FOR THAT REASON, YOU'LL BE DISGUISED, AND I'LL PASS YOU OFF AS TWO DISTANT SPANISH COUSINS.
GOOD EVENING!
YES, THAT REALLY IS MAUD!
AND TH GUILH

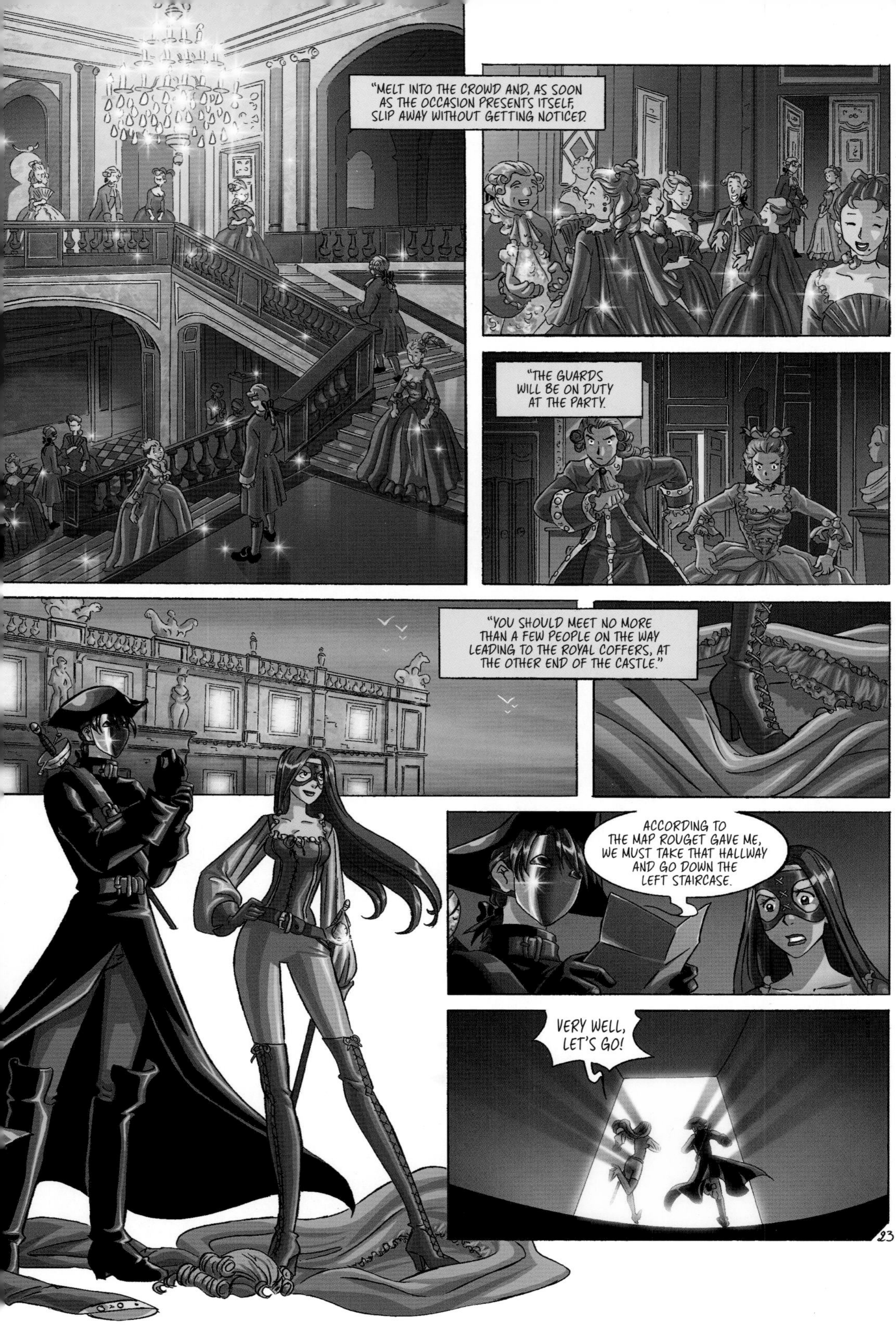
"MELT INTO THE CROWD AND, AS SOON AS THE OCCASION PRESENTS ITSELF, SLIP AWAY WITHOUT GETTING NOTICED.
"THE GUARDS WILL BE ON DUTY AT THE PARTY.
"YOU SHOULD MEET NO MORE THAN A FEW PEOPLE ON THE WAY LEADING TO THE ROYAL COFFERS, AT THE OTHER END OF THE CASTLE."
ACCORDING TO THE MAP ROUGET GAVE ME, WE MUST TAKE THAT HALLWAY AND GO DOWN THE LEFT STAIRCASE.
VERY WELL, LET'S GO!

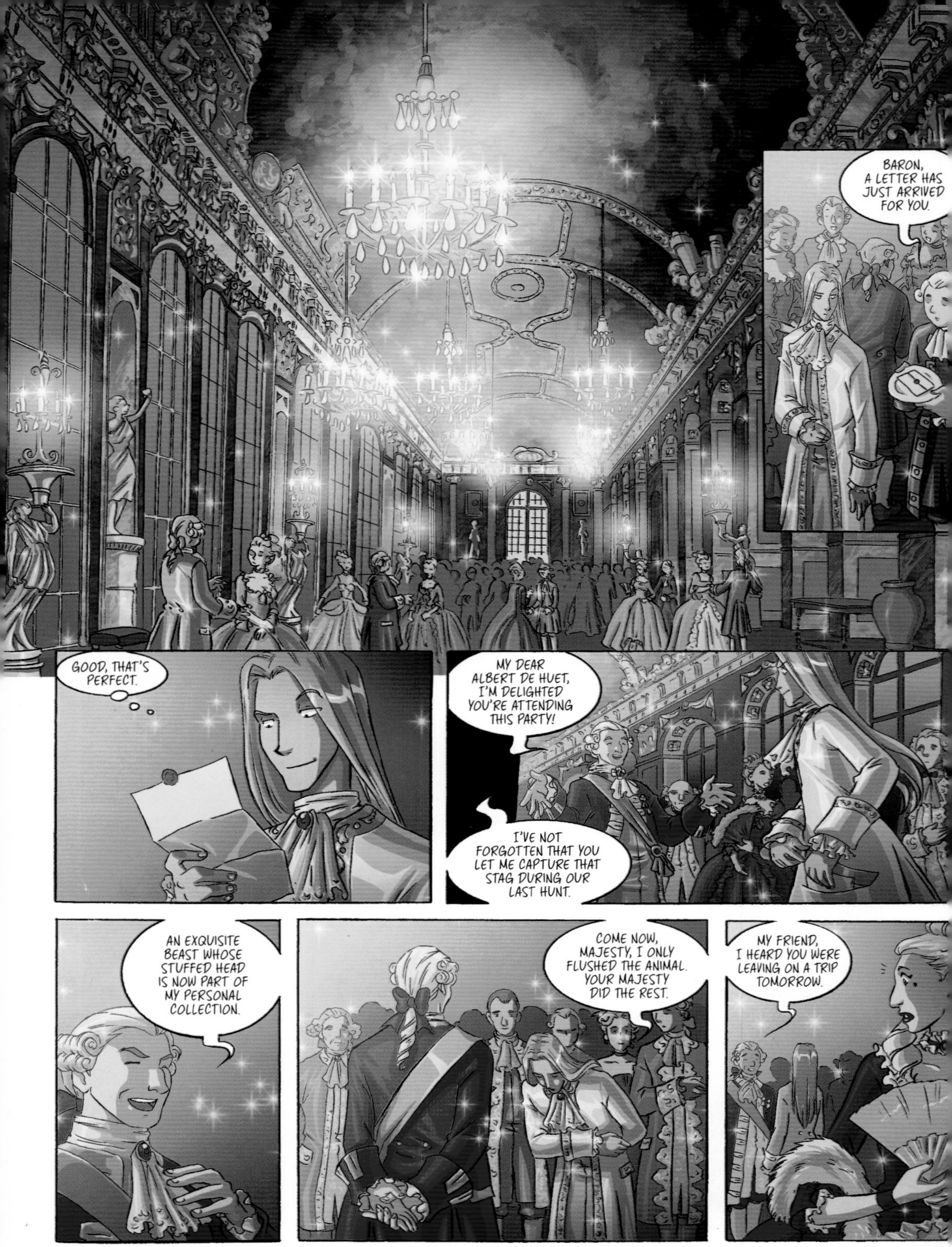
BARON, A LETTER HAS JUST ARRIVED FOR YOU.
GOOD, THAT'S PERFECT.
MY DEAR ALBERT DE HUET, I'M DELIGHTED YOU'RE ATTENDING THIS PARTY!
I'VE NOT FORGOTTEN THAT YOU LET ME CAPTURE THAT STAG DURING OUR LAST HUNT.
AN EXQUISITE BEAST WHOSE STUFFED HEAD IS NOW PART OF MY PERSONAL COLLECTION.
COME NOW, MAJESTY, I ONLY FLUSHED THE ANIMAL. YOUR MAJESTY DID THE REST.
MY FRIEND, I HEARD YOU WERE LEAVING ON A TRIP TOMORROW.

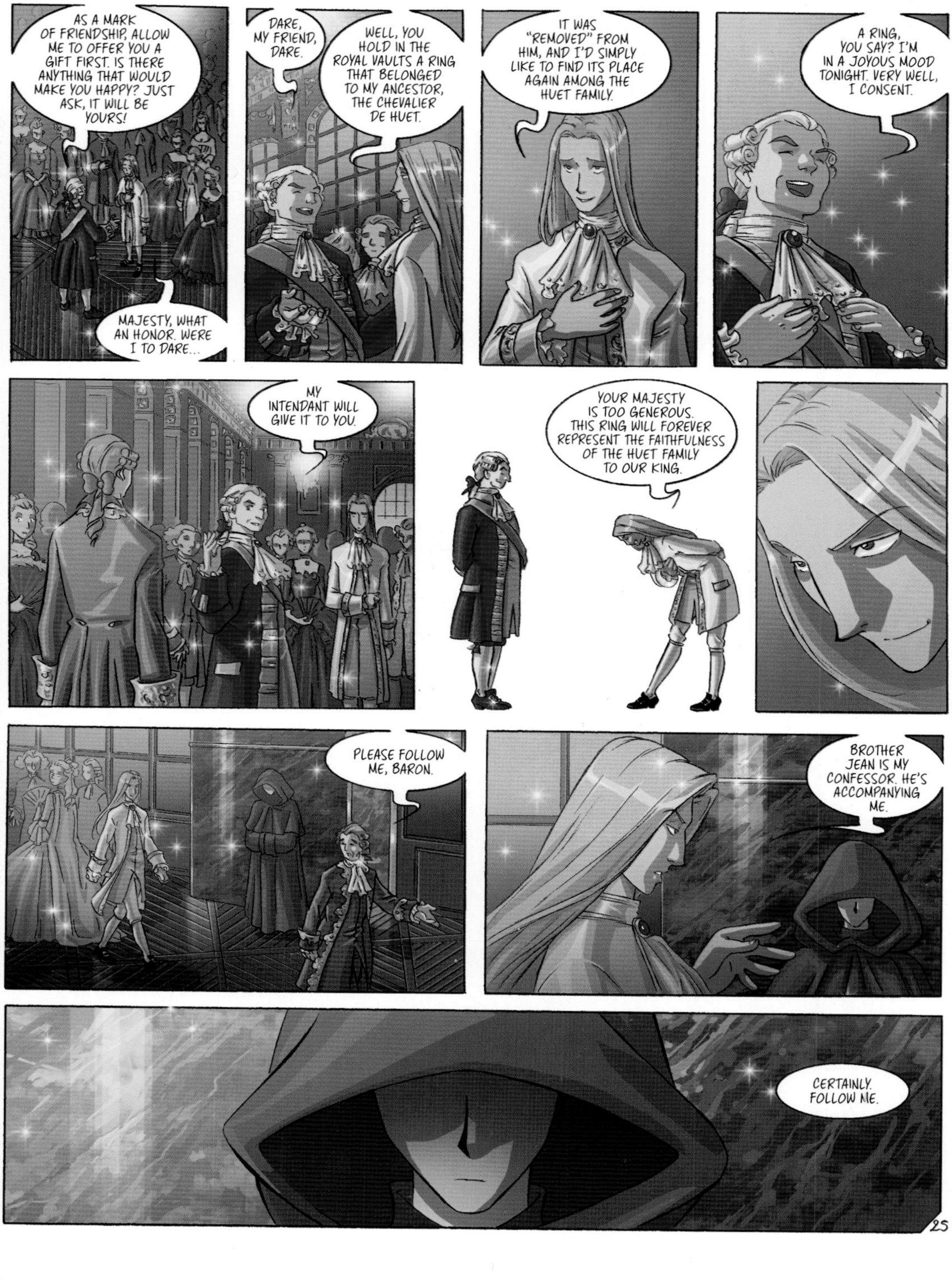
AS A MARK OF FRIENDSHIP, ALLOW ME TO OFFER YOU A GIFT FIRST. IS THERE ANYTHING THAT WOULD MAKE YOU HAPPY? JUST ASK, IT WILL BE YOURS!
MAJESTY, WHAT AN HONOR. WERE I TO DARE...
DARE, MY FRIEND, DARE.
WELL, YOU HOLD IN THE ROYAL VAULTS A RING THAT BELONGED TO MY ANCESTOR, THE CHEVALIER DE HUET.
IT WAS "REMOVED" FROM HIM, AND I'D SIMPLY LIKE TO FIND ITS PLACE AGAIN AMONG THE HUET FAMILY.
A RING, YOU SAY? I'M IN A JOYOUS MOOD TONIGHT. VERY WELL, I CONSENT.
MY INTENDANT WILL GIVE IT TO YOU.
YOUR MAJESTY IS TOO GENEROUS. THIS RING WILL FOREVER REPRESENT THE FAITHFULNESS OF THE HUET FAMILY TO OUR KING.
PLEASE FOLLOW ME, BARON.
BROTHER JEAN IS MY CONFESSOR. HE'S ACCOMPANYING ME.
CERTAINLY. FOLLOW ME.
25

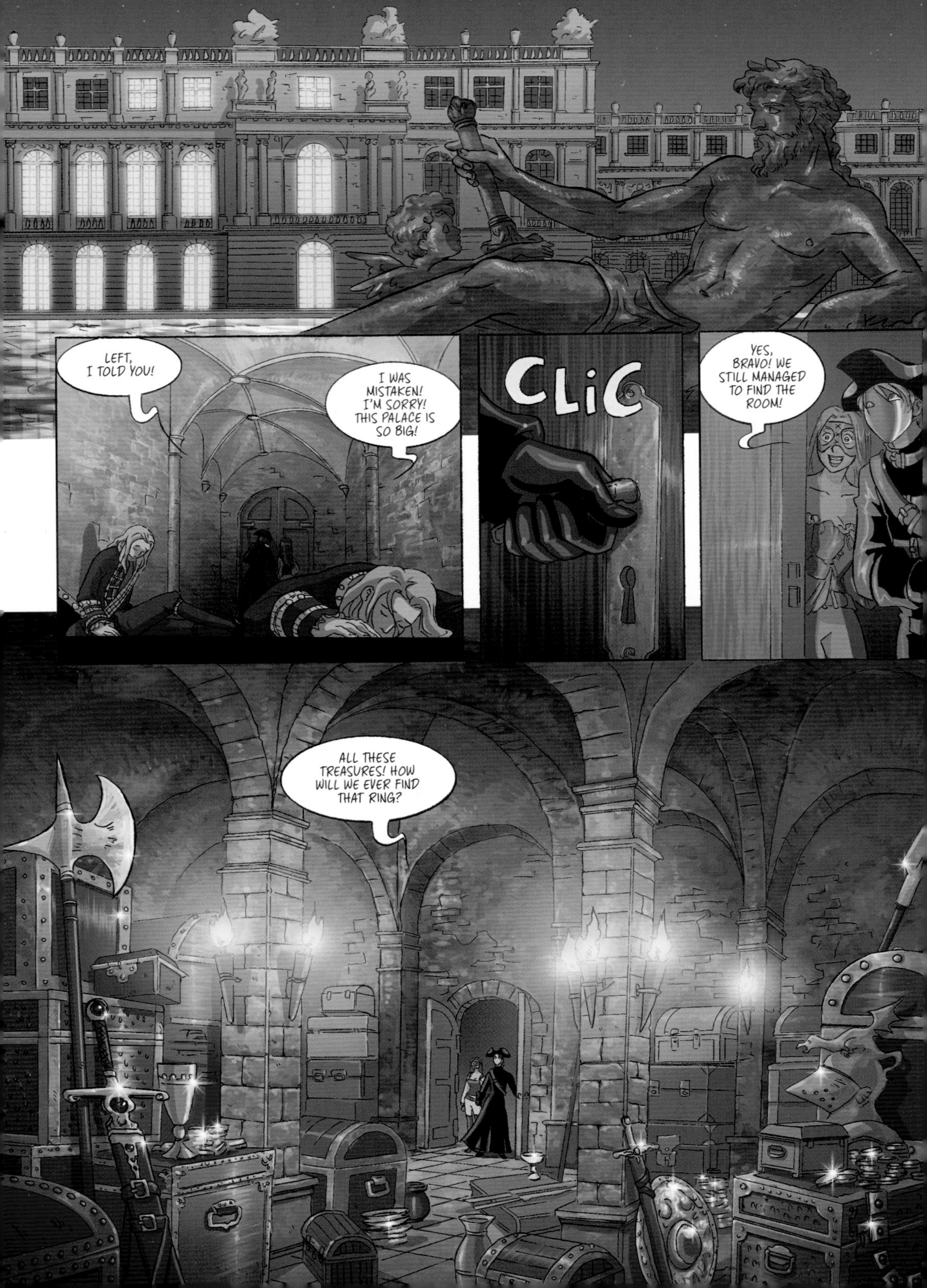
LEFT, I TOLD YOU!
I WAS MISTAKEN! I'M SORRY! THIS PALACE IS SO BIG!
CLIC
YES, BRAVO! WE STILL MANAGED TO FIND THE ROOM!
ALL THESE TREASURES! HOW WILL WE EVER FIND THAT RING?

TRULY, I WONDER HOW YOU MANAGED TO MAKE IT THIS FAR. DON'T YOU KNOW WHAT A PLAN OF ATTACK IS?

A WHAT?

NO, FORGET IT.

ROUGET MADE ME A COPY OF WHAT THE CHESTS CONTAIN. OUR RING IS IN A RED CHEST WITH A LOCK SHAPED LIKE A DRAGON.

IT'S THIS ONE!

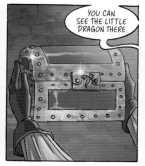

YOU CAN SEE THE LITTLE DRAGON THERE.

VERY WELL, MOVE ASIDE, IT'S GOING TO GET HOT.

I PUT A LITTLE GUN POWDER IN THE LOCK.

SSSSSS

WITH ANY LUCK, WE'RE FAR ENOUGH FROM THE PARTY AND GUARDS THAT NOBODY WILL HEAR US.

27

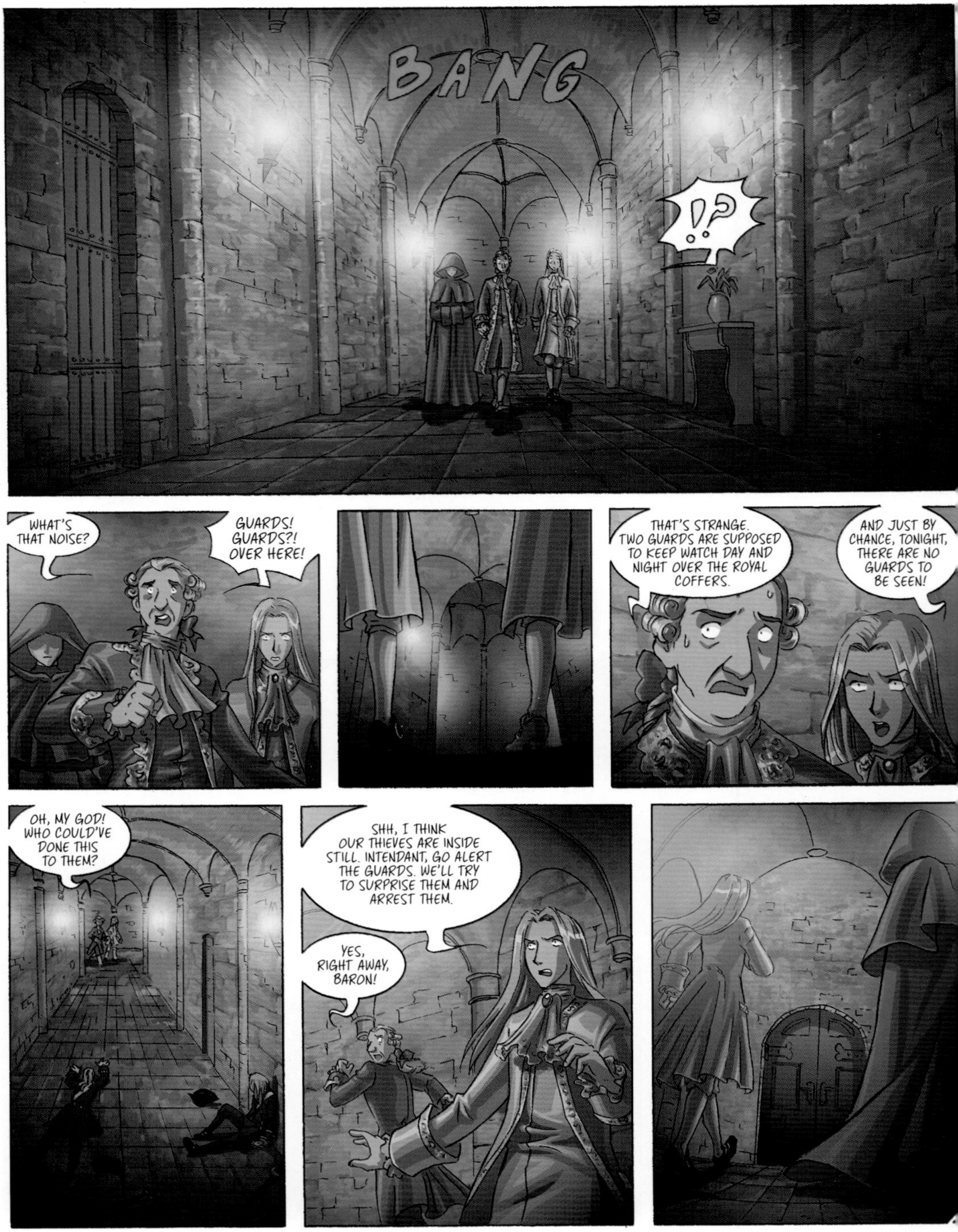
BANG
!?
WHAT'S THAT NOISE?
GUARDS! GUARDS?! OVER HERE!
THAT'S STRANGE. TWO GUARDS ARE SUPPOSED TO KEEP WATCH DAY AND NIGHT OVER THE ROYAL COFFERS.
AND JUST BY CHANCE, TONIGHT, THERE ARE NO GUARDS TO BE SEEN!
OH, MY GOD! WHO COULD'VE DONE THIS TO THEM?
SHH, I THINK OUR THIEVES ARE INSIDE STILL. INTENDANT, GO ALERT THE GUARDS. WE'LL TRY TO SURPRISE THEM AND ARREST THEM.
YES, RIGHT AWAY, BARON!

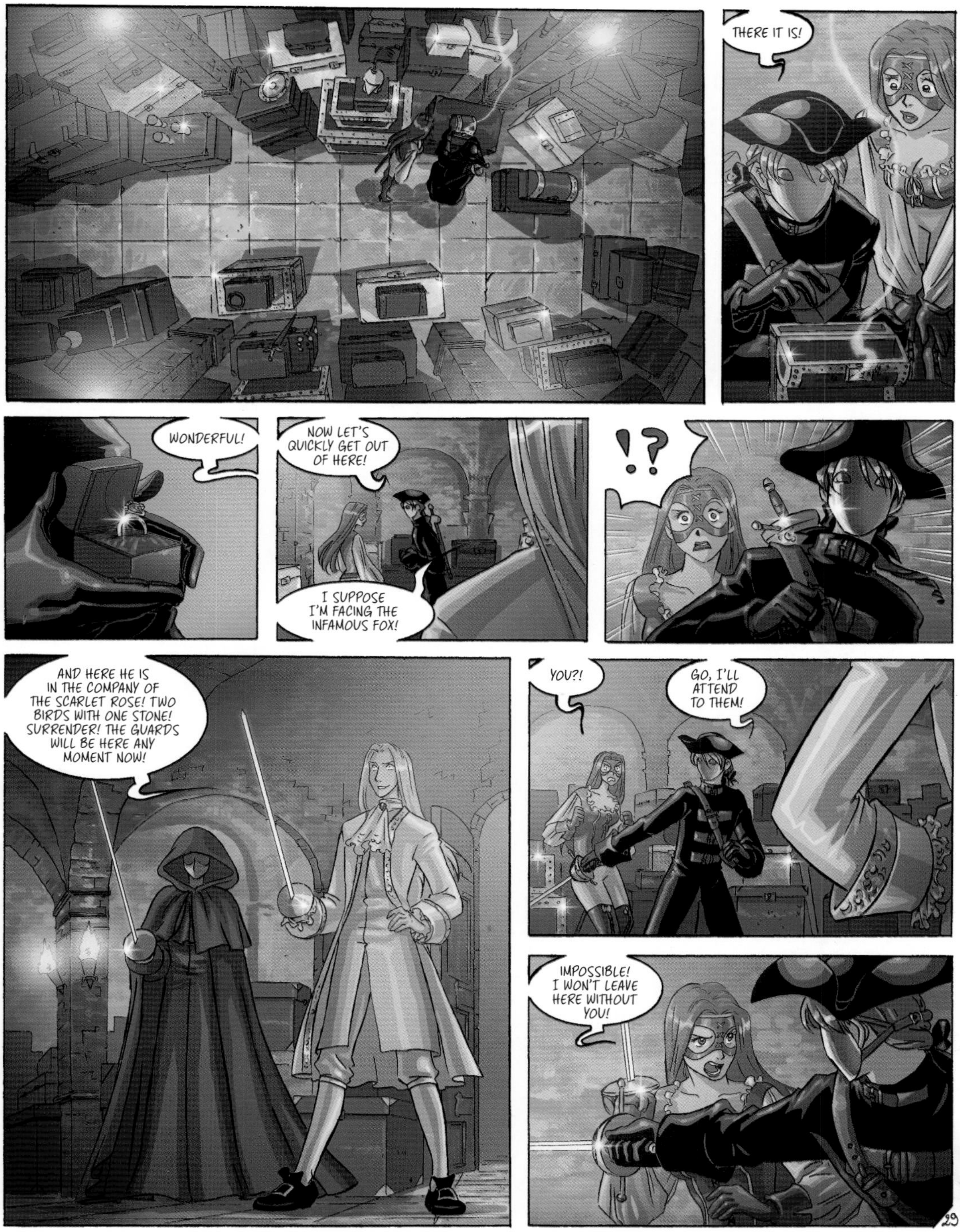

THERE IT IS!
WONDERFUL!
NOW LET'S QUICKLY GET OUT OF HERE!
I SUPPOSE I'M FACING THE INFAMOUS FOX!
!?
AND HERE HE IS IN THE COMPANY OF THE SCARLET ROSE! TWO BIRDS WITH ONE STONE! SURRENDER! THE GUARDS WILL BE HERE ANY MOMENT NOW!
YOU?!
GO, I'LL ATTEND TO THEM!
IMPOSSIBLE! I WON'T LEAVE HERE WITHOUT YOU!
29

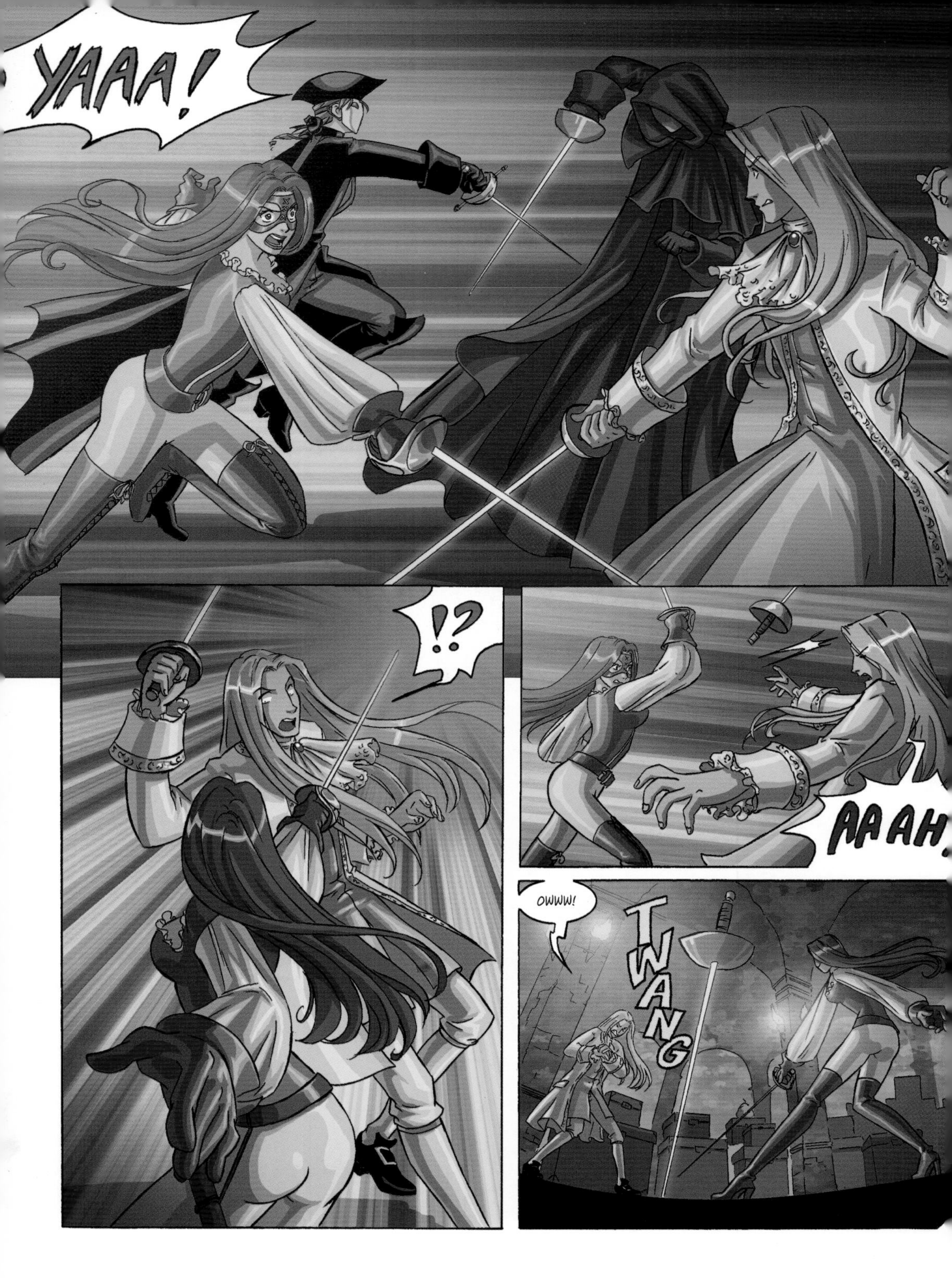
YAAA!
!?
AAAH!
OWWW!
TWANG

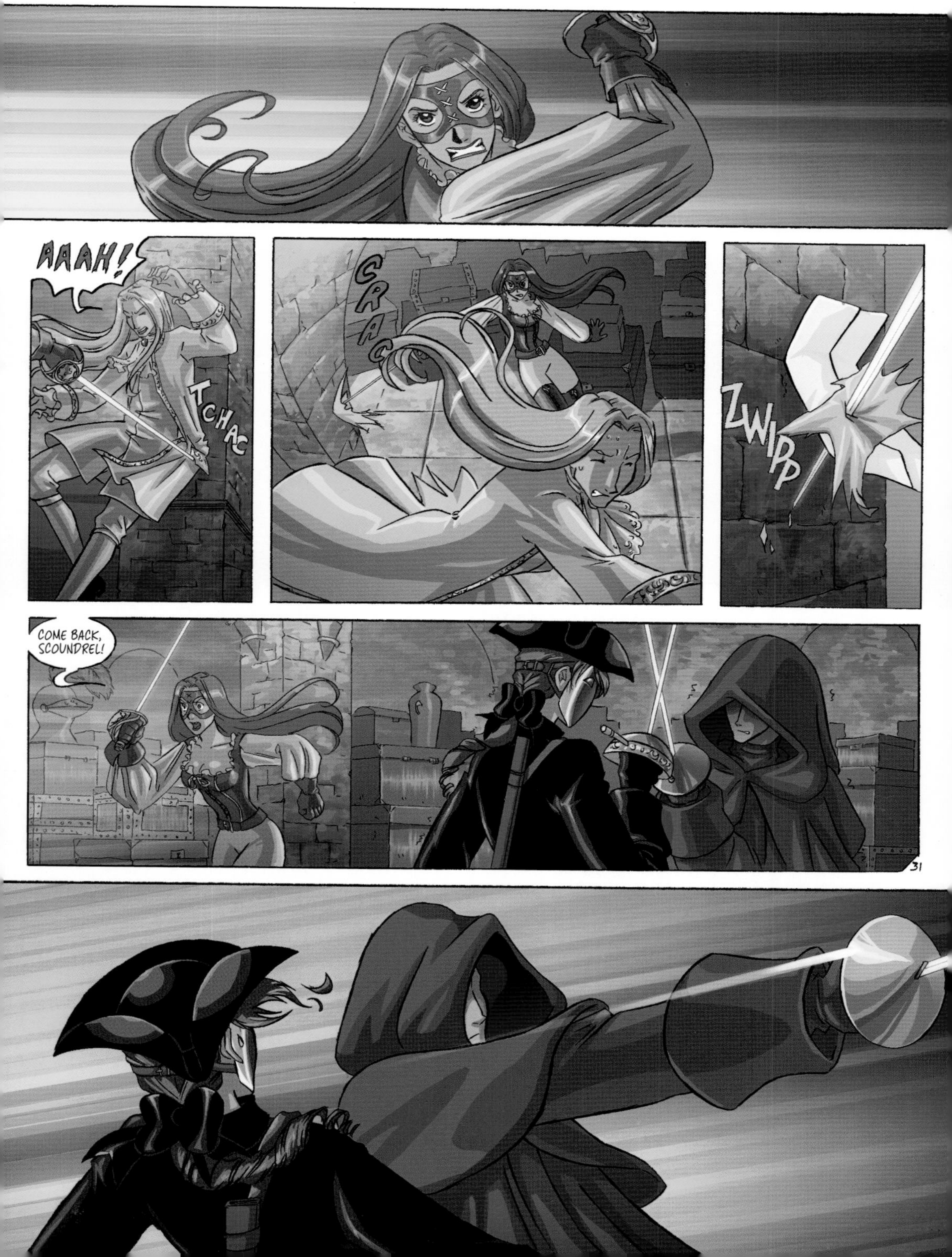
AAAH!
TCHAC
CRAC
ZWIPP
COME BACK, SCOUNDREL!

31

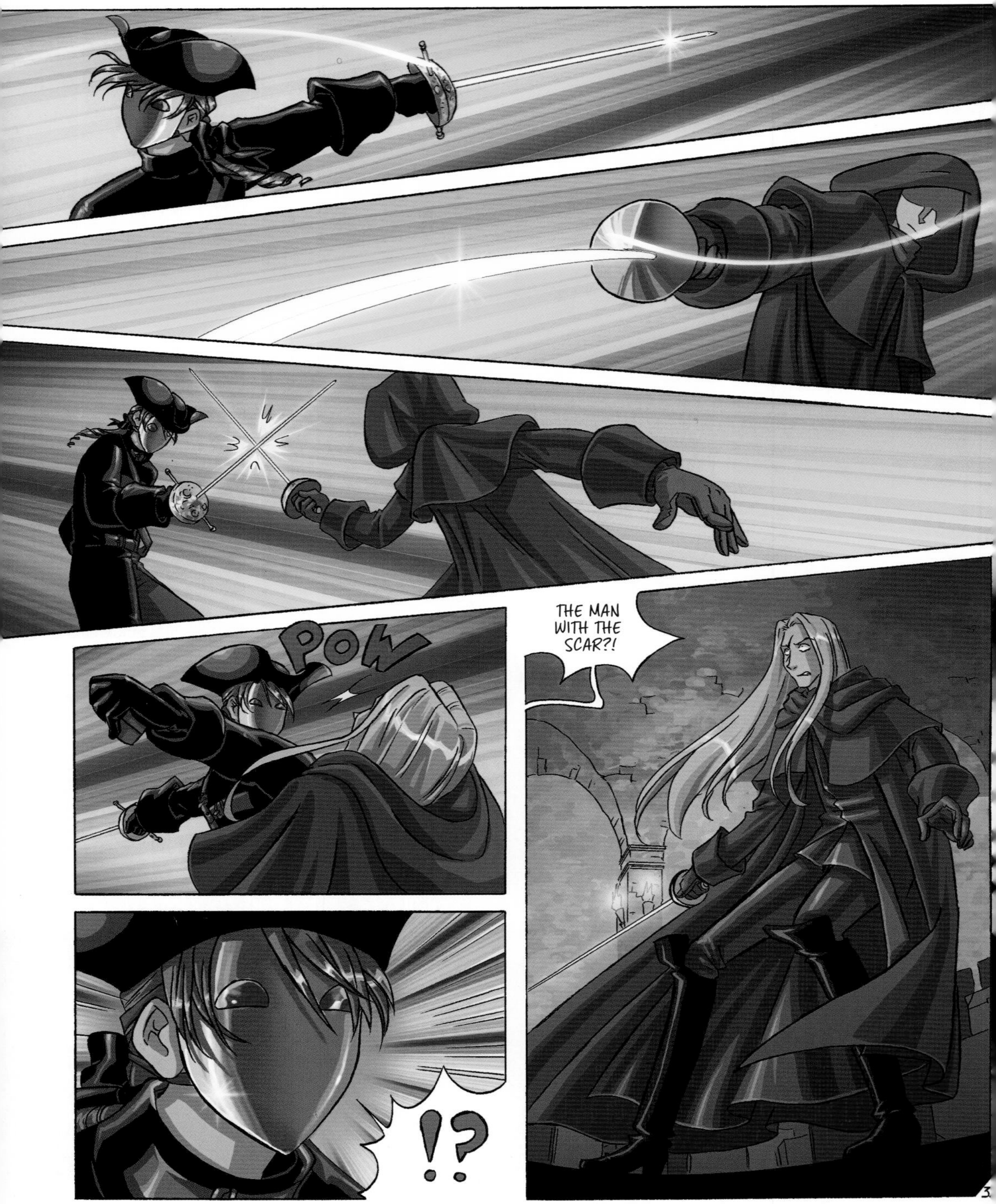
POW
!?
THE MAN WITH THE SCAR?!

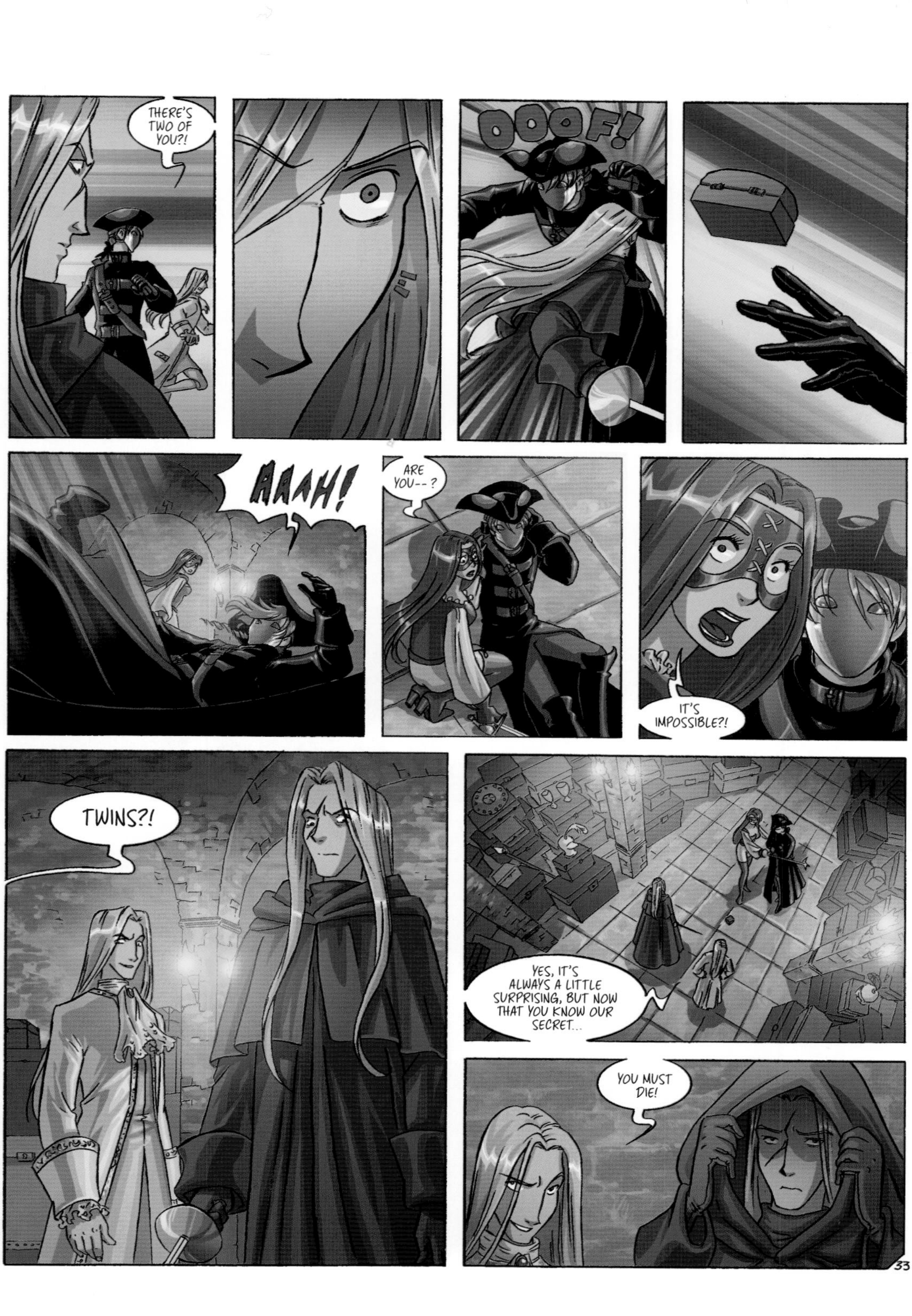
THERE'S TWO OF YOU?!
OOOF!
AAAH!
ARE YOU--?
IT'S IMPOSSIBLE?!
TWINS?!
YES, IT'S ALWAYS A LITTLE SURPRISING, BUT NOW THAT YOU KNOW OUR SECRET...
YOU MUST DIE!
33

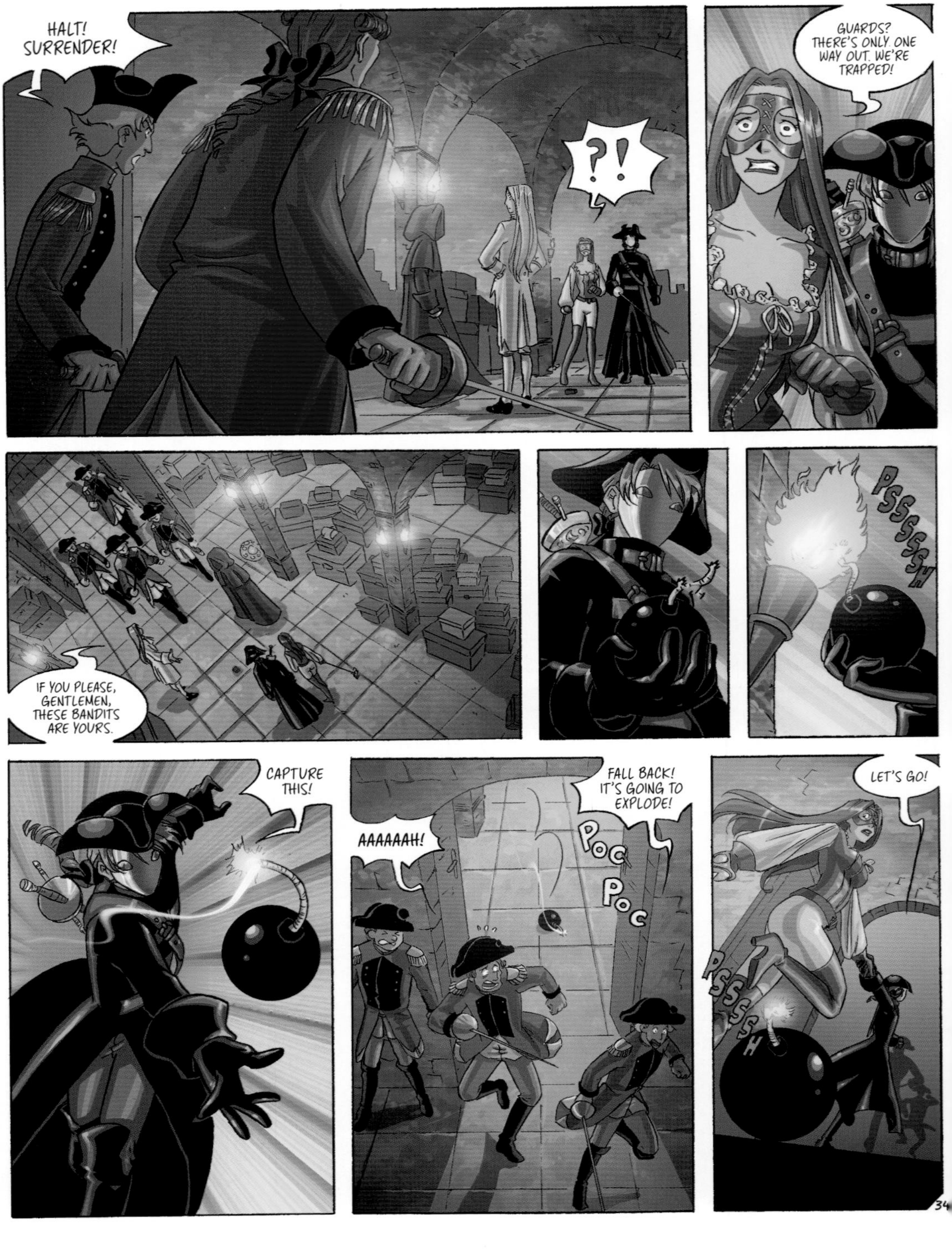
HALT! SURRENDER!
?!
GUARDS? THERE'S ONLY ONE WAY OUT. WE'RE TRAPPED!
IF YOU PLEASE, GENTLEMEN, THESE BANDITS ARE YOURS.
PSSSSSH
CAPTURE THIS!
AAAAAAH!
FALL BACK! IT'S GOING TO EXPLODE!
POC POC
LET'S GO!
PSSSSH
34

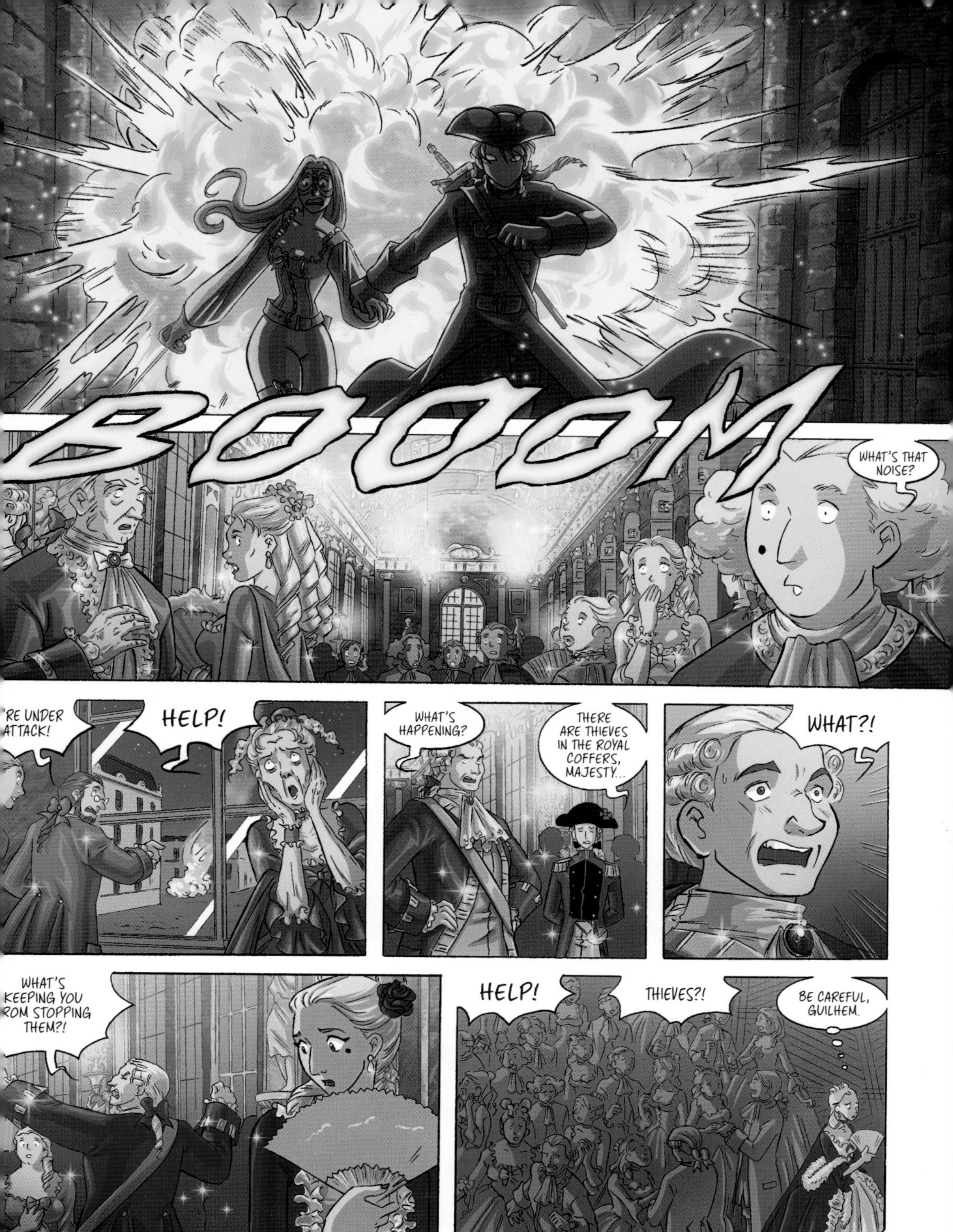
BOOM
WHAT'S THAT NOISE?
'RE UNDER ATTACK!
HELP!
WHAT'S HAPPENING?
THERE ARE THIEVES IN THE ROYAL COFFERS, MAJESTY...
WHAT?!
WHAT'S KEEPING YOU ROM STOPPING THEM?!
HELP!
THIEVES?!
BE CAREFUL, GUILHEM.
35

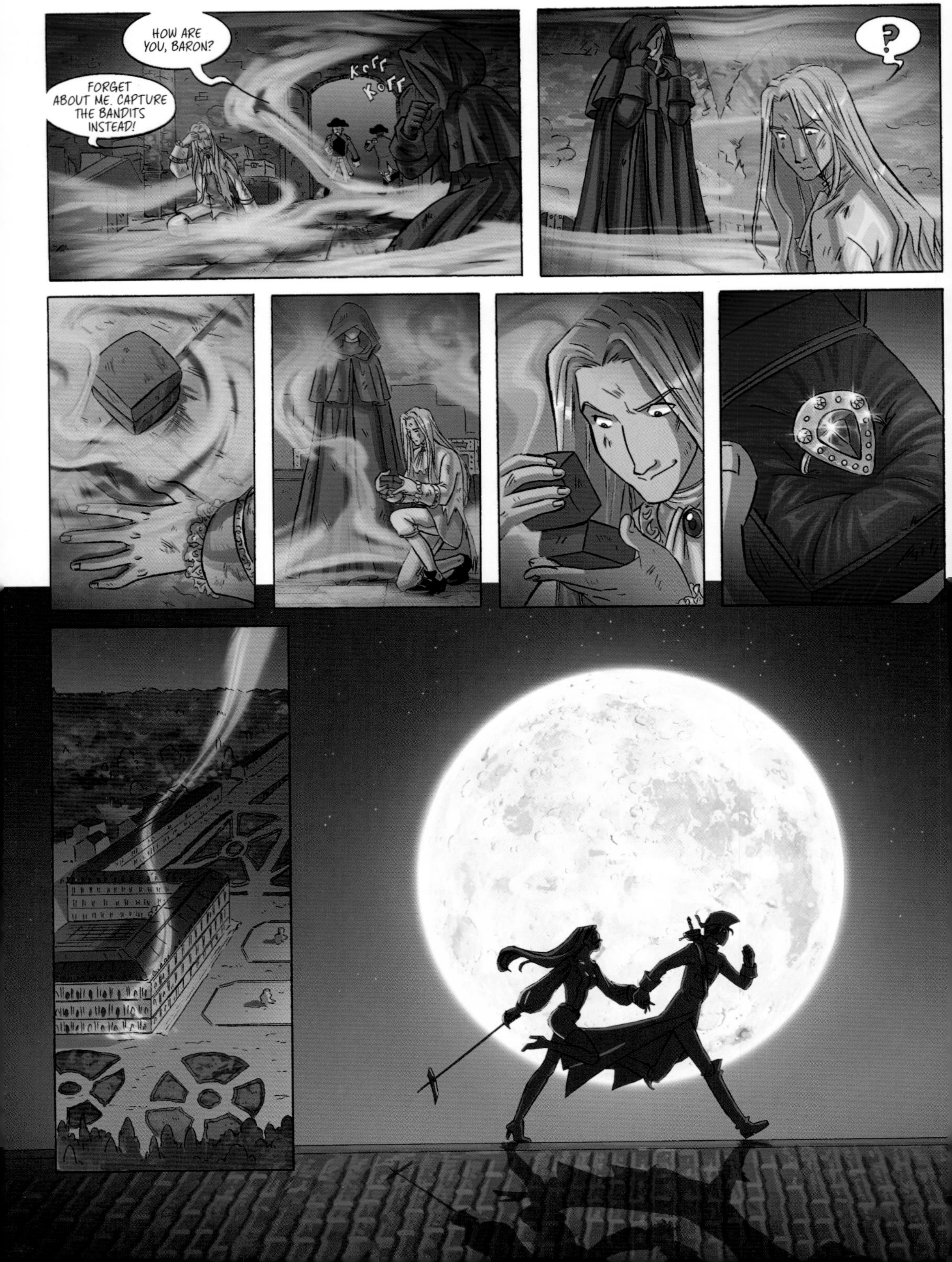
HOW ARE YOU, BARON?
FORGET ABOUT ME. CAPTURE THE BANDITS INSTEAD!
KOFF KOFF
?

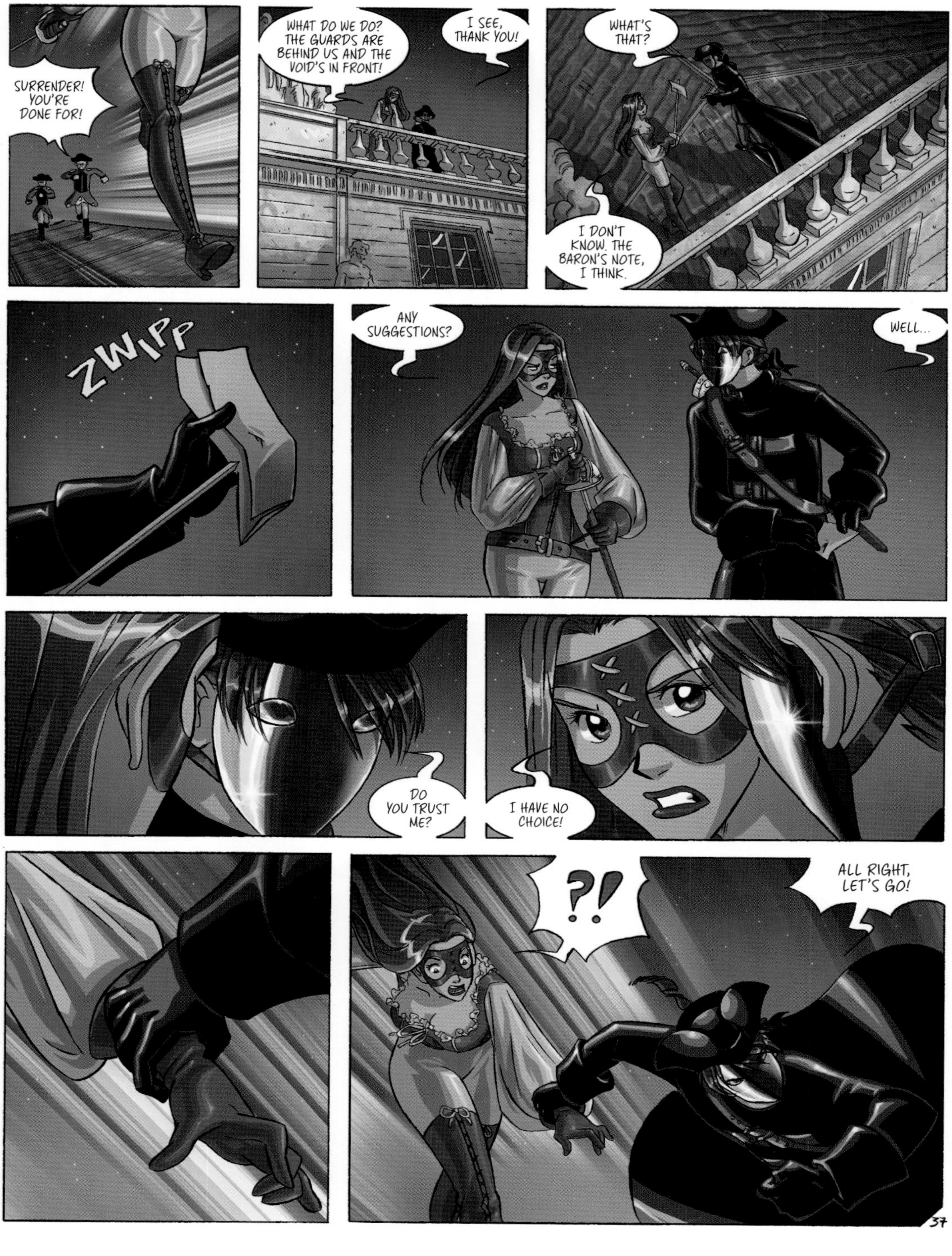
SURRENDER! YOU'RE DONE FOR!
WHAT DO WE DO? THE GUARDS ARE BEHIND US AND THE VOID'S IN FRONT!
I SEE, THANK YOU!
WHAT'S THAT?
I DON'T KNOW. THE BARON'S NOTE, I THINK.
ZWIPP
ANY SUGGESTIONS?
WELL...
DO YOU TRUST ME?
I HAVE NO CHOICE!
?!
ALL RIGHT, LET'S GO!
37

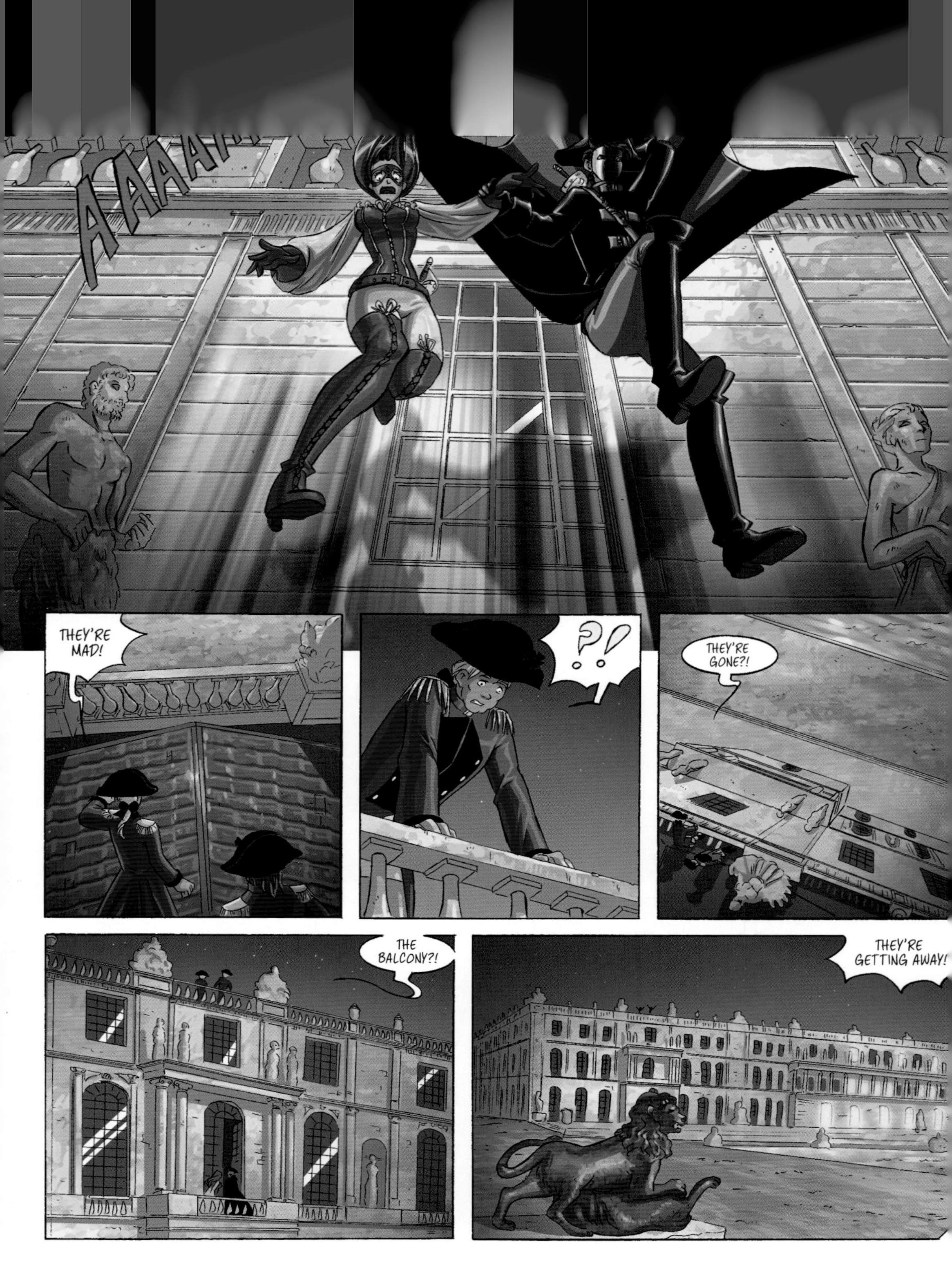
AAAAAH!
THEY'RE MAD!
?!
THEY'RE GONE?!
THE BALCONY?!
THEY'RE GETTING AWAY!

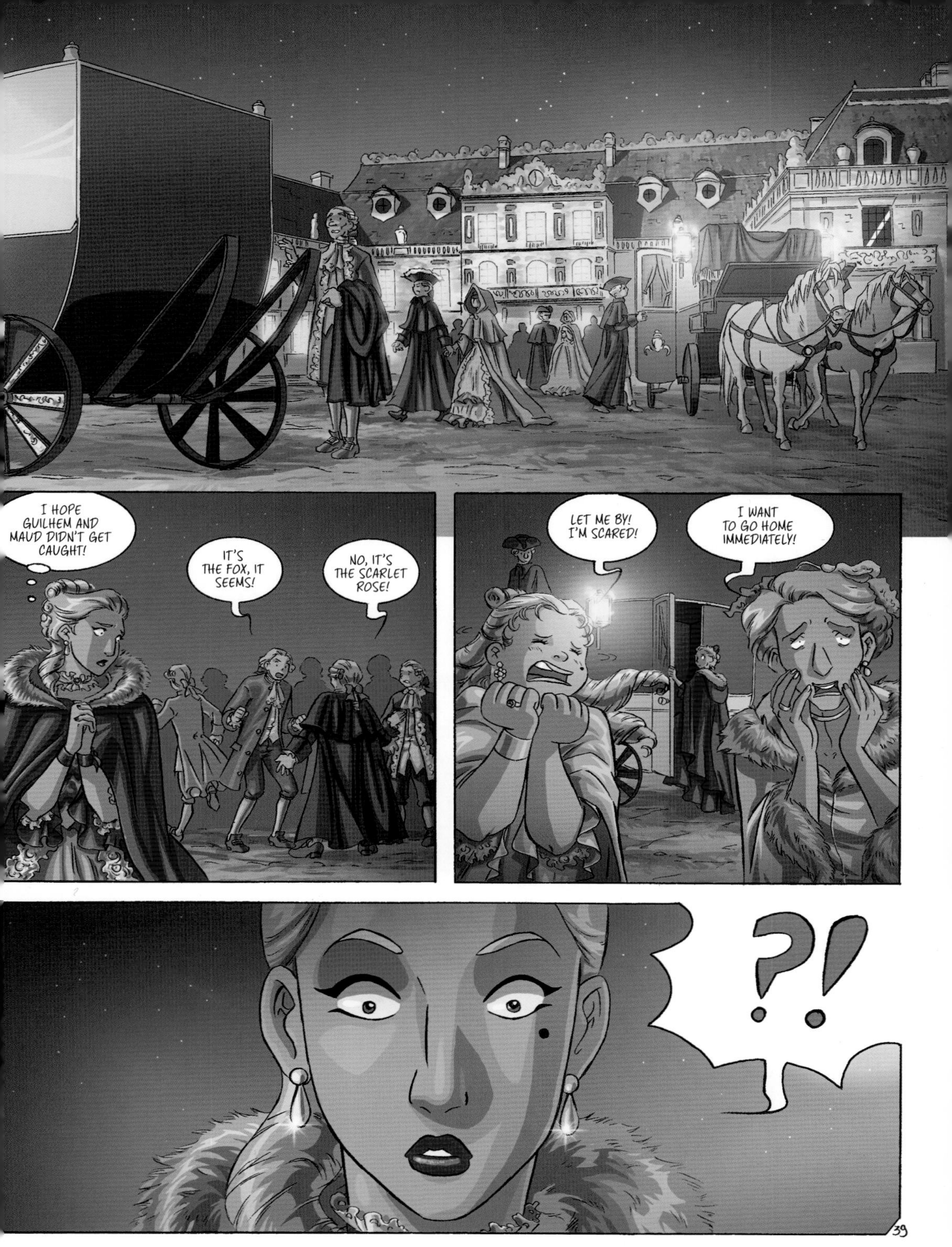
I HOPE GUILHEM AND MAUD DIDN'T GET CAUGHT!
IT'S THE FOX, IT SEEMS!
NO, IT'S THE SCARLET ROSE!
LET ME BY! I'M SCARED!
I WANT TO GO HOME IMMEDIATELY!
?!
39

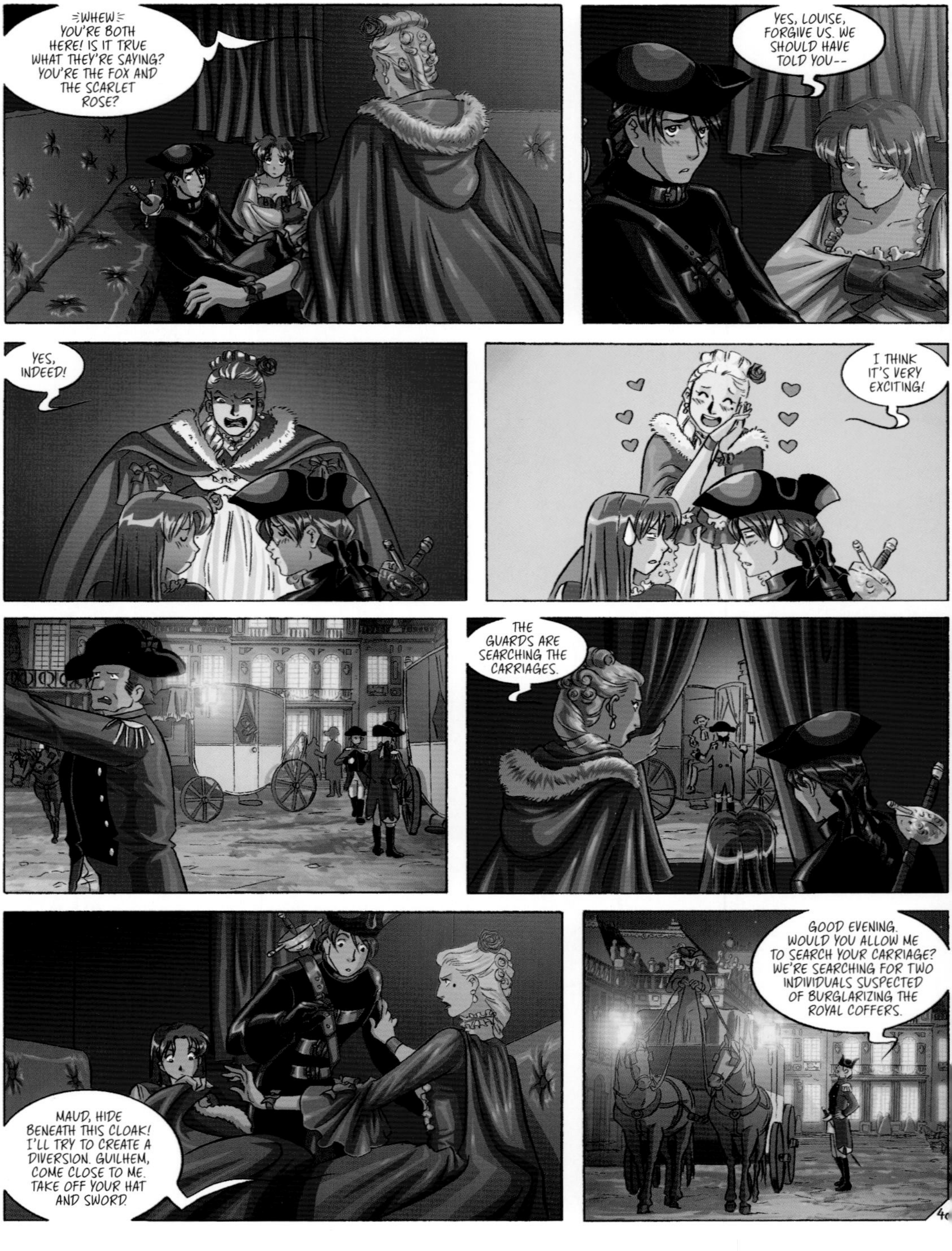
WHEW
YOU'RE BOTH HERE! IS IT TRUE WHAT THEY'RE SAYING? YOU'RE THE FOX AND THE SCARLET ROSE?
YES, LOUISE, FORGIVE US. WE SHOULD HAVE TOLD YOU--
YES, INDEED!
I THINK IT'S VERY EXCITING!
THE GUARDS ARE SEARCHING THE CARRIAGES.
MAUD, HIDE BENEATH THIS CLOAK! I'LL TRY TO CREATE A DIVERSION. GUILHEM, COME CLOSE TO ME. TAKE OFF YOUR HAT AND SWORD.
GOOD EVENING. WOULD YOU ALLOW ME TO SEARCH YOUR CARRIAGE? WE'RE SEARCHING FOR TWO INDIVIDUALS SUSPECTED OF BURGLARIZING THE ROYAL COFFERS.

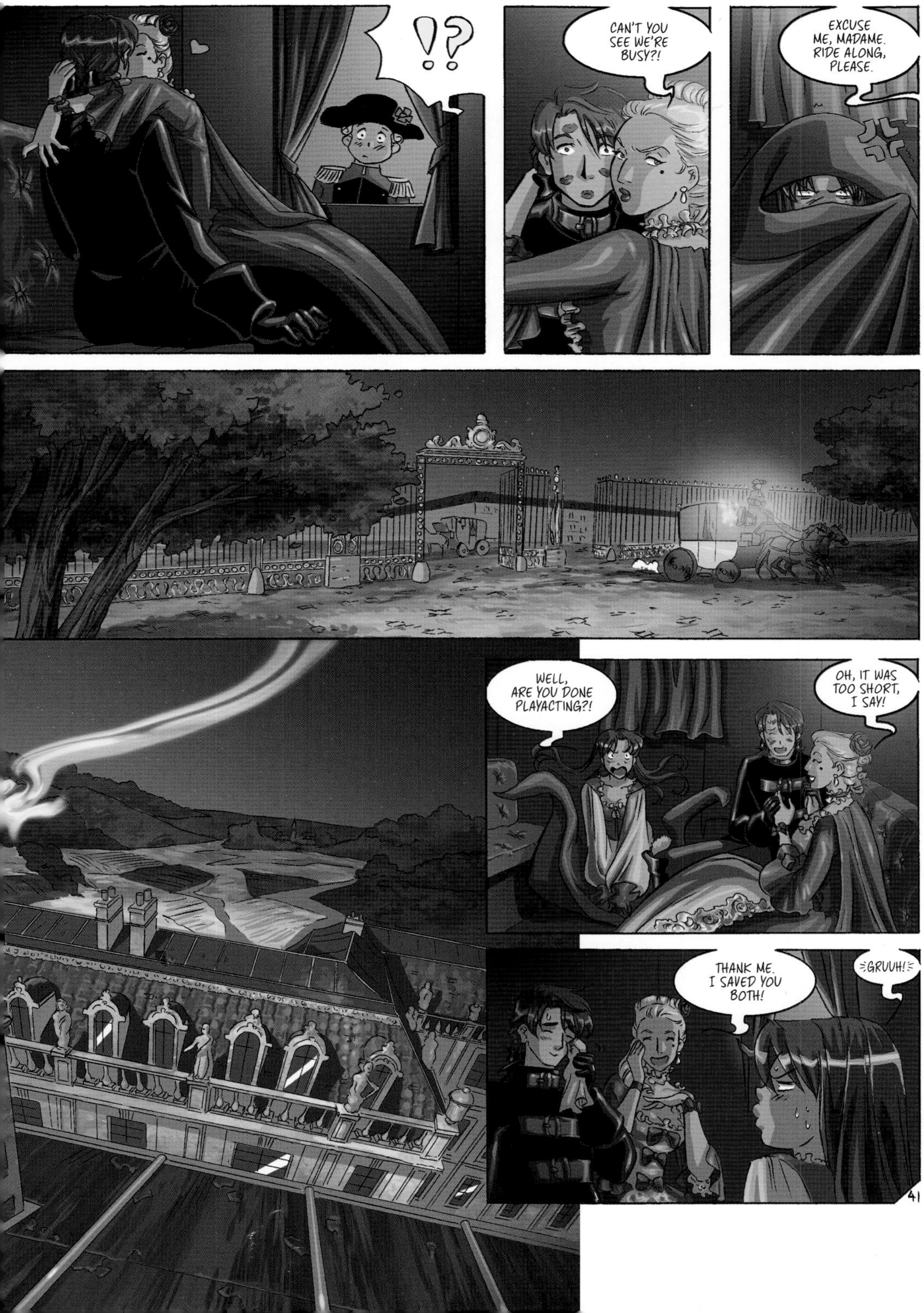
!?
CAN'T YOU SEE WE'RE BUSY?!
EXCUSE ME, MADAME. RIDE ALONG, PLEASE.
WELL, ARE YOU DONE PLAYACTING?!
OH, IT WAS TOO SHORT, I SAY!
THANK ME. I SAVED YOU BOTH!
GRUUH!
41

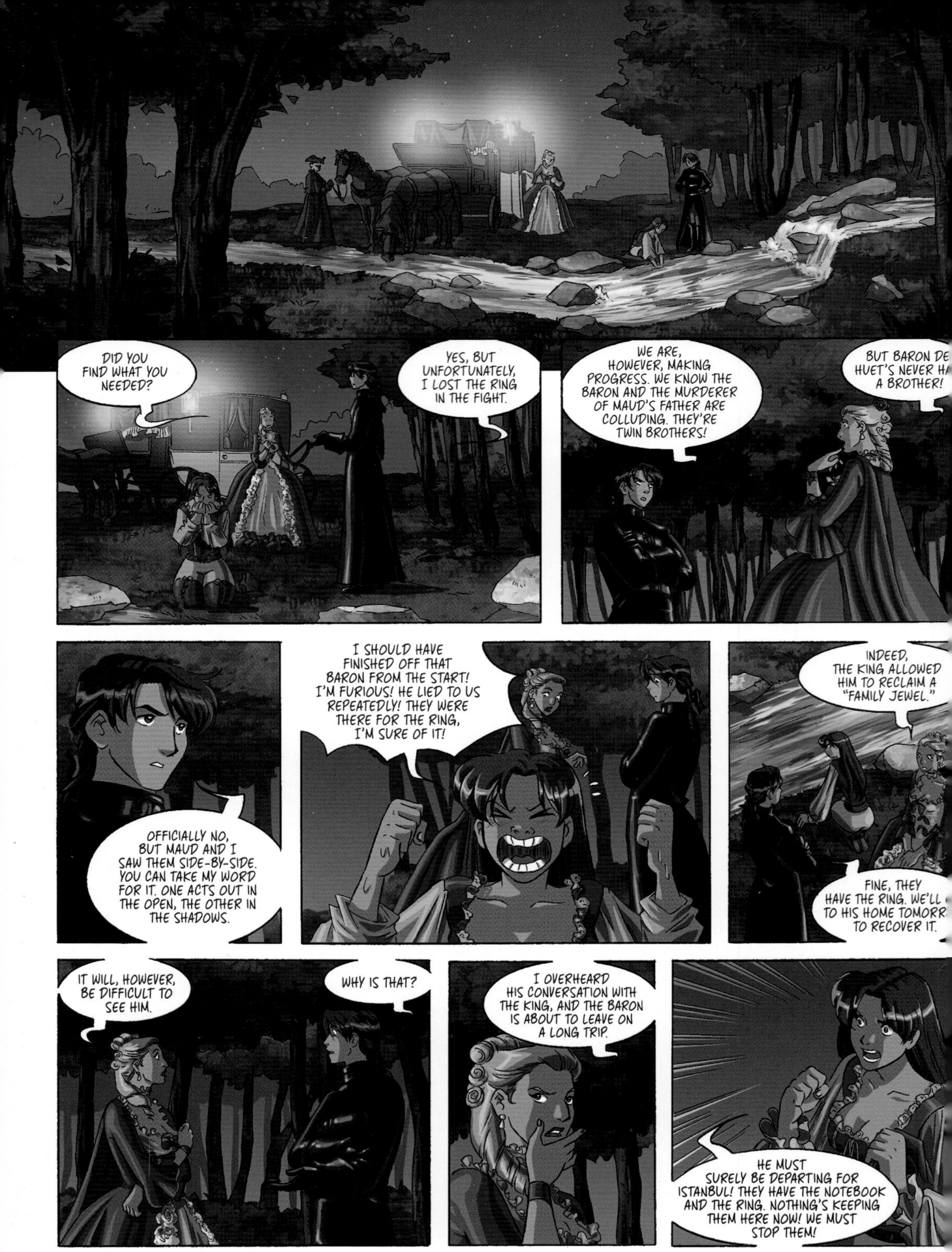
DID YOU FIND WHAT YOU NEEDED?
YES, BUT UNFORTUNATELY, I LOST THE RING IN THE FIGHT.
WE ARE, HOWEVER, MAKING PROGRESS. WE KNOW THE BARON AND THE MURDERER OF MAUD'S FATHER ARE COLLUDING. THEY'RE TWIN BROTHERS!
BUT BARON DE HUET'S NEVER HA A BROTHER!
OFFICIALLY NO, BUT MAUD AND I SAW THEM SIDE-BY-SIDE. YOU CAN TAKE MY WORD FOR IT. ONE ACTS OUT IN THE OPEN, THE OTHER IN THE SHADOWS.
I SHOULD HAVE FINISHED OFF THAT BARON FROM THE START! I'M FURIOUS! HE LIED TO US REPEATEDLY! THEY WERE THERE FOR THE RING, I'M SURE OF IT!
INDEED, THE KING ALLOWED HIM TO RECLAIM A "FAMILY JEWEL."
FINE, THEY HAVE THE RING. WE'LL TO HIS HOME TOMORR TO RECOVER IT.
IT WILL, HOWEVER, BE DIFFICULT TO SEE HIM.
WHY IS THAT?
I OVERHEARD HIS CONVERSATION WITH THE KING, AND THE BARON IS ABOUT TO LEAVE ON A LONG TRIP.
HE MUST SURELY BE DEPARTING FOR ISTANBUL! THEY HAVE THE NOTEBOOK AND THE RING. NOTHING'S KEEPING THEM HERE NOW! WE MUST STOP THEM!

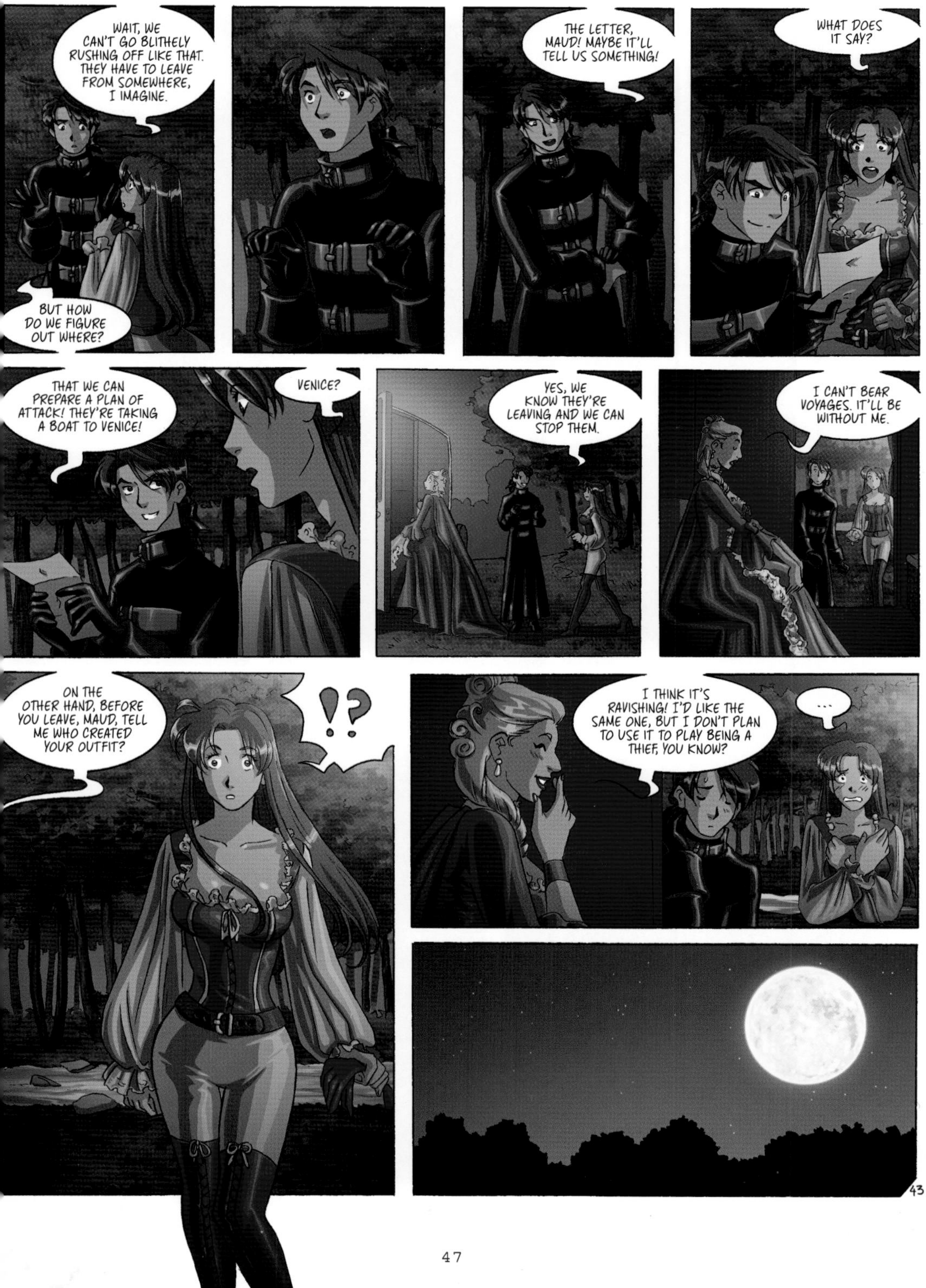
WAIT, WE CAN'T GO BLITHELY RUSHING OFF LIKE THAT. THEY HAVE TO LEAVE FROM SOMEWHERE, I IMAGINE.
BUT HOW DO WE FIGURE OUT WHERE?
THE LETTER, MAUD! MAYBE IT'LL TELL US SOMETHING!
WHAT DOES IT SAY?
THAT WE CAN PREPARE A PLAN OF ATTACK! THEY'RE TAKING A BOAT TO VENICE!
VENICE?
YES, WE KNOW THEY'RE LEAVING AND WE CAN STOP THEM.
I CAN'T BEAR VOYAGES. IT'LL BE WITHOUT ME.
ON THE OTHER HAND, BEFORE YOU LEAVE, MAUD, TELL ME WHO CREATED YOUR OUTFIT?
!?
I THINK IT'S RAVISHING! I'D LIKE THE SAME ONE, BUT I DON'T PLAN TO USE IT TO PLAY BEING A THIEF, YOU KNOW?
...
43

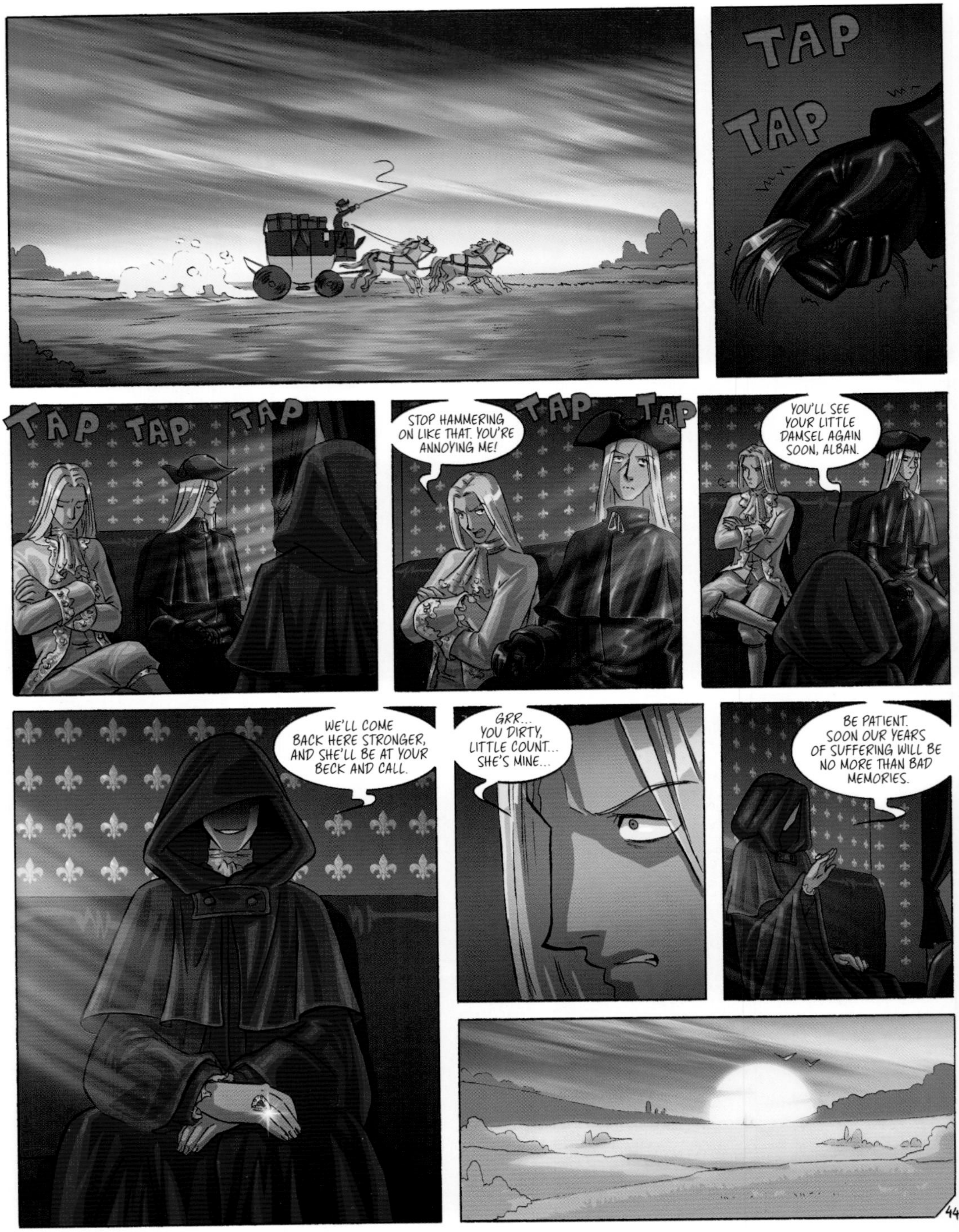
TAP
TAP
TAP TAP TAP
TAP TAP
STOP HAMMERING ON LIKE THAT. YOU'RE ANNOYING ME!
YOU'LL SEE YOUR LITTLE DAMSEL AGAIN SOON, ALBAN.
WE'LL COME BACK HERE STRONGER, AND SHE'LL BE AT YOUR BECK AND CALL.
GRR... YOU DIRTY, LITTLE COUNT... SHE'S MINE...
BE PATIENT. SOON OUR YEARS OF SUFFERING WILL BE NO MORE THAN BAD MEMORIES.
44

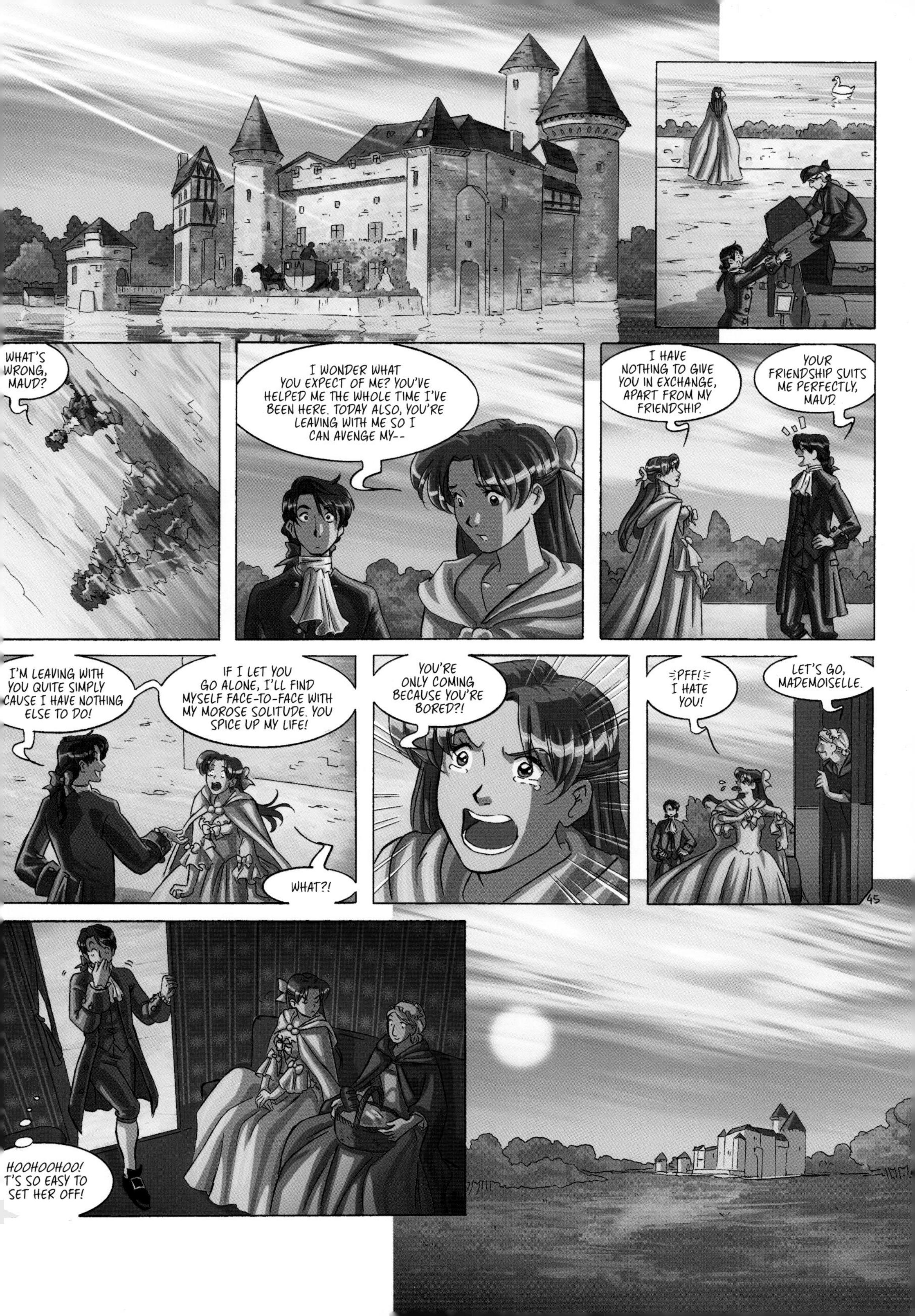
WHAT'S WRONG, MAUD?
I WONDER WHAT YOU EXPECT OF ME? YOU'VE HELPED ME THE WHOLE TIME I'VE BEEN HERE. TODAY ALSO, YOU'RE LEAVING WITH ME SO I CAN AVENGE MY--
I HAVE NOTHING TO GIVE YOU IN EXCHANGE, APART FROM MY FRIENDSHIP.
YOUR FRIENDSHIP SUITS ME PERFECTLY, MAUD.
I'M LEAVING WITH YOU QUITE SIMPLY CAUSE I HAVE NOTHING ELSE TO DO!
IF I LET YOU GO ALONE, I'LL FIND MYSELF FACE-TO-FACE WITH MY MOROSE SOLITUDE. YOU SPICE UP MY LIFE!
WHAT?!
YOU'RE ONLY COMING BECAUSE YOU'RE BORED?!
PFF! I HATE YOU!
LET'S GO, MADEMOISELLE.
HOOHOOHOO! IT'S SO EASY TO SET HER OFF!

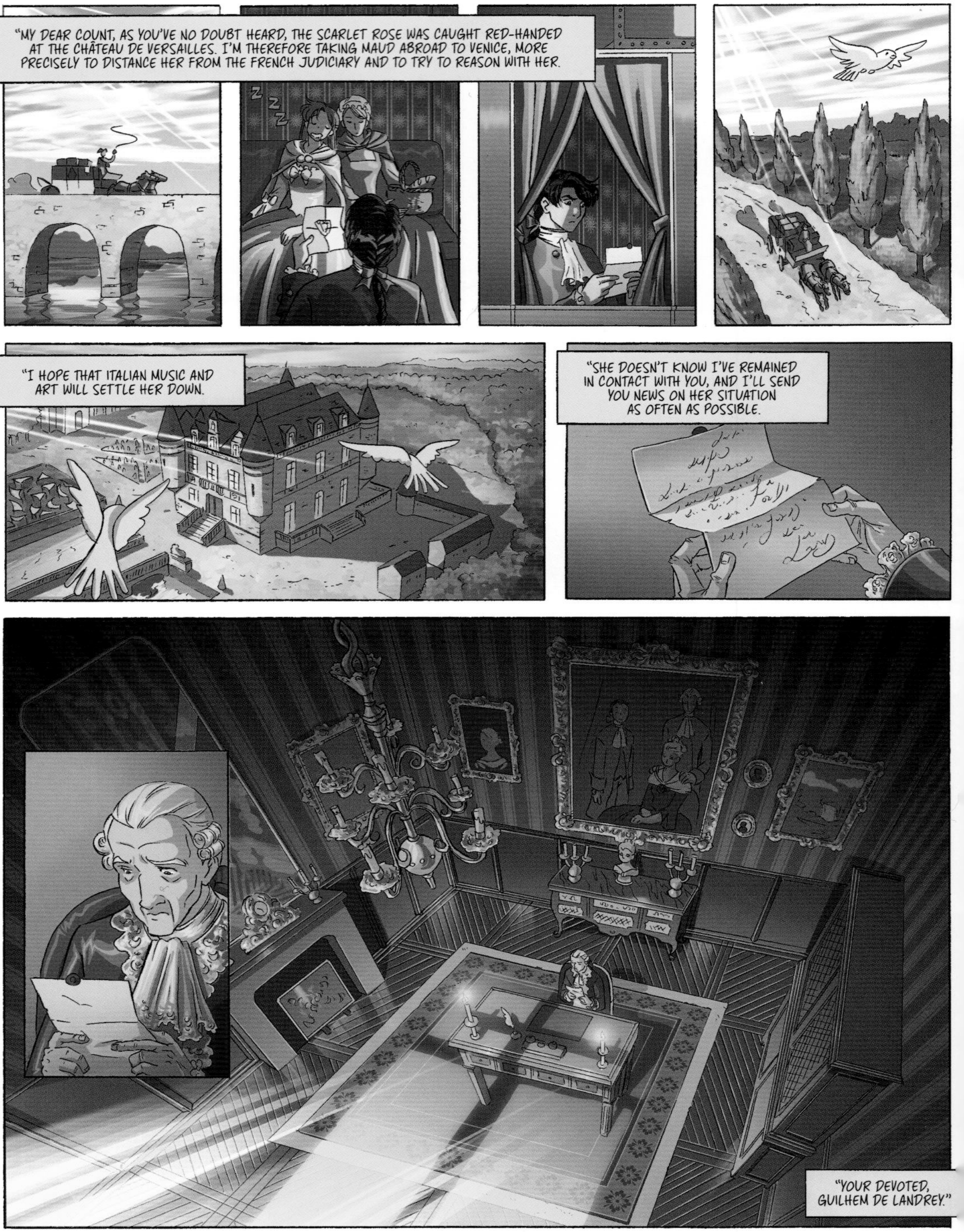
"MY DEAR COUNT, AS YOU'VE NO DOUBT HEARD, THE SCARLET ROSE WAS CAUGHT RED-HANDED AT THE CHÂTEAU DE VERSAILLES. I'M THEREFORE TAKING MAUD ABROAD TO VENICE, MORE PRECISELY TO DISTANCE HER FROM THE FRENCH JUDICIARY AND TO TRY TO REASON WITH HER.
ZZZ
"I HOPE THAT ITALIAN MUSIC AND ART WILL SETTLE HER DOWN.
"SHE DOESN'T KNOW I'VE REMAINED IN CONTACT WITH YOU, AND I'LL SEND YOU NEWS ON HER SITUATION AS OFTEN AS POSSIBLE.
"YOUR DEVOTED, GUILHEM DE LANDREY."

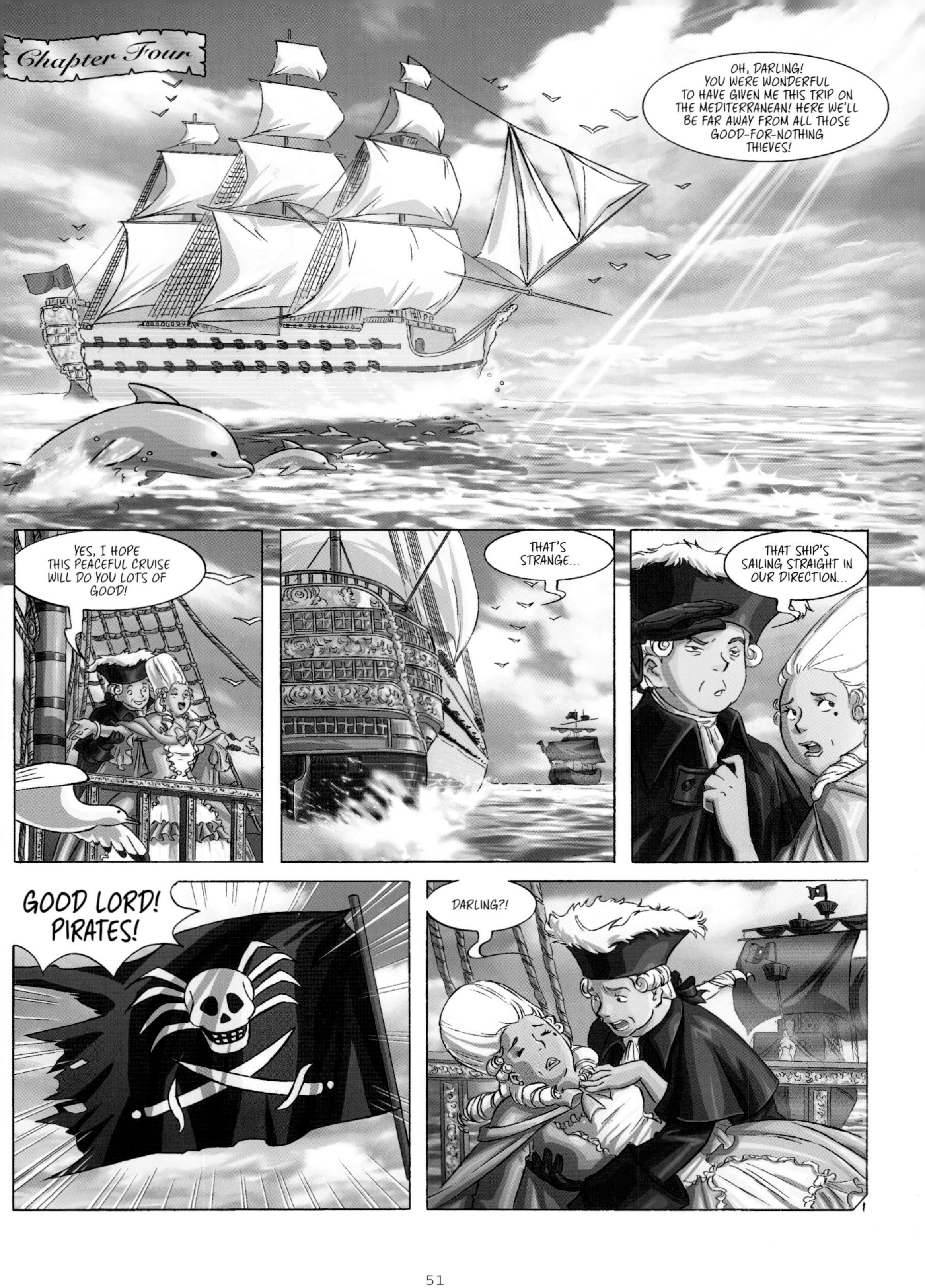
Chapter Four
OH, DARLING! YOU WERE WONDERFUL TO HAVE GIVEN ME THIS TRIP ON THE MEDITERRANEAN! HERE WE'LL BE FAR AWAY FROM ALL THOSE GOOD-FOR-NOTHING THIEVES!
YES, I HOPE THIS PEACEFUL CRUISE WILL DO YOU LOTS OF GOOD!
THAT'S STRANGE...
THAT SHIP'S SAILING STRAIGHT IN OUR DIRECTION...
GOOD LORD! PIRATES!
DARLING?!

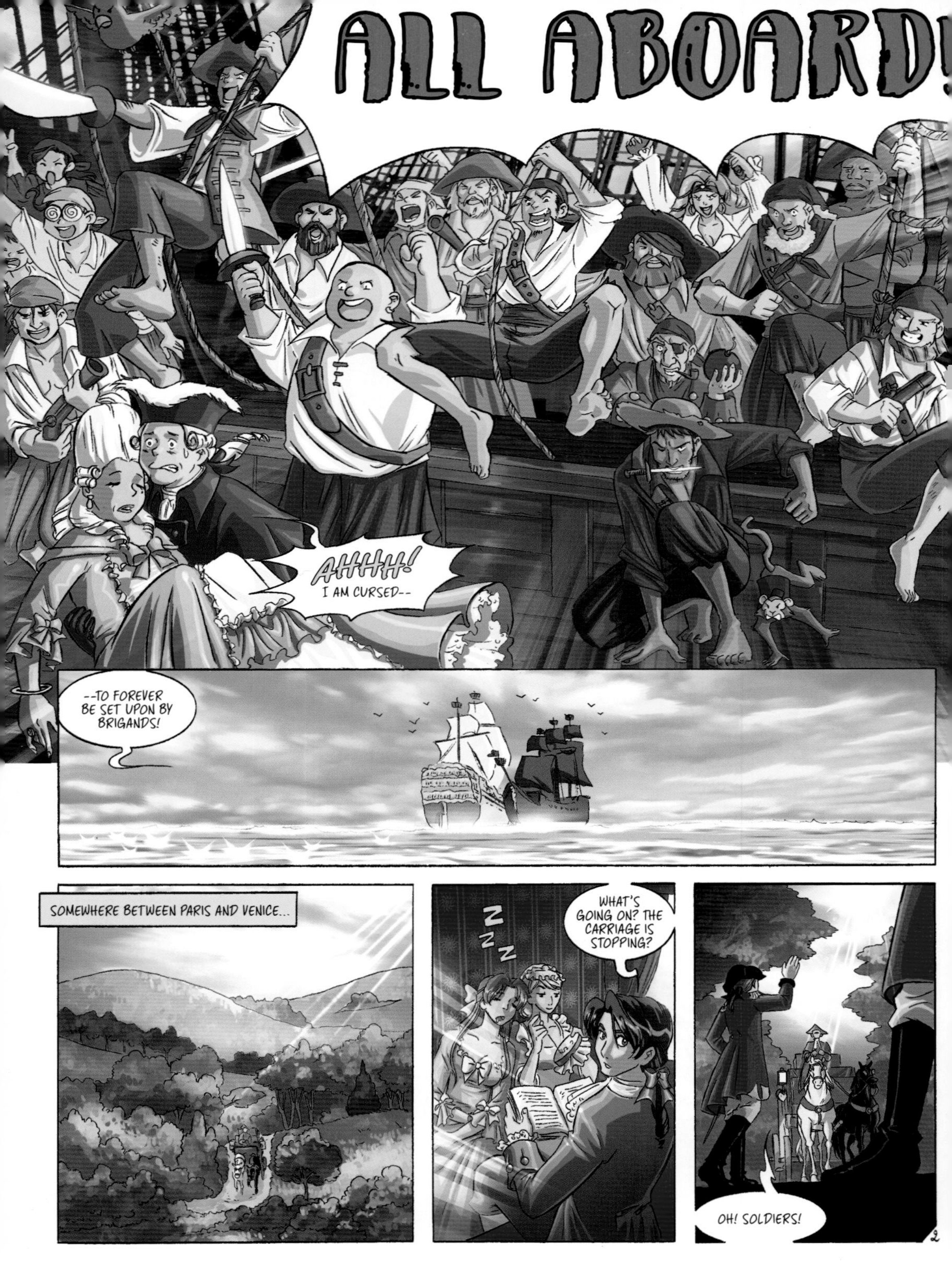
ALL ABOARD!
AHHH! I AM CURSED--
--TO FOREVER BE SET UPON BY BRIGANDS!
SOMEWHERE BETWEEN PARIS AND VENICE...
Z Z Z
WHAT'S GOING ON? THE CARRIAGE IS STOPPING?
OH! SOLDIERS!

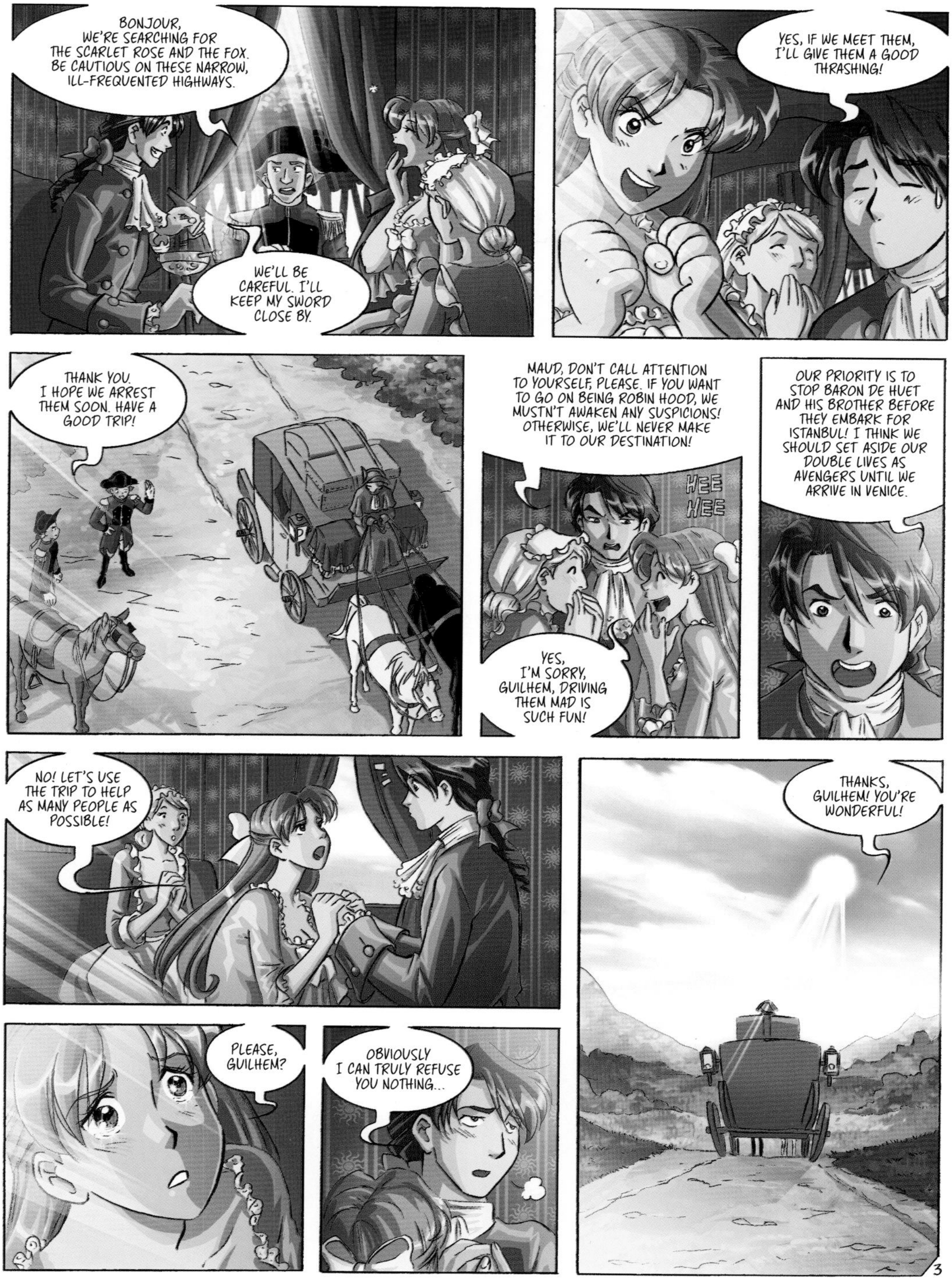
BONJOUR, WE'RE SEARCHING FOR THE SCARLET ROSE AND THE FOX. BE CAUTIOUS ON THESE NARROW, ILL-FREQUENTED HIGHWAYS.
WE'LL BE CAREFUL. I'LL KEEP MY SWORD CLOSE BY.
YES, IF WE MEET THEM, I'LL GIVE THEM A GOOD THRASHING!
THANK YOU. I HOPE WE ARREST THEM SOON. HAVE A GOOD TRIP!
MAUD, DON'T CALL ATTENTION TO YOURSELF, PLEASE. IF YOU WANT TO GO ON BEING ROBIN HOOD, WE MUSTN'T AWAKEN ANY SUSPICIONS! OTHERWISE, WE'LL NEVER MAKE IT TO OUR DESTINATION!
HEE HEE
YES, I'M SORRY, GUILHEM, DRIVING THEM MAD IS SUCH FUN!
OUR PRIORITY IS TO STOP BARON DE HUET AND HIS BROTHER BEFORE THEY EMBARK FOR ISTANBUL! I THINK WE SHOULD SET ASIDE OUR DOUBLE LIVES AS AVENGERS UNTIL WE ARRIVE IN VENICE.
NO! LET'S USE THE TRIP TO HELP AS MANY PEOPLE AS POSSIBLE!
PLEASE, GUILHEM?
OBVIOUSLY I CAN TRULY REFUSE YOU NOTHING...
THANKS, GUILHEM! YOU'RE WONDERFUL!
3

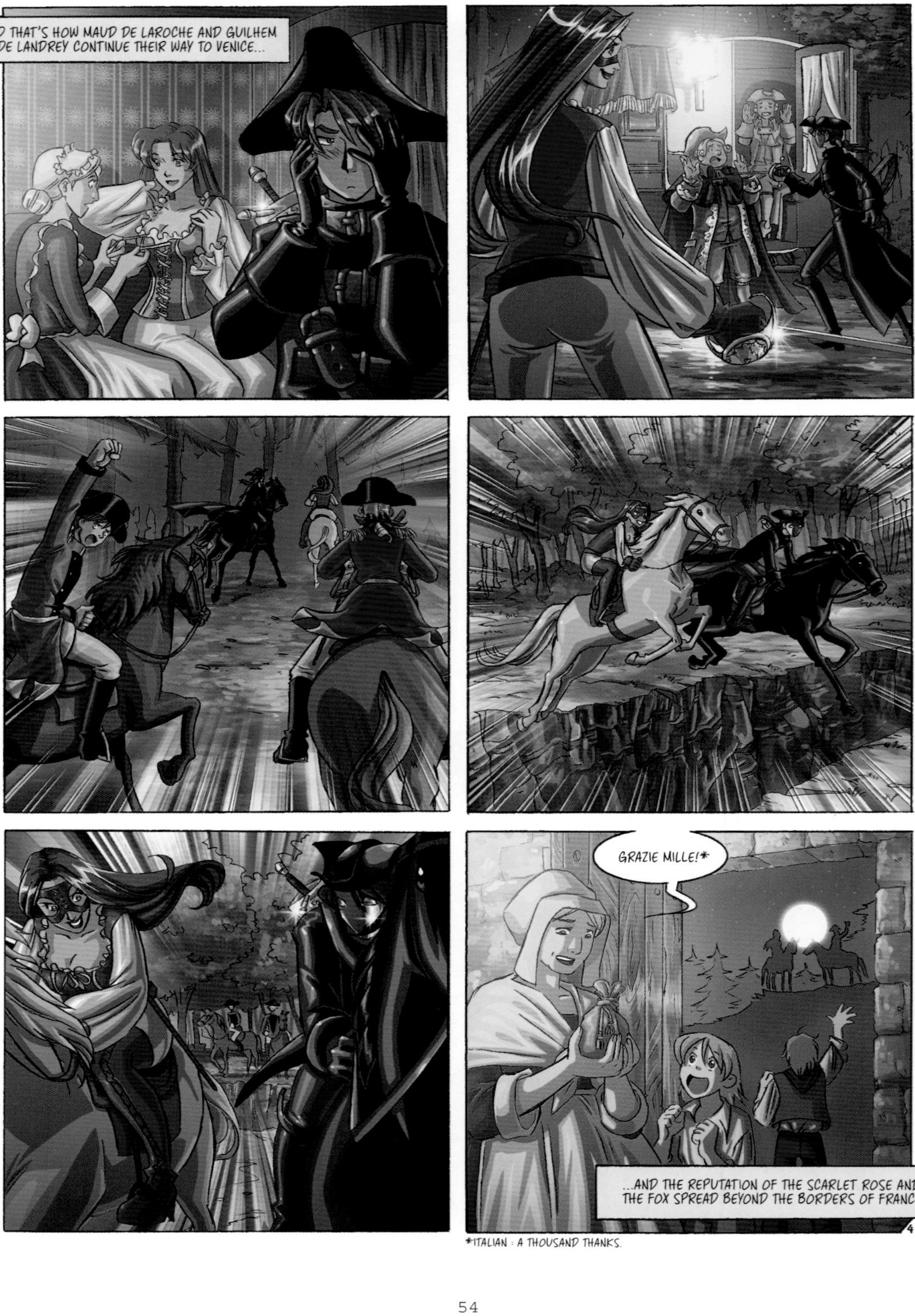
AND THAT'S HOW MAUD DE LAROCHE AND GUILHEM DE LANDREY CONTINUE THEIR WAY TO VENICE...
GRAZIE MILLE!*
...AND THE REPUTATION OF THE SCARLET ROSE AND THE FOX SPREAD BEYOND THE BORDERS OF FRANCE.
4

*ITALIAN : A THOUSAND THANKS.

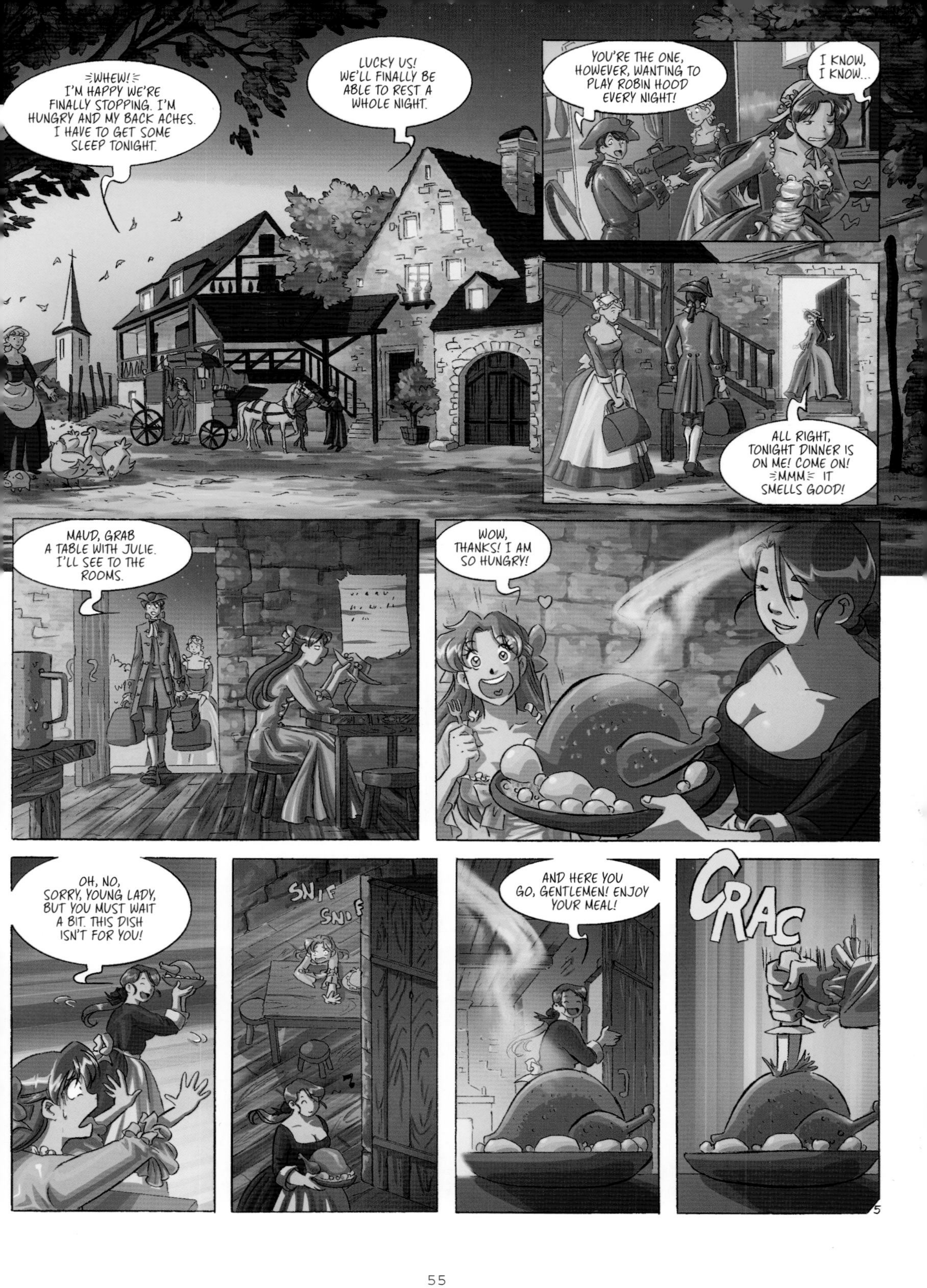

≡WHEW!≡ I'M HAPPY WE'RE FINALLY STOPPING. I'M HUNGRY AND MY BACK ACHES. I HAVE TO GET SOME SLEEP TONIGHT.
LUCKY US! WE'LL FINALLY BE ABLE TO REST A WHOLE NIGHT.
YOU'RE THE ONE, HOWEVER, WANTING TO PLAY ROBIN HOOD EVERY NIGHT!
I KNOW, I KNOW...
ALL RIGHT, TONIGHT DINNER IS ON ME! COME ON! ≡MMM≡ IT SMELLS GOOD!
MAUD, GRAB A TABLE WITH JULIE. I'LL SEE TO THE ROOMS.
WOW, THANKS! I AM SO HUNGRY!
OH, NO, SORRY, YOUNG LADY, BUT YOU MUST WAIT A BIT. THIS DISH ISN'T FOR YOU!
SNIF
SNIF
AND HERE YOU GO, GENTLEMEN! ENJOY YOUR MEAL!
CRAC
5

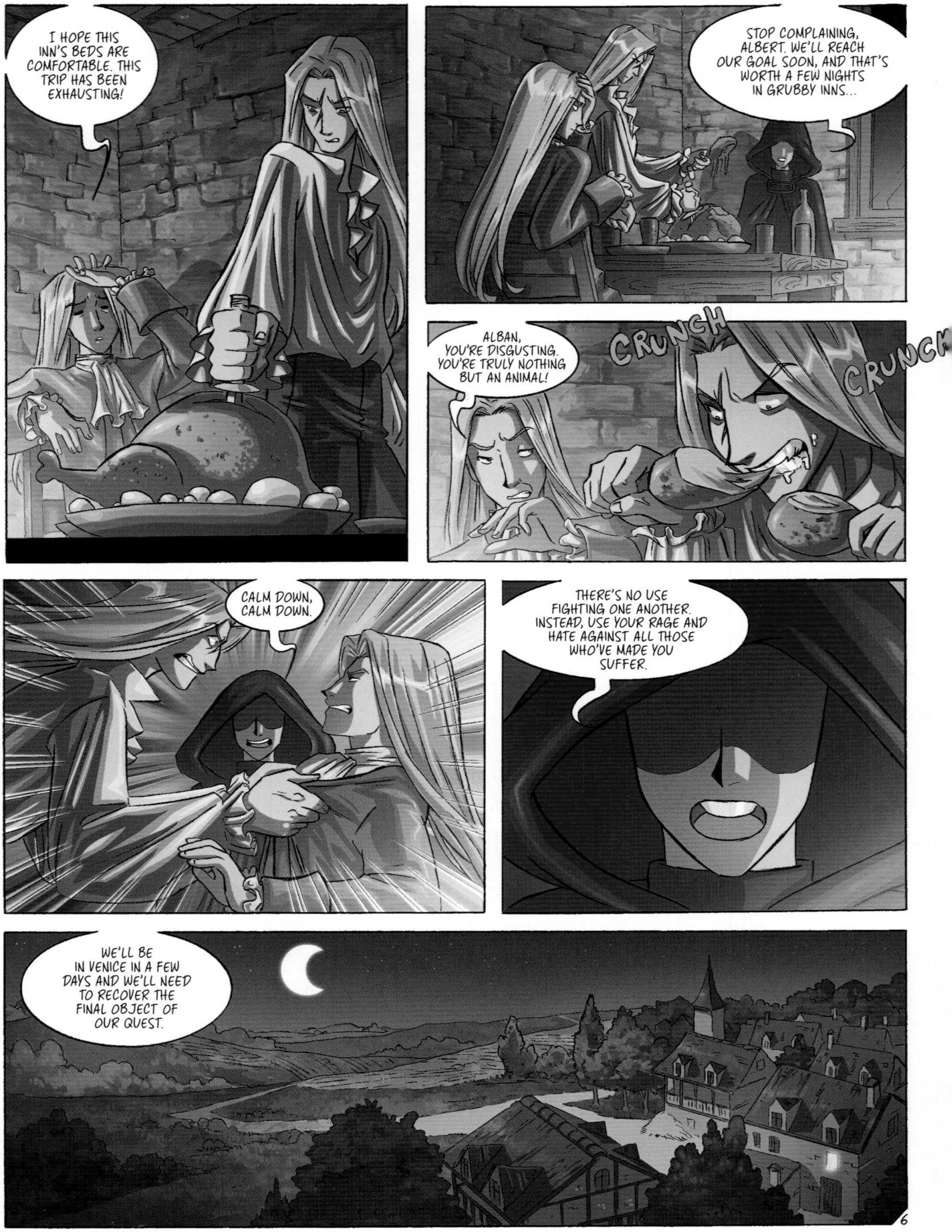
I HOPE THIS INN'S BEDS ARE COMFORTABLE. THIS TRIP HAS BEEN EXHAUSTING!
STOP COMPLAINING, ALBERT. WE'LL REACH OUR GOAL SOON, AND THAT'S WORTH A FEW NIGHTS IN GRUBBY INNS...
ALBAN, YOU'RE DISGUSTING. YOU'RE TRULY NOTHING BUT AN ANIMAL!
CRUNCH
CRUNCH
CALM DOWN, CALM DOWN.
THERE'S NO USE FIGHTING ONE ANOTHER. INSTEAD, USE YOUR RAGE AND HATE AGAINST ALL THOSE WHO'VE MADE YOU SUFFER.
WE'LL BE IN VENICE IN A FEW DAYS AND WE'LL NEED TO RECOVER THE FINAL OBJECT OF OUR QUEST.
6

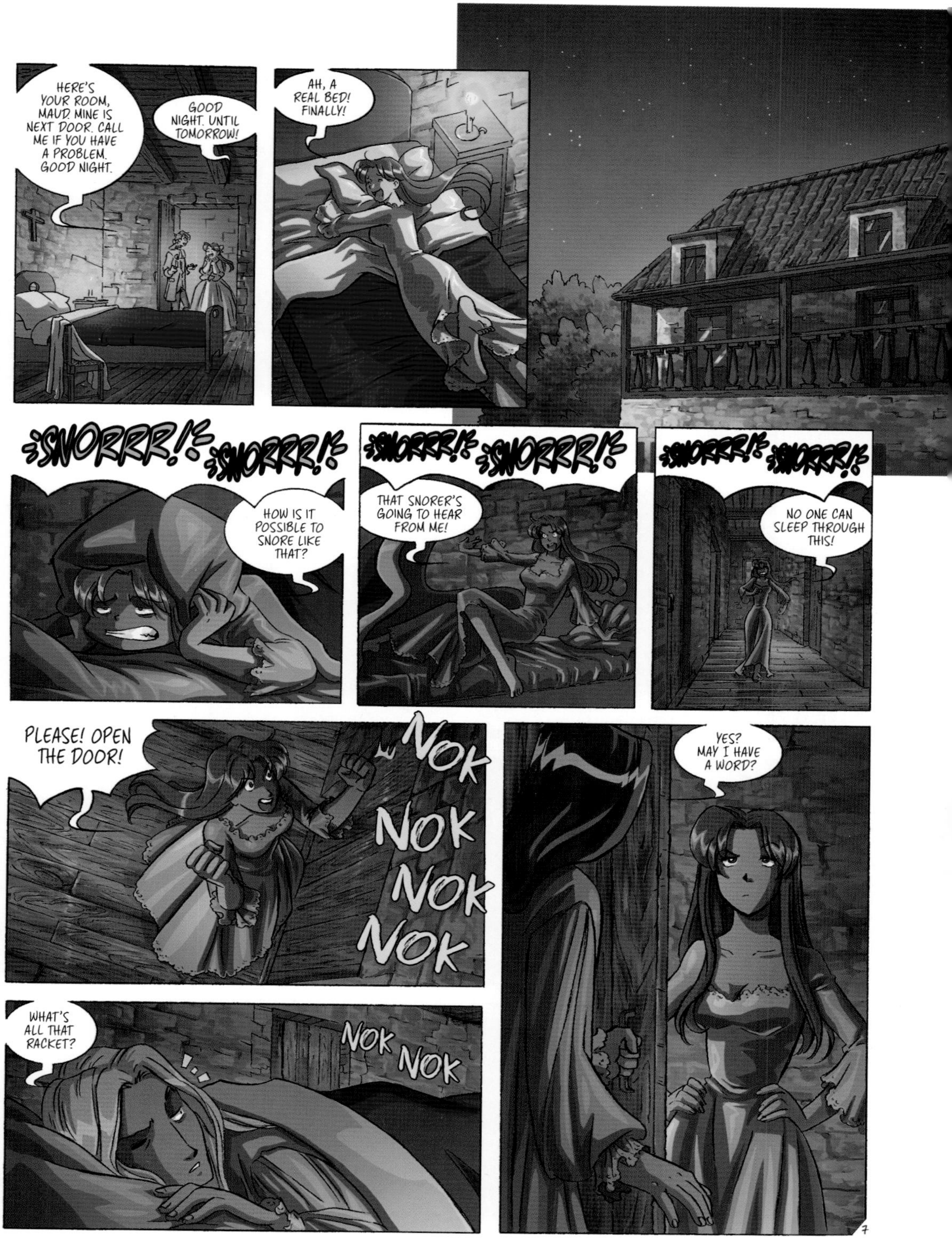
HERE'S YOUR ROOM, MAUD. MINE IS NEXT DOOR. CALL ME IF YOU HAVE A PROBLEM. GOOD NIGHT.
GOOD NIGHT. UNTIL TOMORROW!
AH, A REAL BED! FINALLY!
SNORRR! SNORRR!
HOW IS IT POSSIBLE TO SNORE LIKE THAT?
SNORRR! SNORRR!
THAT SNORER'S GOING TO HEAR FROM ME!
SNORRR! SNORRR!
NO ONE CAN SLEEP THROUGH THIS!
PLEASE! OPEN THE DOOR!
NOK NOK NOK NOK
WHAT'S ALL THAT RACKET?
NOK NOK
YES? MAY I HAVE A WORD?
7

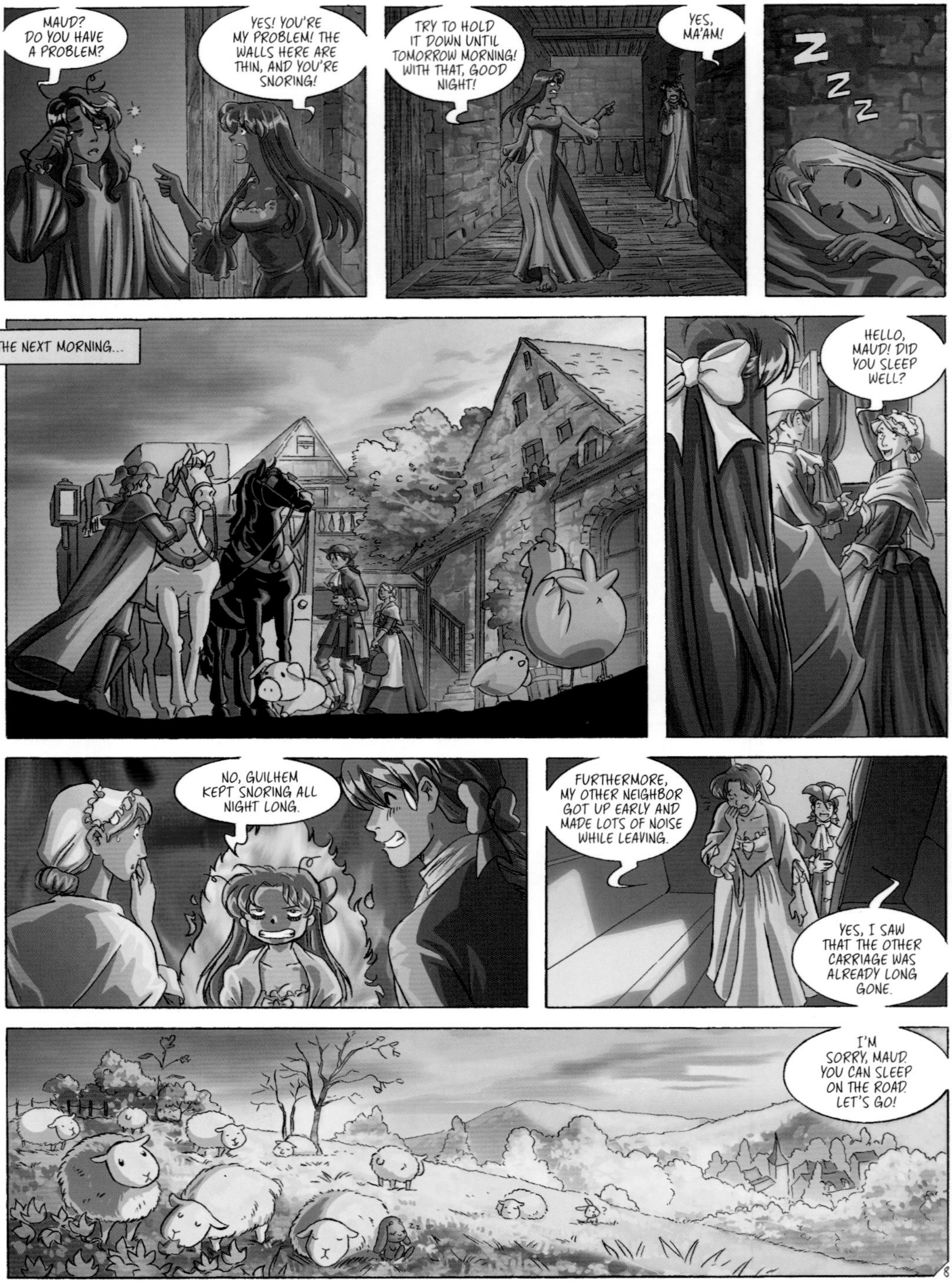
MAUD? DO YOU HAVE A PROBLEM?
YES! YOU'RE MY PROBLEM! THE WALLS HERE ARE THIN, AND YOU'RE SNORING!
TRY TO HOLD IT DOWN UNTIL TOMORROW MORNING! WITH THAT, GOOD NIGHT!
YES, MA'AM!
Z Z Z
THE NEXT MORNING...
HELLO, MAUD! DID YOU SLEEP WELL?
NO, GUILHEM KEPT SNORING ALL NIGHT LONG.
FURTHERMORE, MY OTHER NEIGHBOR GOT UP EARLY AND MADE LOTS OF NOISE WHILE LEAVING.
YES, I SAW THAT THE OTHER CARRIAGE WAS ALREADY LONG GONE.
I'M SORRY, MAUD. YOU CAN SLEEP ON THE ROAD. LET'S GO!
8

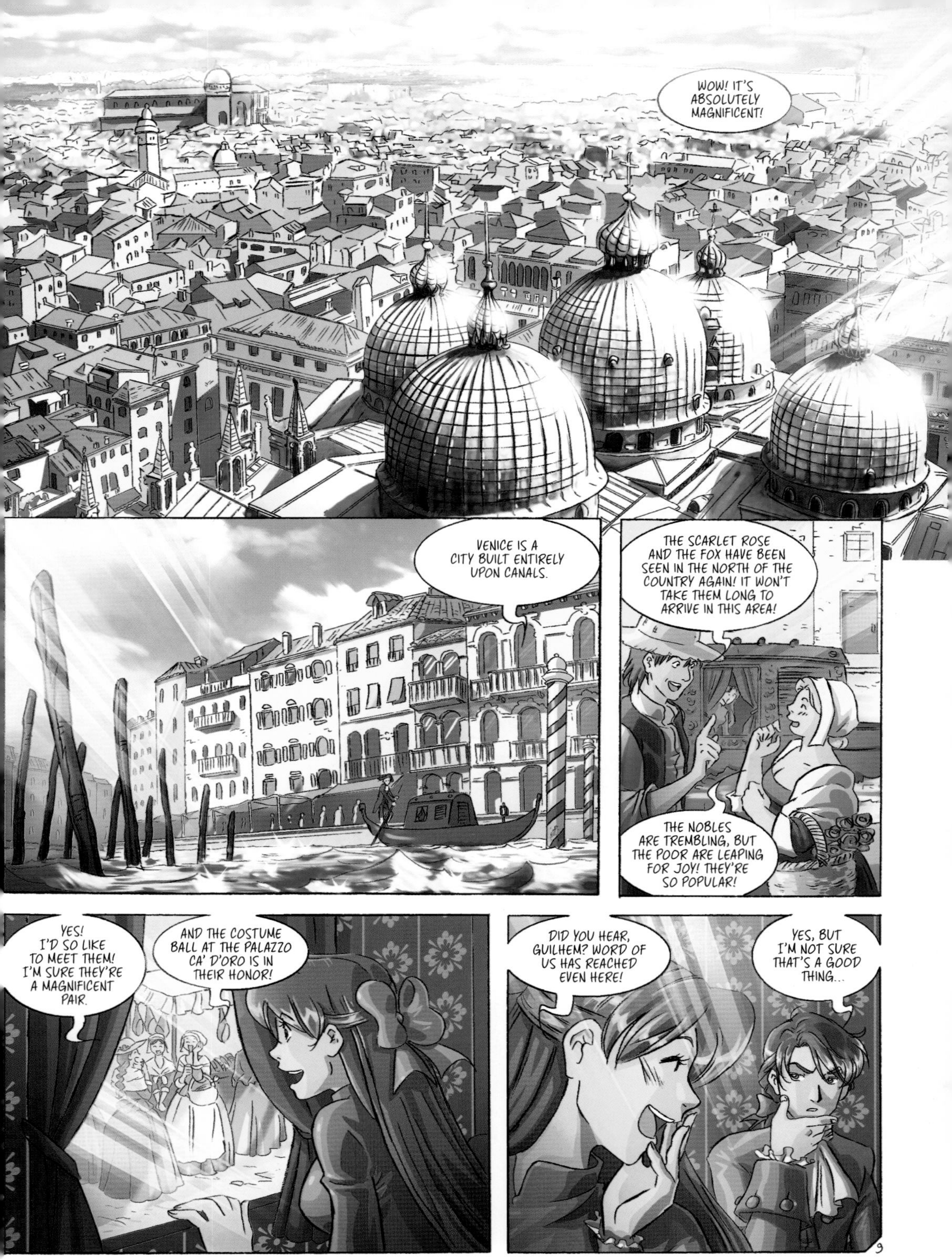

WOW! IT'S ABSOLUTELY MAGNIFICENT!
VENICE IS A CITY BUILT ENTIRELY UPON CANALS.
THE SCARLET ROSE AND THE FOX HAVE BEEN SEEN IN THE NORTH OF THE COUNTRY AGAIN! IT WON'T TAKE THEM LONG TO ARRIVE IN THIS AREA!
THE NOBLES ARE TREMBLING, BUT THE POOR ARE LEAPING FOR JOY! THEY'RE SO POPULAR!
YES! I'D SO LIKE TO MEET THEM! I'M SURE THEY'RE A MAGNIFICENT PAIR.
AND THE COSTUME BALL AT THE PALAZZO CA' D'ORO IS IN THEIR HONOR!
DID YOU HEAR, GUILHEM? WORD OF US HAS REACHED EVEN HERE!
YES, BUT I'M NOT SURE THAT'S A GOOD THING...
9

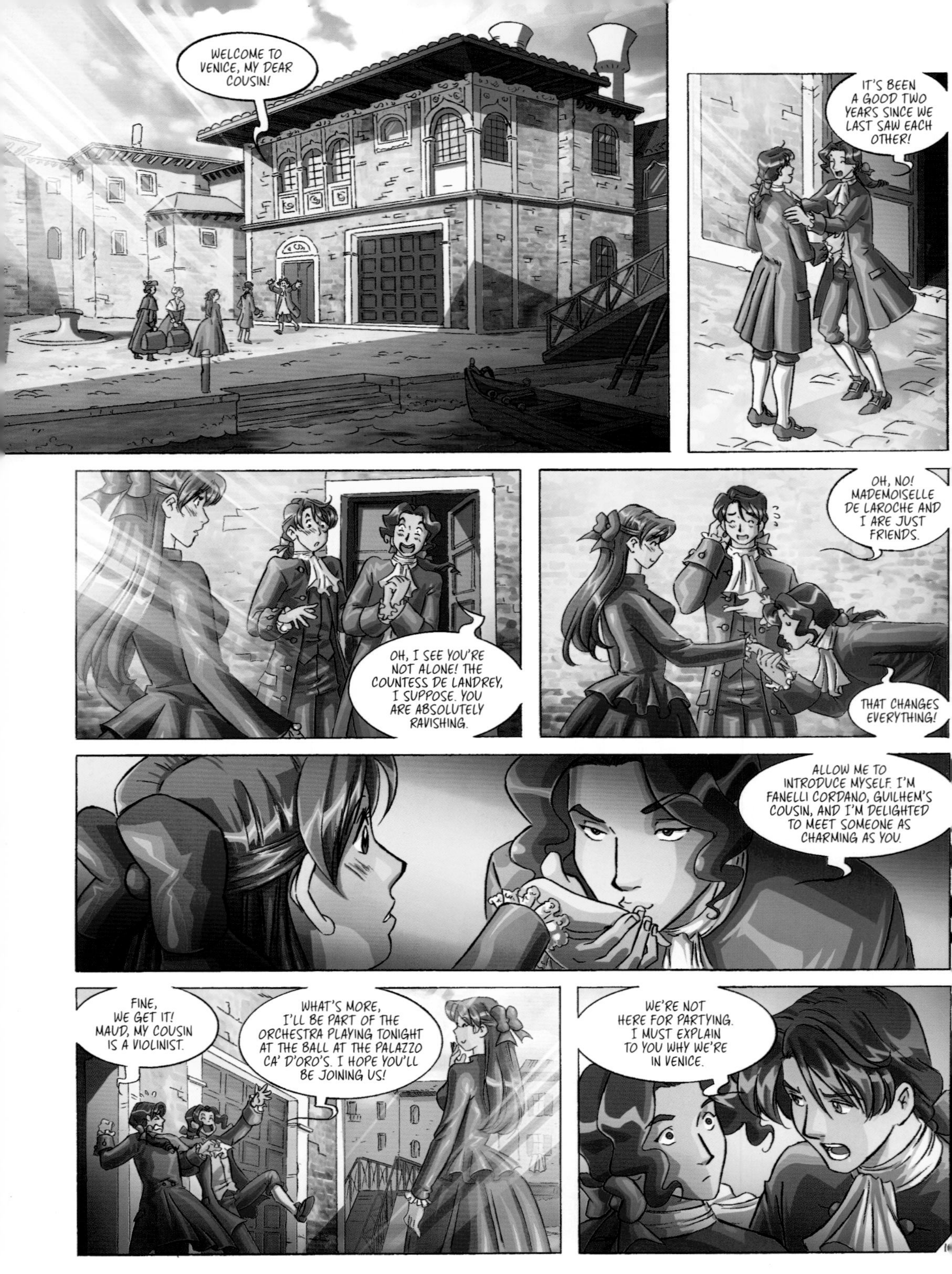
WELCOME TO VENICE, MY DEAR COUSIN!
IT'S BEEN A GOOD TWO YEARS SINCE WE LAST SAW EACH OTHER!
OH, I SEE YOU'RE NOT ALONE! THE COUNTESS DE LANDREY, I SUPPOSE. YOU ARE ABSOLUTELY RAVISHING.
OH, NO! MADEMOISELLE DE LAROCHE AND I ARE JUST FRIENDS.
THAT CHANGES EVERYTHING!
ALLOW ME TO INTRODUCE MYSELF. I'M FANELLI CORDANO, GUILHEM'S COUSIN, AND I'M DELIGHTED TO MEET SOMEONE AS CHARMING AS YOU.
FINE, WE GET IT! MAUD, MY COUSIN IS A VIOLINIST.
WHAT'S MORE, I'LL BE PART OF THE ORCHESTRA PLAYING TONIGHT AT THE BALL AT THE PALAZZO CA' D'ORO'S. I HOPE YOU'LL BE JOINING US!
WE'RE NOT HERE FOR PARTYING. I MUST EXPLAIN TO YOU WHY WE'RE IN VENICE.

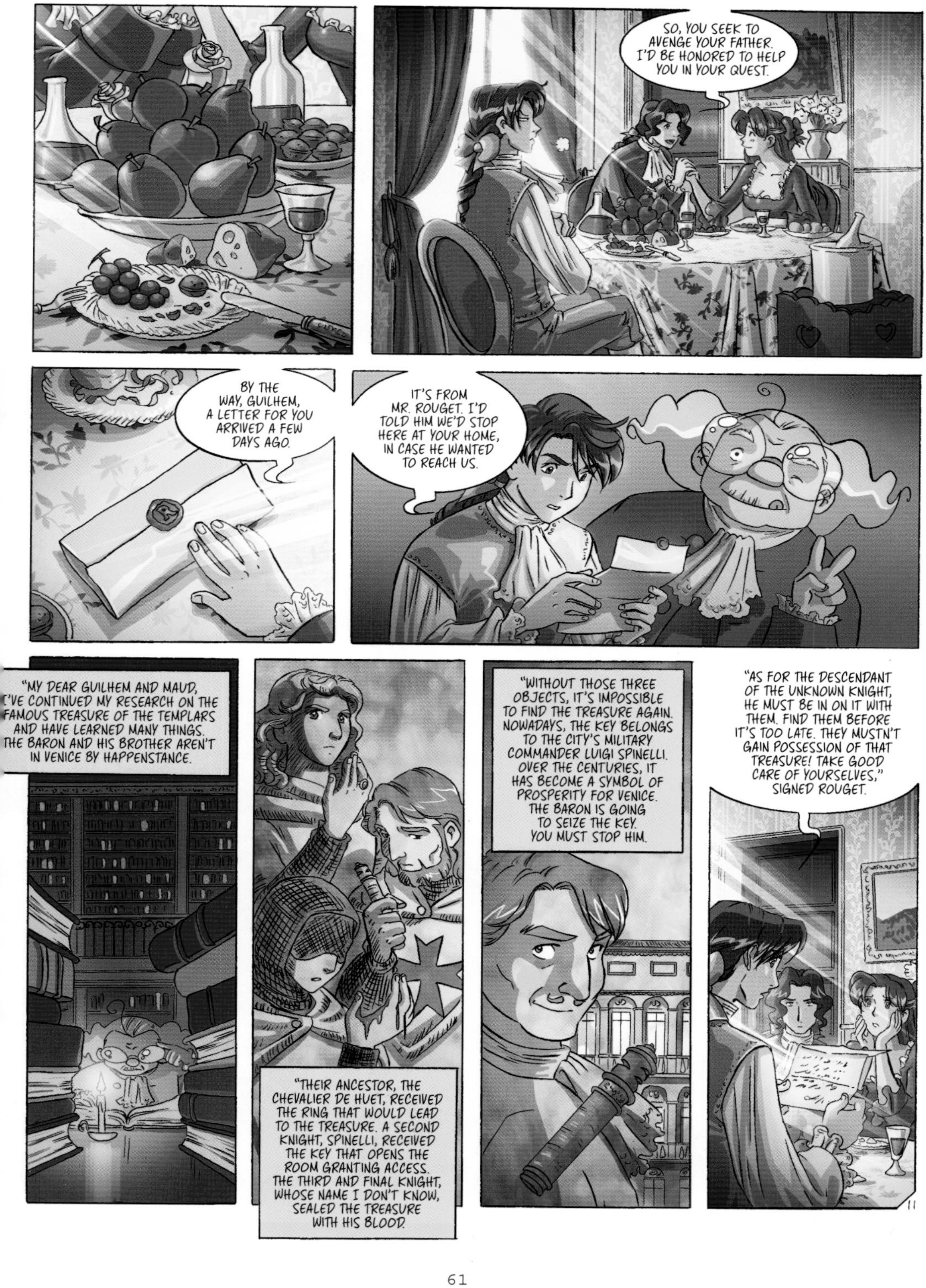

SO, YOU SEEK TO AVENGE YOUR FATHER. I'D BE HONORED TO HELP YOU IN YOUR QUEST.
BY THE WAY, GUILHEM, A LETTER FOR YOU ARRIVED A FEW DAYS AGO.
IT'S FROM MR. ROUGET. I'D TOLD HIM WE'D STOP HERE AT YOUR HOME, IN CASE HE WANTED TO REACH US.
"MY DEAR GUILHEM AND MAUD, I'VE CONTINUED MY RESEARCH ON THE FAMOUS TREASURE OF THE TEMPLARS AND HAVE LEARNED MANY THINGS. THE BARON AND HIS BROTHER AREN'T IN VENICE BY HAPPENSTANCE.
"THEIR ANCESTOR, THE CHEVALIER DE HUET, RECEIVED THE RING THAT WOULD LEAD TO THE TREASURE. A SECOND KNIGHT, SPINELLI, RECEIVED THE KEY THAT OPENS THE ROOM GRANTING ACCESS. THE THIRD AND FINAL KNIGHT, WHOSE NAME I DON'T KNOW, SEALED THE TREASURE WITH HIS BLOOD.
"WITHOUT THOSE THREE OBJECTS, IT'S IMPOSSIBLE TO FIND THE TREASURE AGAIN. NOWADAYS, THE KEY BELONGS TO THE CITY'S MILITARY COMMANDER LUIGI SPINELLI. OVER THE CENTURIES, IT HAS BECOME A SYMBOL OF PROSPERITY FOR VENICE. THE BARON IS GOING TO SEIZE THE KEY. YOU MUST STOP HIM.
"AS FOR THE DESCENDANT OF THE UNKNOWN KNIGHT, HE MUST BE IN ON IT WITH THEM. FIND THEM BEFORE IT'S TOO LATE. THEY MUSTN'T GAIN POSSESSION OF THAT TREASURE! TAKE GOOD CARE OF YOURSELVES," SIGNED ROUGET.
11

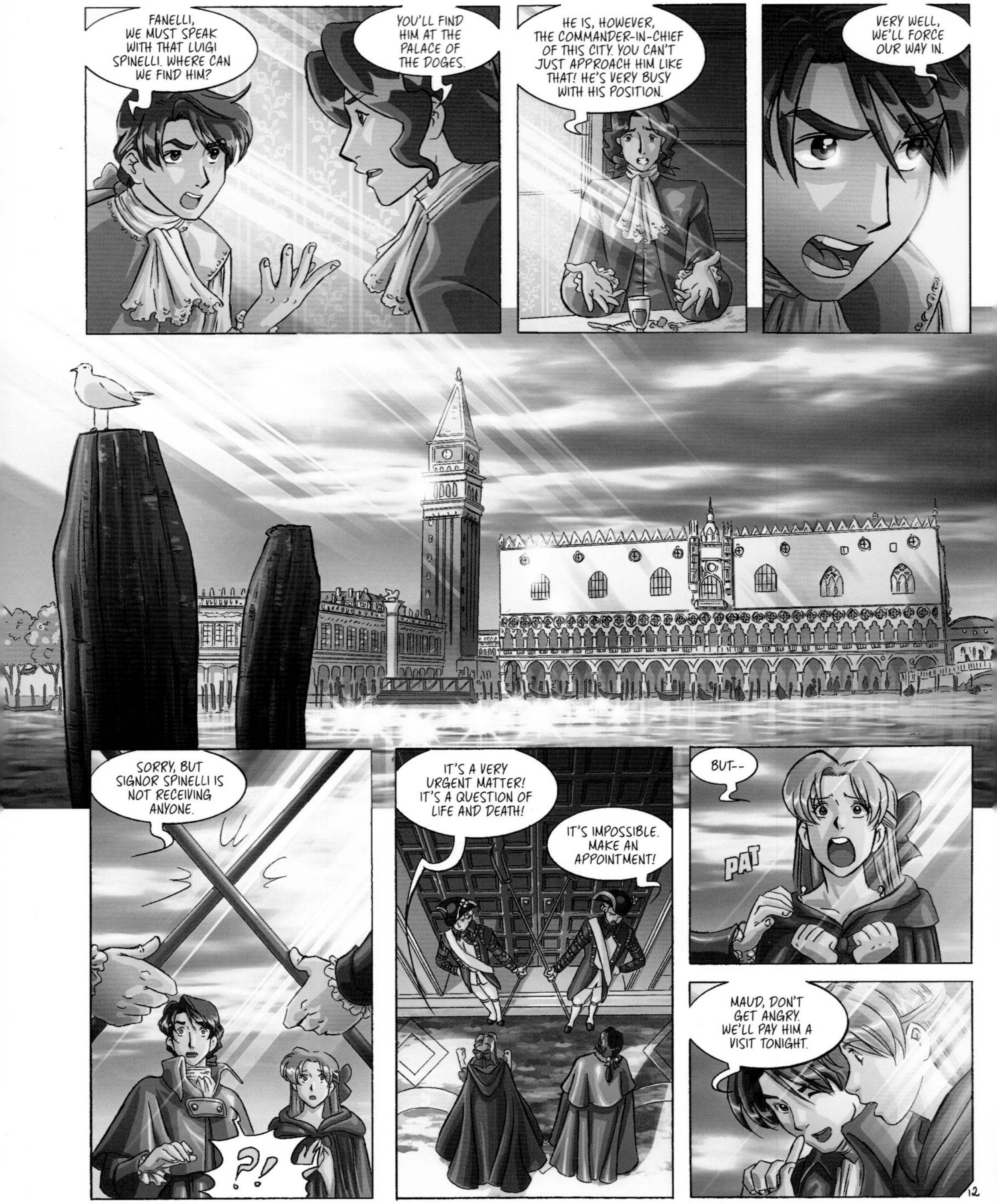
FANELLI, WE MUST SPEAK WITH THAT LUIGI SPINELLI. WHERE CAN WE FIND HIM?
YOU'LL FIND HIM AT THE PALACE OF THE DOGES.
HE IS, HOWEVER, THE COMMANDER-IN-CHIEF OF THIS CITY. YOU CAN'T JUST APPROACH HIM LIKE THAT! HE'S VERY BUSY WITH HIS POSITION.
VERY WELL, WE'LL FORCE OUR WAY IN.
SORRY, BUT SIGNOR SPINELLI IS NOT RECEIVING ANYONE.
?!
IT'S A VERY URGENT MATTER! IT'S A QUESTION OF LIFE AND DEATH!
IT'S IMPOSSIBLE. MAKE AN APPOINTMENT!
BUT--
PAT
MAUD, DON'T GET ANGRY. WE'LL PAY HIM A VISIT TONIGHT.
12

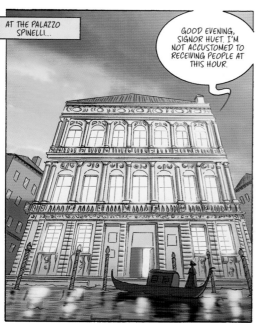

AT THE PALAZZO SPINELLI...

GOOD EVENING, SIGNOR HUET. I'M NOT ACCUSTOMED TO RECEIVING PEOPLE AT THIS HOUR.

AS I KNEW YOUR FATHER WELL, I'LL DO YOU A FAVOR. BE BRIEF, MY GUESTS AWAIT ME AT THE BALL.

THE SPINELLI KEY?!

SIGNOR SPINELLI, WE'RE HONORED YOU'VE ACCORDED US A BIT OF YOUR INVALUABLE TIME. I'LL GET STRAIGHT TO THE POINT. I'VE COME IN SEARCH OF THE SPINELLI KEY.

13

BUT WHY DO YOU WANT THAT KEY?

COME NOW, SIGNOR SPINELLI. YOU KNOW FULL WELL WHY WE WANT THAT KEY...

YOU KNOW ABOUT THE TREASURE?! THAT KEY'S BEEN UNDER THE PROTECTION OF THE SPINELLI FAMILY FOR CENTURIES!

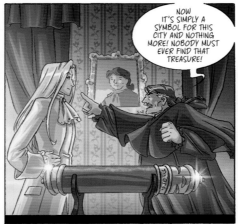

NOW IT'S SIMPLY A SYMBOL FOR THIS CITY AND NOTHING MORE! NOBODY MUST EVER FIND THAT TREASURE!

NEVER WILL YOU HAVE THAT KEY! I'M CALLING MY GUARDS!

!?

AAAAH!

TCHAC

SINCE YOU REFUSE TO GIVE IT TO US, WE'LL TAKE IT BY FORCE!

14

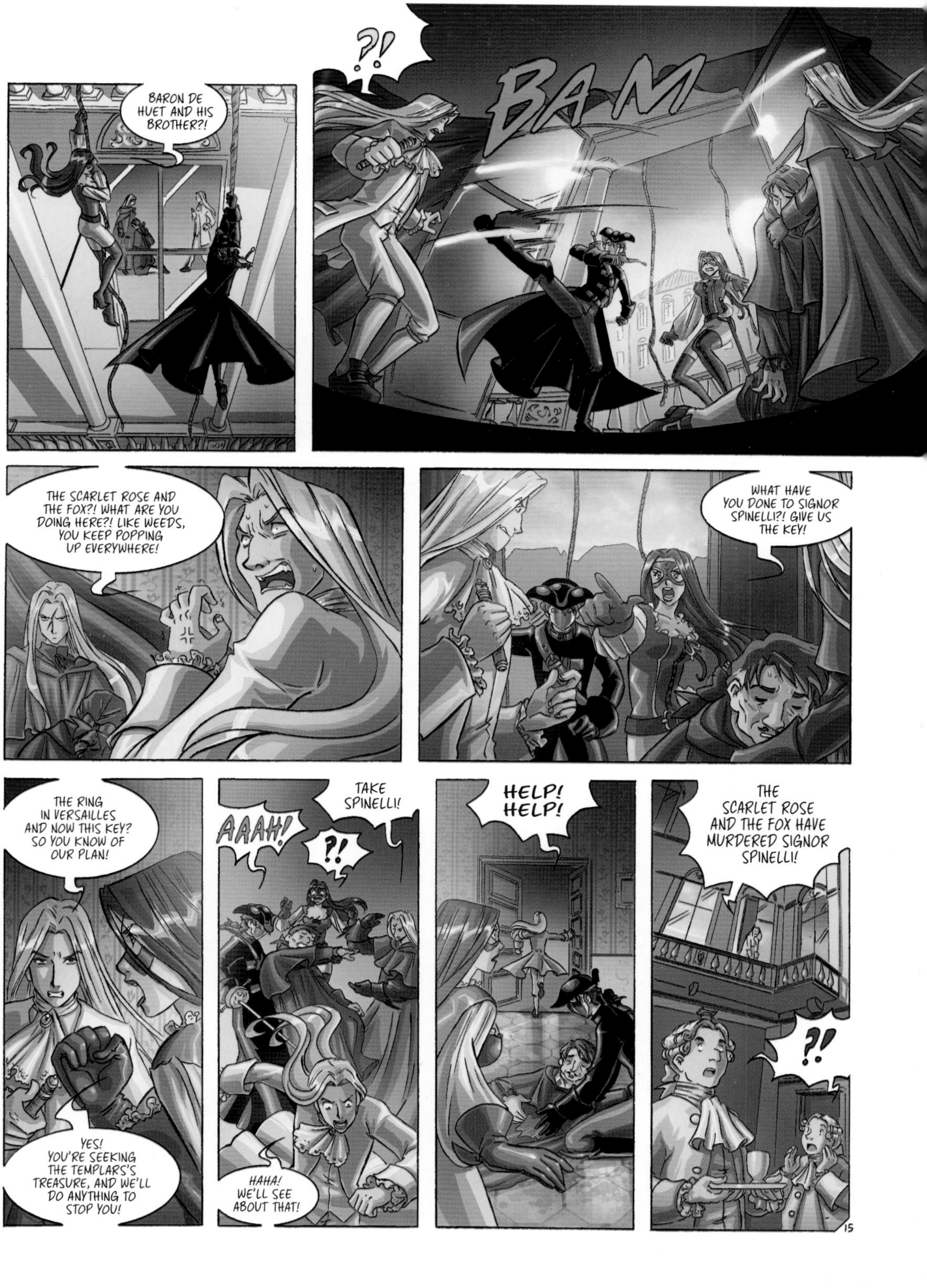

BARON DE HUET AND HIS BROTHER?!
?!
BAM
THE SCARLET ROSE AND THE FOX?! WHAT ARE YOU DOING HERE?! LIKE WEEDS, YOU KEEP POPPING UP EVERYWHERE!
WHAT HAVE YOU DONE TO SIGNOR SPINELLI?! GIVE US THE KEY!
THE RING IN VERSAILLES AND NOW THIS KEY? SO YOU KNOW OF OUR PLAN!
YES! YOU'RE SEEKING THE TEMPLARS'S TREASURE, AND WE'LL DO ANYTHING TO STOP YOU!
TAKE SPINELLI!
AAAH!
?!
HAHA! WE'LL SEE ABOUT THAT!
HELP! HELP!
THE SCARLET ROSE AND THE FOX HAVE MURDERED SIGNOR SPINELLI!
?!
15

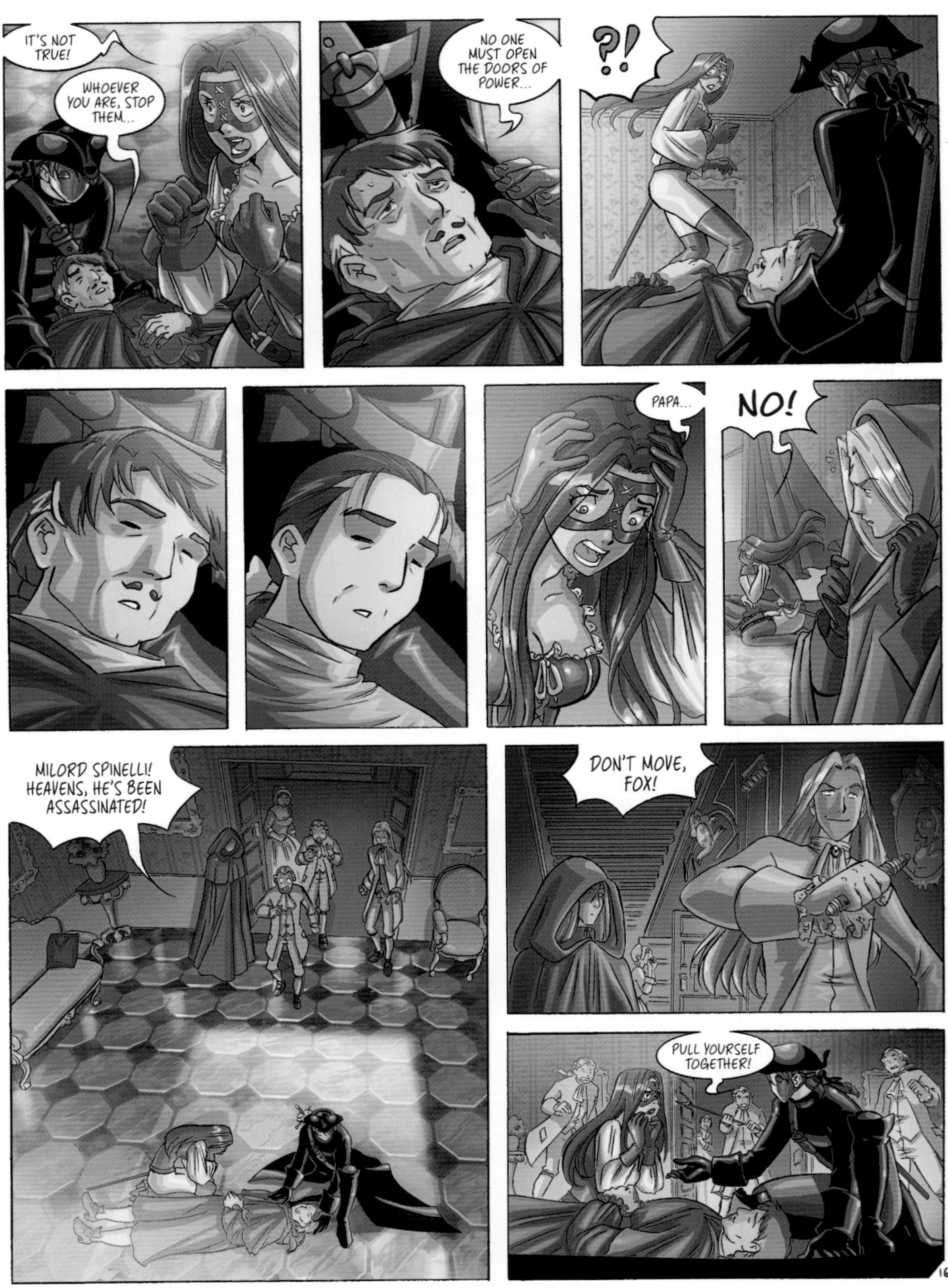
IT'S NOT TRUE!
WHOEVER YOU ARE, STOP THEM...
NO ONE MUST OPEN THE DOORS OF POWER...
?!
PAPA...
NO!
MILORD SPINELLI! HEAVENS, HE'S BEEN ASSASSINATED!
DON'T MOVE, FOX!
PULL YOURSELF TOGETHER!
16

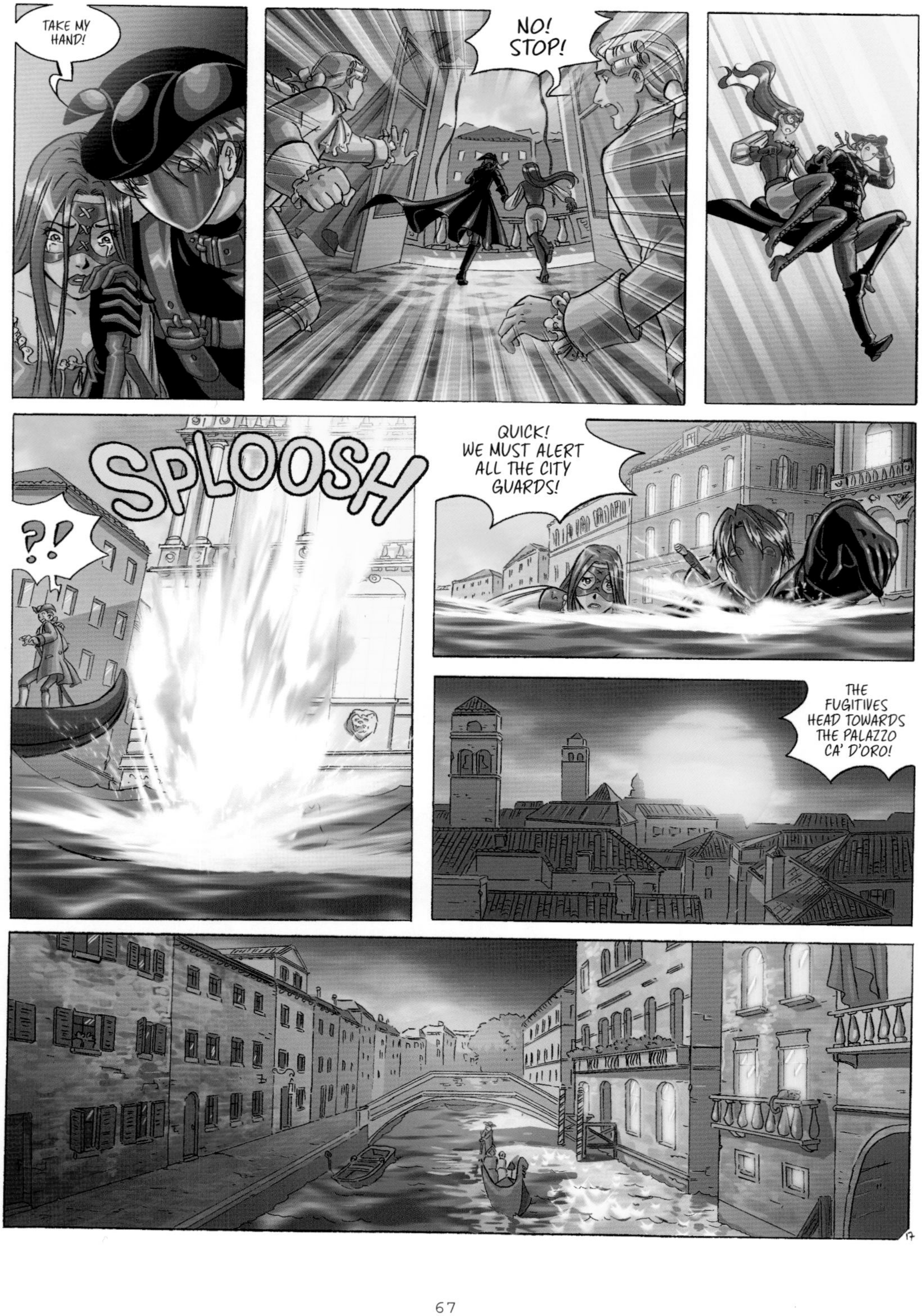
TAKE MY HAND!
NO! STOP!
SPLOOSH
?!
QUICK! WE MUST ALERT ALL THE CITY GUARDS!
THE FUGITIVES HEAD TOWARDS THE PALAZZO CA' D'ORO!
17

VERY WELL, YOU'VE SUCCEEDED. WE CAN RAISE ANCHOR.

WE ENCOUNTERED THE SCARLET ROSE AND THE FOX. THEY'RE AWARE OF OUR PLANS. I DON'T UNDERSTAND HOW THEY KNOW OF THE TREASURE'S EXISTENCE.

I RECOGNIZED HER. IT WAS MAUD DE LAROCHE!

WHAT?!

I'D RECOGNIZE THAT PERFUME ANYWHERE. AND THE MAN IS GUILHEM DE LANDREY.

WHAT A SURPRISE! AND I THOUGHT HE WAS ONLY A COMMON LIBERTINE. HE IS ALSO A HERO OF THE PEOPLE! NOW BOTH ACCUSED OF SPINELLI'S MURDER, AND VENICE WON'T LET THEM ESCAPE ALIVE! WE'RE RID OF THEM.

TOO BAD FOR YOU, MY FOPPISH BROTHER! YOUR PRINCESS WILL END UP WITH A ROPE AROUND HER NECK!

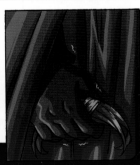

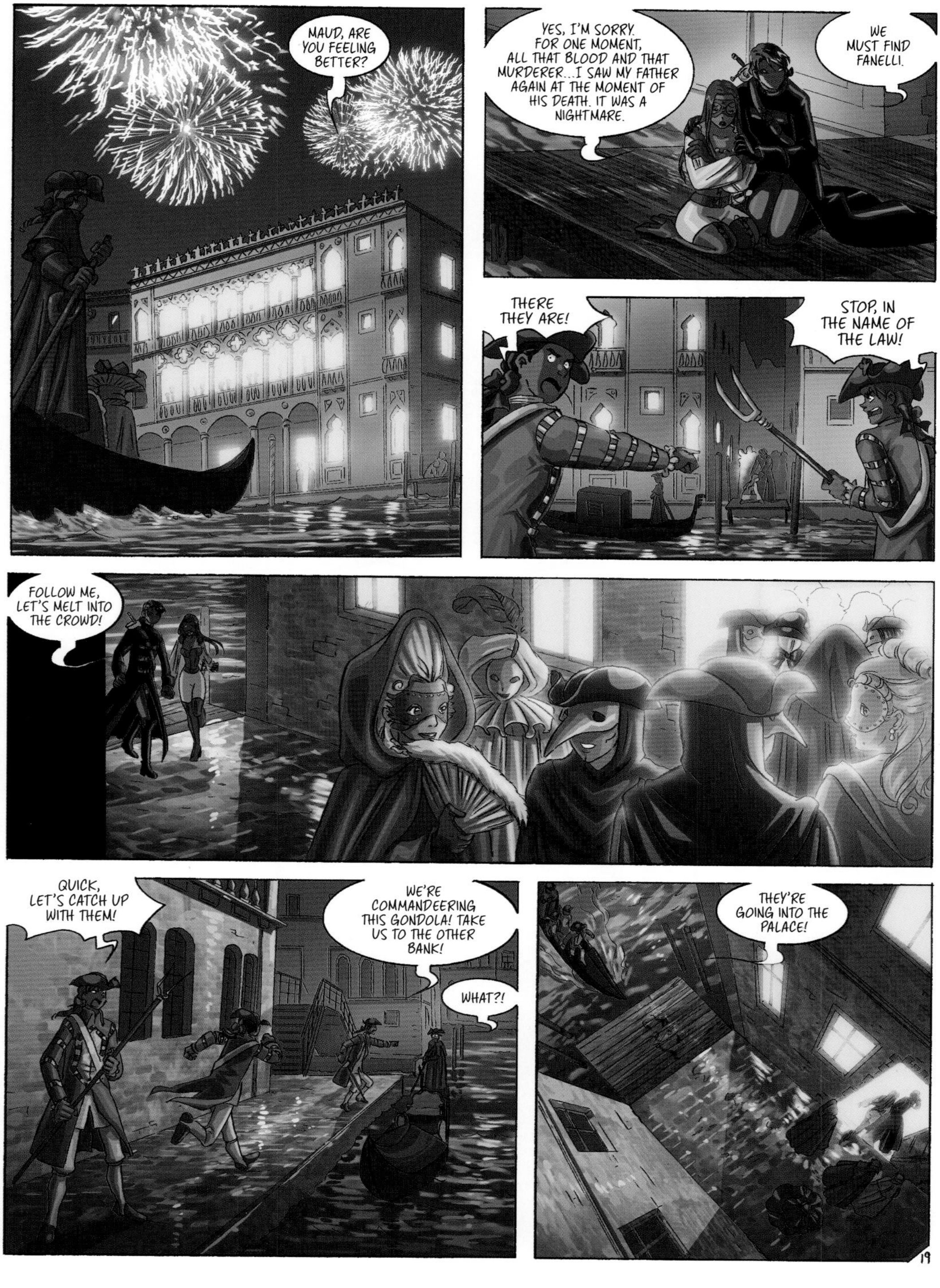
MAUD, ARE YOU FEELING BETTER?
YES, I'M SORRY. FOR ONE MOMENT, ALL THAT BLOOD AND THAT MURDERER...I SAW MY FATHER AGAIN AT THE MOMENT OF HIS DEATH. IT WAS A NIGHTMARE.
WE MUST FIND FANELLI.
THERE THEY ARE!
STOP, IN THE NAME OF THE LAW!
FOLLOW ME, LET'S MELT INTO THE CROWD!
QUICK, LET'S CATCH UP WITH THEM!
WE'RE COMMANDEERING THIS GONDOLA! TAKE US TO THE OTHER BANK!
WHAT?!
THEY'RE GOING INTO THE PALACE!
19

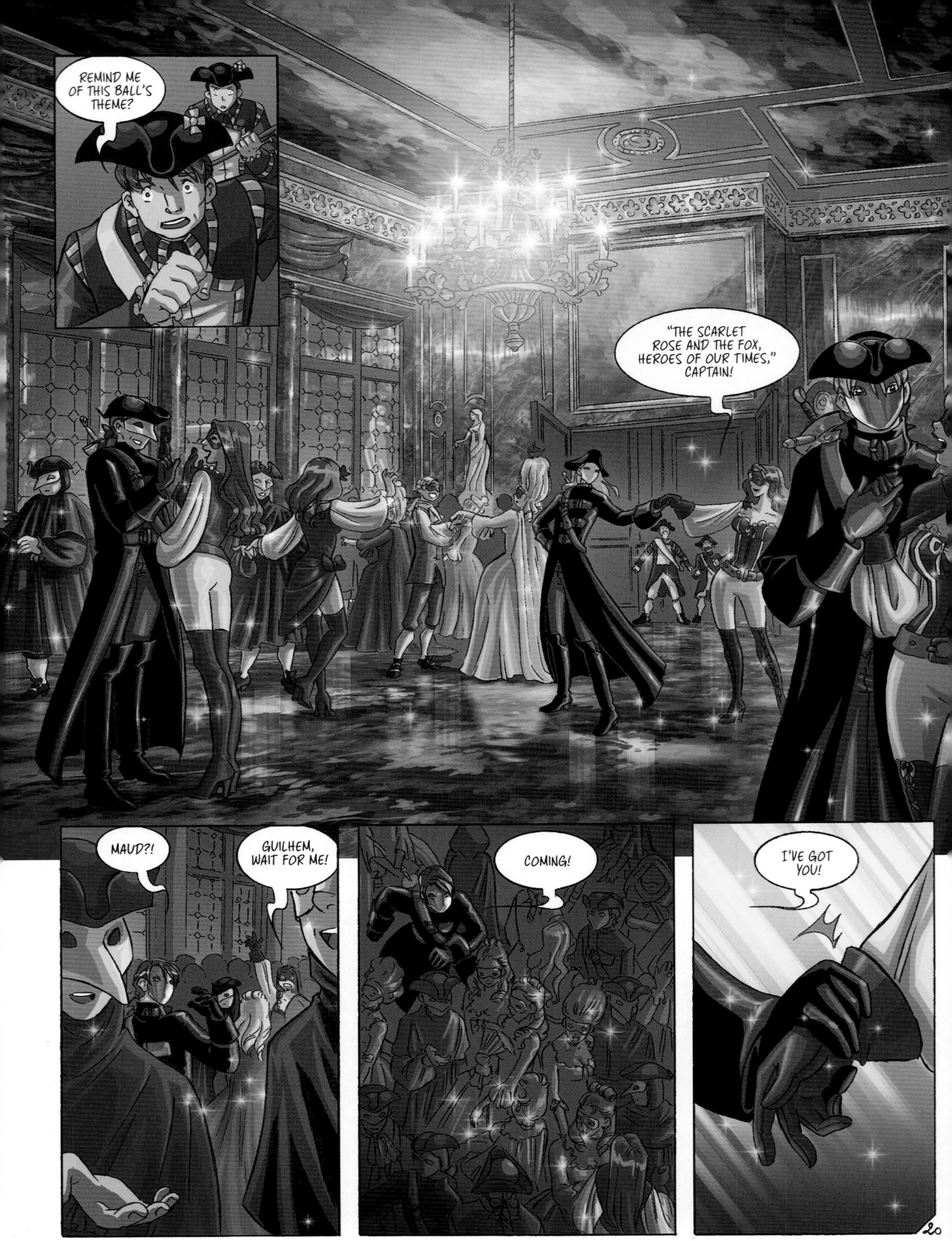
REMIND ME OF THIS BALL'S THEME?
"THE SCARLET ROSE AND THE FOX, HEROES OF OUR TIMES," CAPTAIN!
MAUD?!
GUILHEM, WAIT FOR ME!
COMING!
I'VE GOT YOU!
20

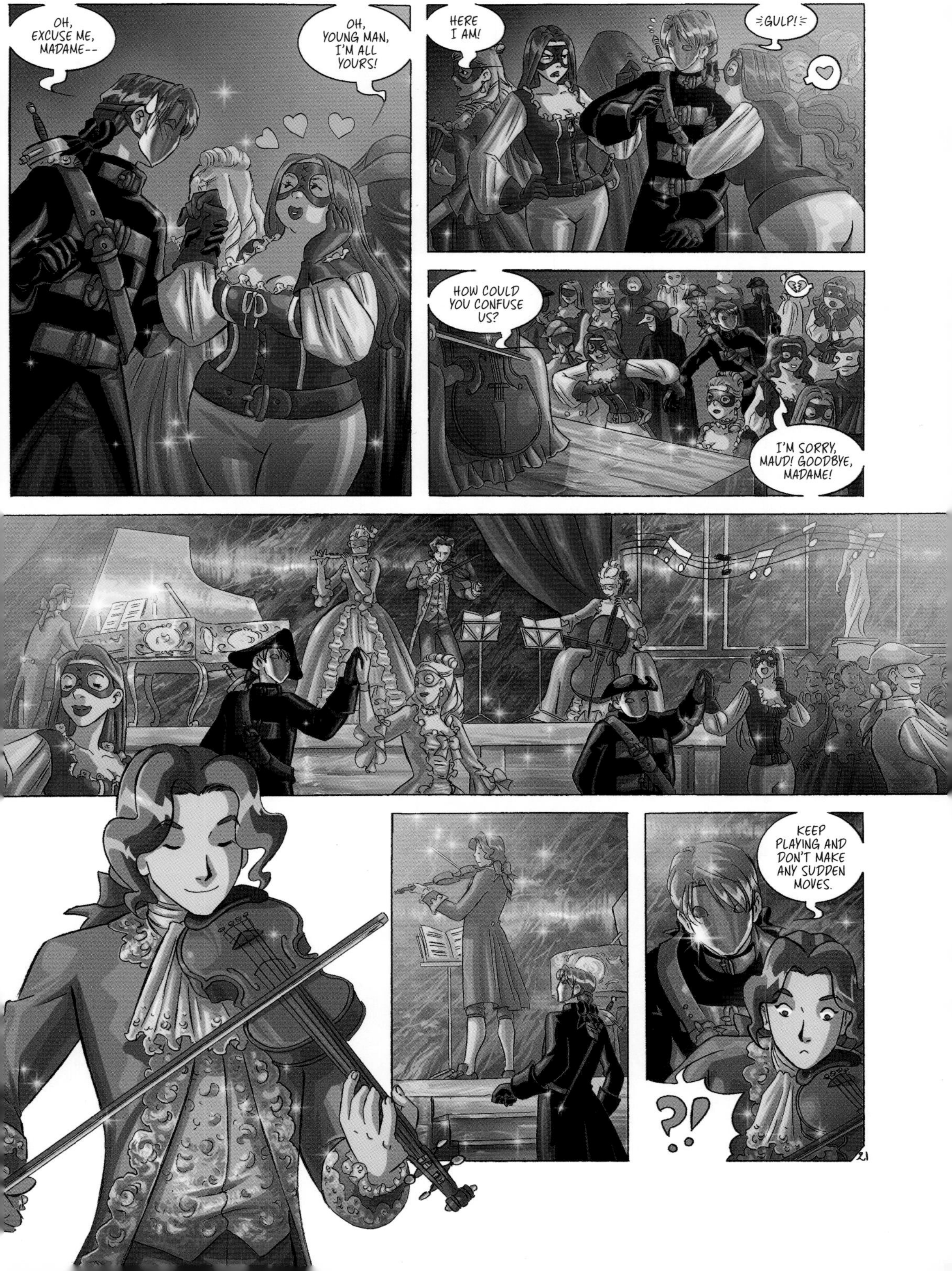
OH, EXCUSE ME, MADAME--
OH, YOUNG MAN, I'M ALL YOURS!
HERE I AM!
GULP!
HOW COULD YOU CONFUSE US?
I'M SORRY, MAUD! GOODBYE, MADAME!
KEEP PLAYING AND DON'T MAKE ANY SUDDEN MOVES.
?!

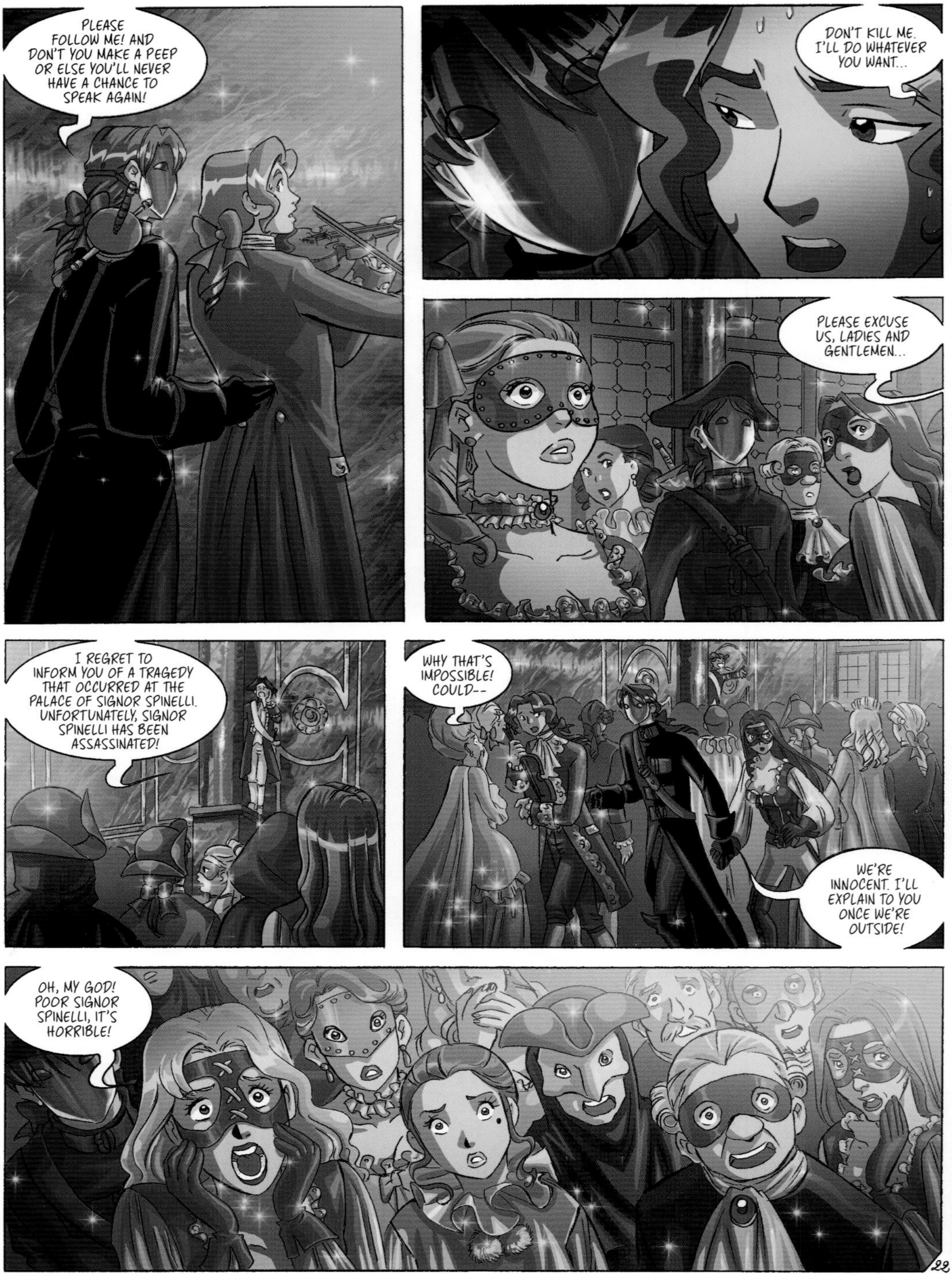

PLEASE FOLLOW ME! AND DON'T YOU MAKE A PEEP OR ELSE YOU'LL NEVER HAVE A CHANCE TO SPEAK AGAIN!
DON'T KILL ME. I'LL DO WHATEVER YOU WANT...
PLEASE EXCUSE US, LADIES AND GENTLEMEN...
I REGRET TO INFORM YOU OF A TRAGEDY THAT OCCURRED AT THE PALACE OF SIGNOR SPINELLI. UNFORTUNATELY, SIGNOR SPINELLI HAS BEEN ASSASSINATED!
WHY THAT'S IMPOSSIBLE! COULD--
WE'RE INNOCENT. I'LL EXPLAIN TO YOU ONCE WE'RE OUTSIDE!
OH, MY GOD! POOR SIGNOR SPINELLI, IT'S HORRIBLE!
22

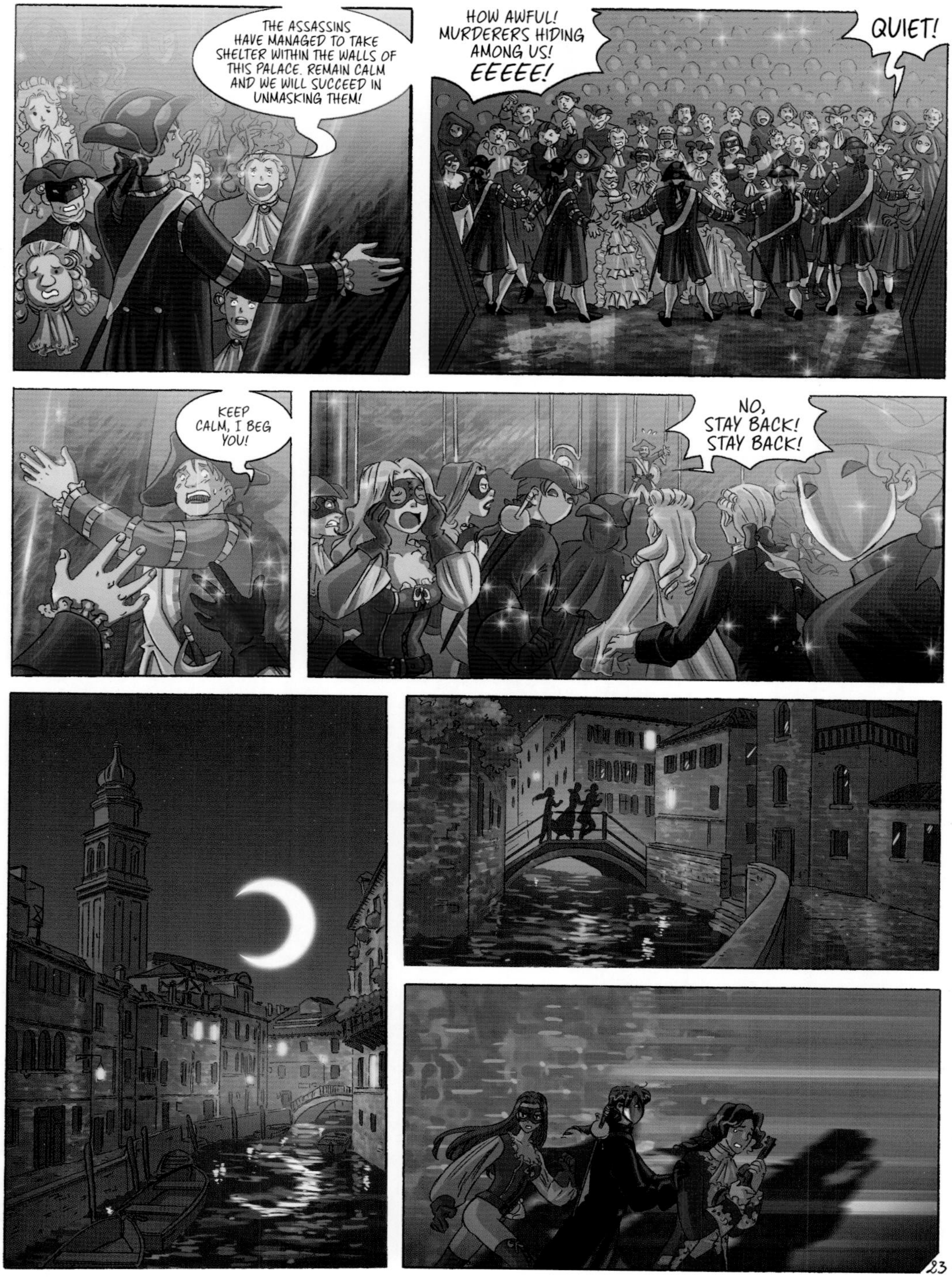
THE ASSASSINS HAVE MANAGED TO TAKE SHELTER WITHIN THE WALLS OF THIS PALACE. REMAIN CALM AND WE WILL SUCCEED IN UNMASKING THEM!
HOW AWFUL! MURDERERS HIDING AMONG US! EEEEE!
QUIET!
KEEP CALM, I BEG YOU!
NO, STAY BACK! STAY BACK!
23

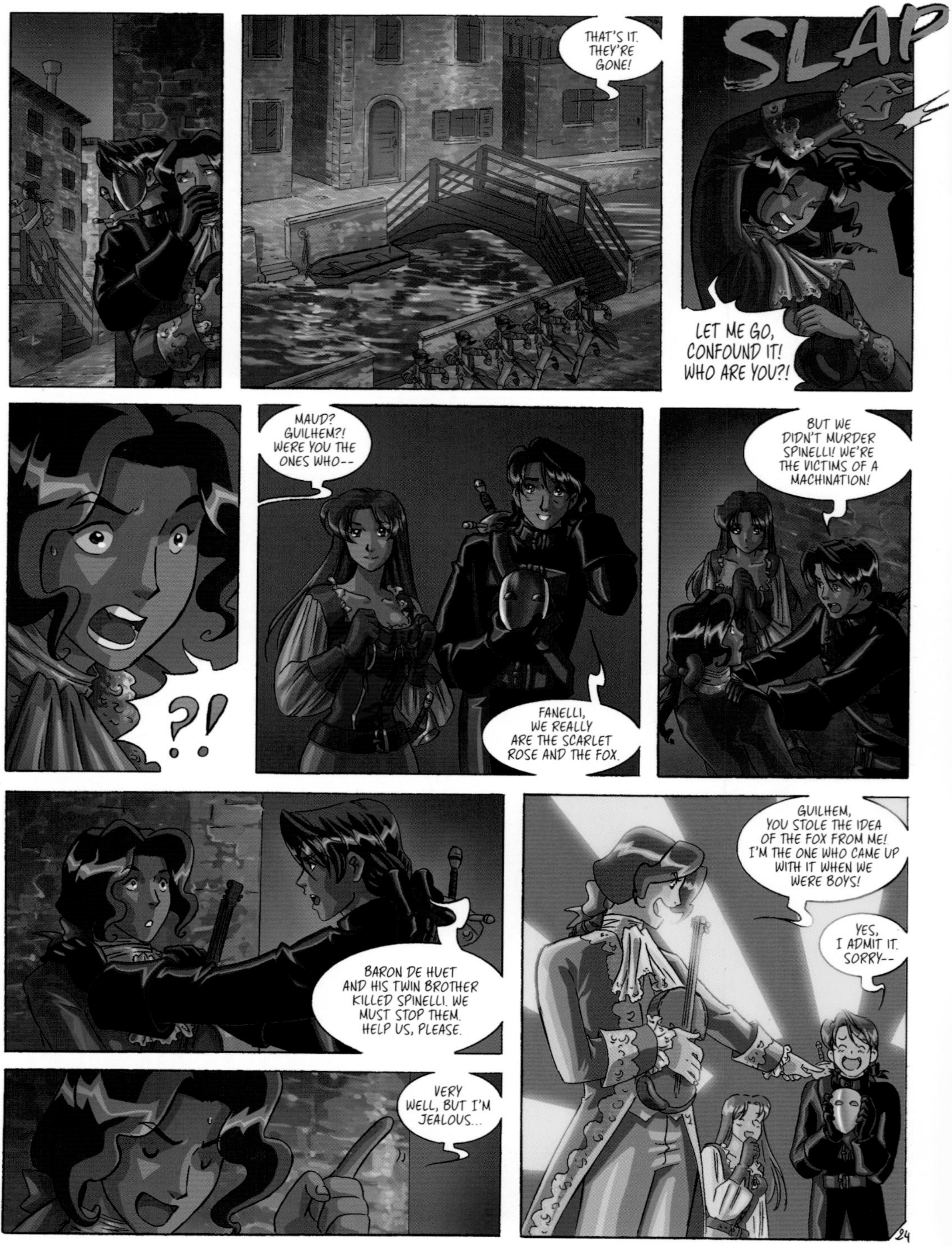
THAT'S IT. THEY'RE GONE!
SLAP
LET ME GO, CONFOUND IT! WHO ARE YOU?!
?!
MAUD? GUILHEM?! WERE YOU THE ONES WHO--
FANELLI, WE REALLY ARE THE SCARLET ROSE AND THE FOX.
BUT WE DIDN'T MURDER SPINELLI! WE'RE THE VICTIMS OF A MACHINATION!
BARON DE HUET AND HIS TWIN BROTHER KILLED SPINELLI. WE MUST STOP THEM. HELP US, PLEASE.
VERY WELL, BUT I'M JEALOUS...
GUILHEM, YOU STOLE THE IDEA OF THE FOX FROM ME! I'M THE ONE WHO CAME UP WITH IT WHEN WE WERE BOYS!
YES, I ADMIT IT. SORRY--
24

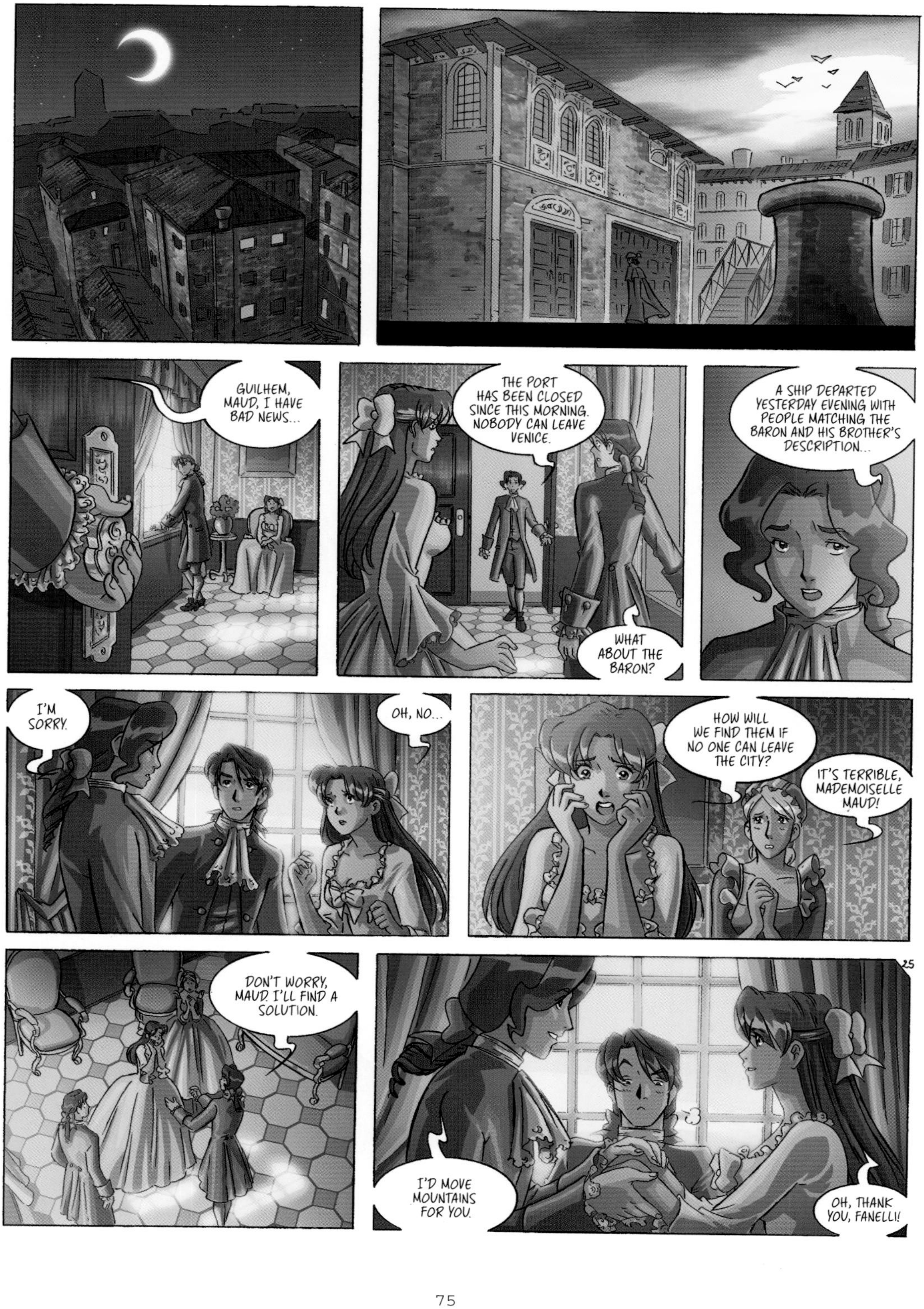
GUILHEM, MAUD, I HAVE BAD NEWS...
THE PORT HAS BEEN CLOSED SINCE THIS MORNING. NOBODY CAN LEAVE VENICE.
WHAT ABOUT THE BARON?
A SHIP DEPARTED YESTERDAY EVENING WITH PEOPLE MATCHING THE BARON AND HIS BROTHER'S DESCRIPTION...
I'M SORRY.
OH, NO...
HOW WILL WE FIND THEM IF NO ONE CAN LEAVE THE CITY?
IT'S TERRIBLE, MADEMOISELLE MAUD!
DON'T WORRY, MAUD. I'LL FIND A SOLUTION.
25
I'D MOVE MOUNTAINS FOR YOU.
OH, THANK YOU, FANELLI!

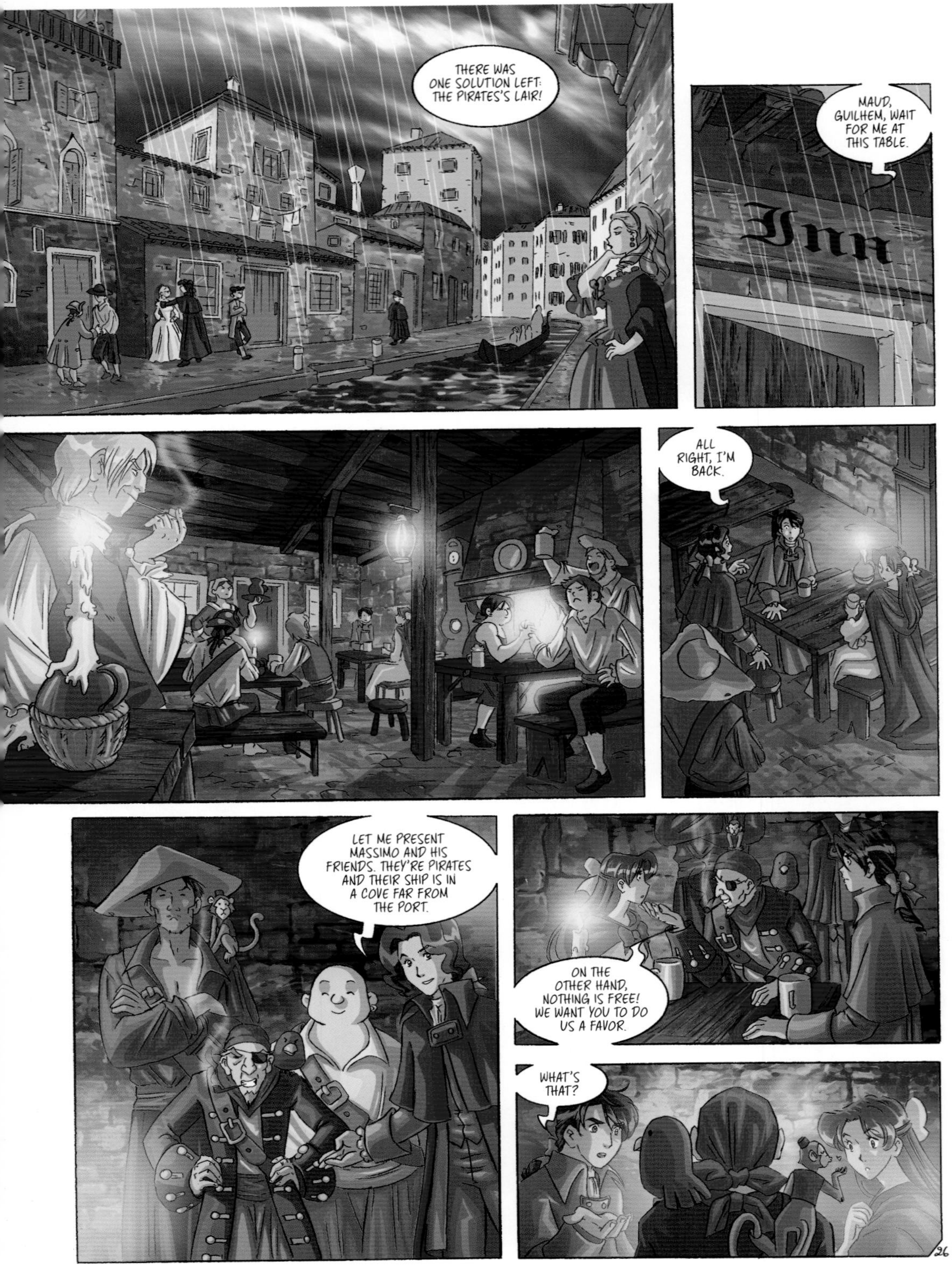
THERE WAS ONE SOLUTION LEFT: THE PIRATES'S LAIR!
MAUD, GUILHEM, WAIT FOR ME AT THIS TABLE.
Inn
ALL RIGHT, I'M BACK.
LET ME PRESENT MASSIMO AND HIS FRIENDS. THEY'RE PIRATES AND THEIR SHIP IS IN A COVE FAR FROM THE PORT.
ON THE OTHER HAND, NOTHING IS FREE! WE WANT YOU TO DO US A FAVOR.
WHAT'S THAT?
26

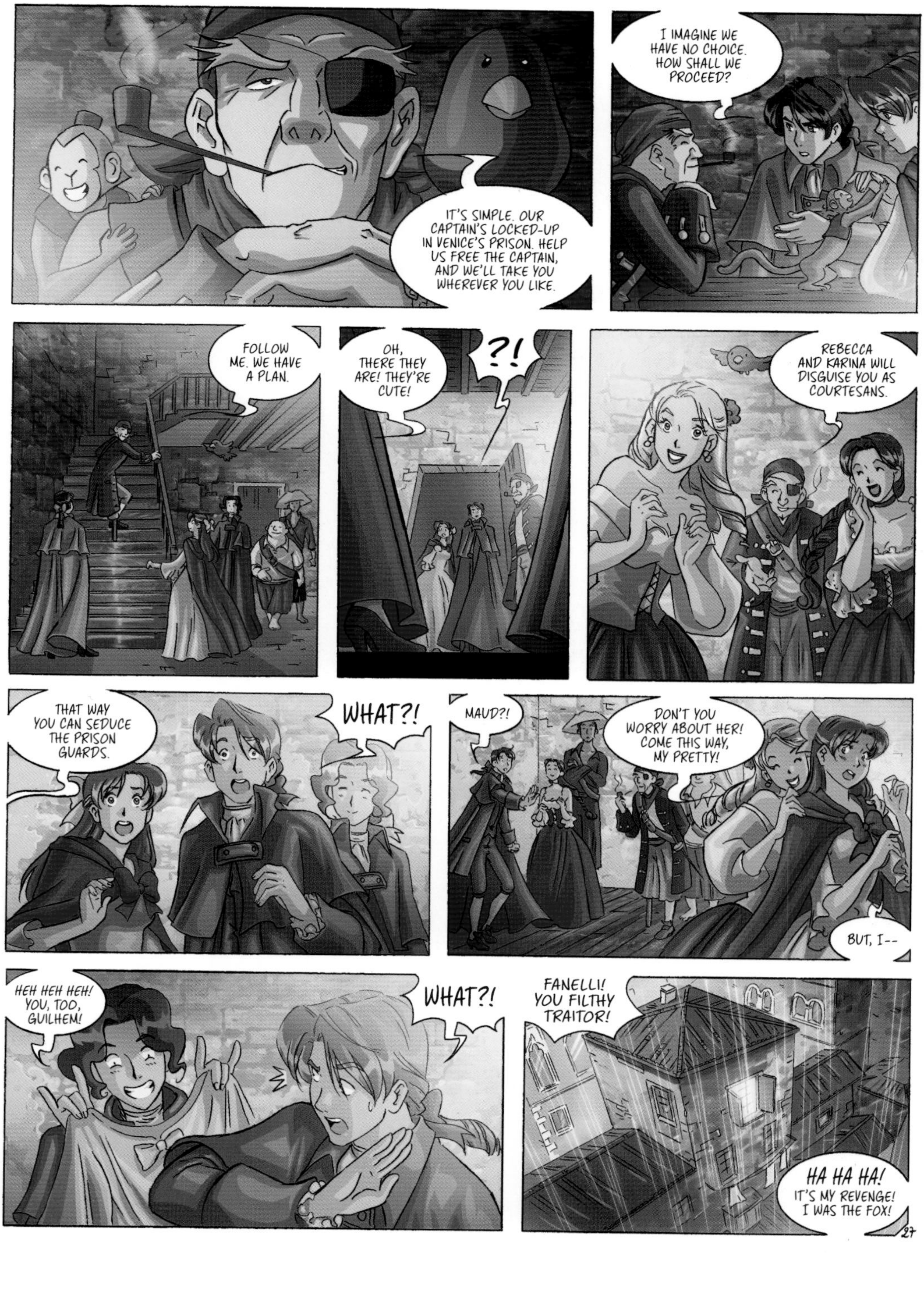

IT'S SIMPLE. OUR CAPTAIN'S LOCKED-UP IN VENICE'S PRISON. HELP US FREE THE CAPTAIN, AND WE'LL TAKE YOU WHEREVER YOU LIKE.
I IMAGINE WE HAVE NO CHOICE. HOW SHALL WE PROCEED?
FOLLOW ME. WE HAVE A PLAN.
OH, THERE THEY ARE! THEY'RE CUTE!
?!
REBECCA AND KARINA WILL DISGUISE YOU AS COURTESANS.
THAT WAY YOU CAN SEDUCE THE PRISON GUARDS.
WHAT?!
MAUD?!
DON'T YOU WORRY ABOUT HER! COME THIS WAY, MY PRETTY!
BUT, I--
HEH HEH HEH! YOU, TOO, GUILHEM!
WHAT?!
FANELLI! YOU FILTHY TRAITOR!
HA HA HA! IT'S MY REVENGE! I WAS THE FOX!
27

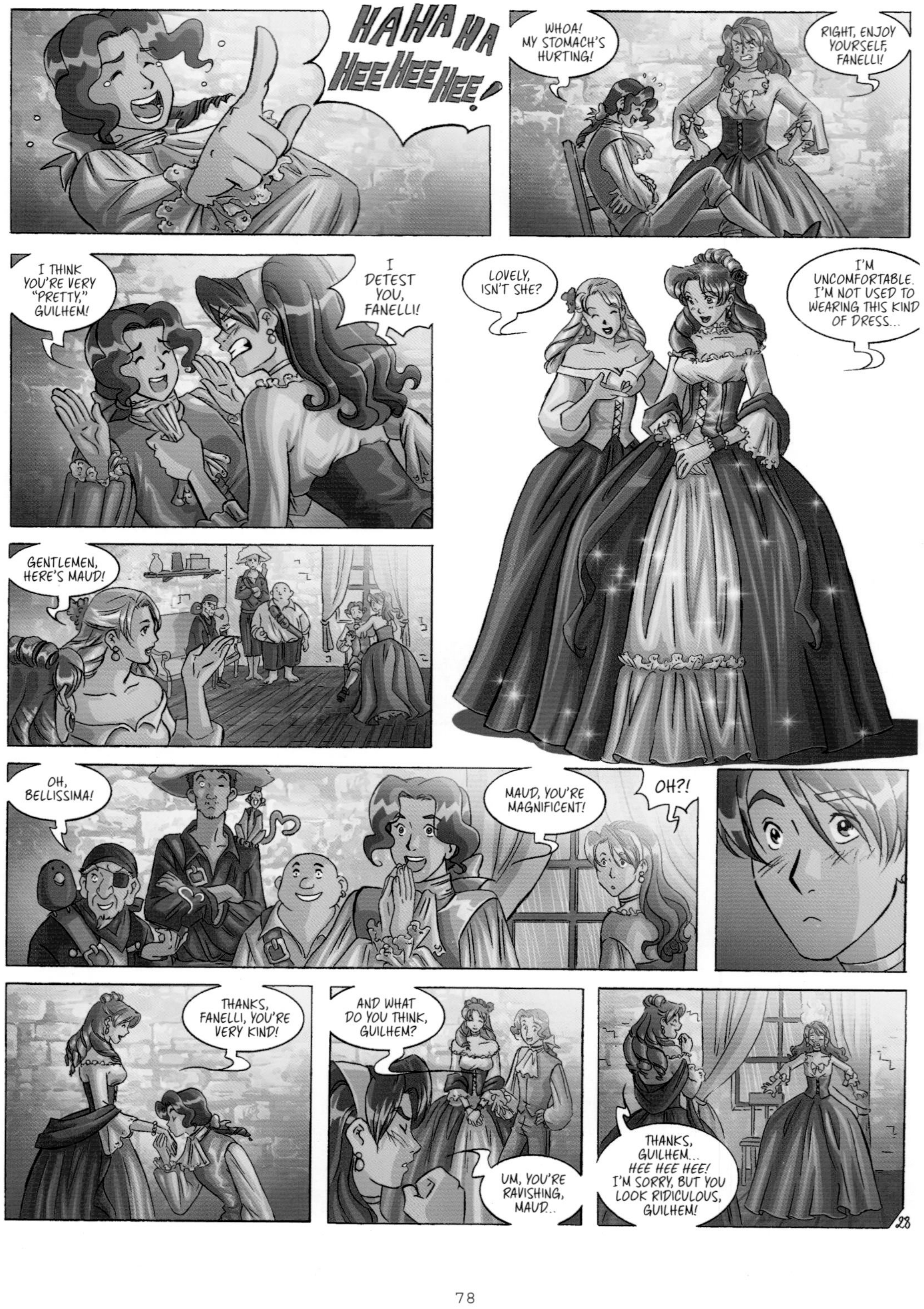
HAHAHA HA
HEEHEEHEE!
WHOA! MY STOMACH'S HURTING!
RIGHT, ENJOY YOURSELF, FANELLI!
I THINK YOU'RE VERY "PRETTY," GUILHEM!
I DETEST YOU, FANELLI!
GENTLEMEN, HERE'S MAUD!
LOVELY, ISN'T SHE?
I'M UNCOMFORTABLE. I'M NOT USED TO WEARING THIS KIND OF DRESS...
OH, BELLISSIMA!
MAUD, YOU'RE MAGNIFICENT!
OH?!
THANKS, FANELLI, YOU'RE VERY KIND!
AND WHAT DO YOU THINK, GUILHEM?
UM, YOU'RE RAVISHING, MAUD...
THANKS, GUILHEM... HEE HEE HEE! I'M SORRY, BUT YOU LOOK RIDICULOUS, GUILHEM!
28

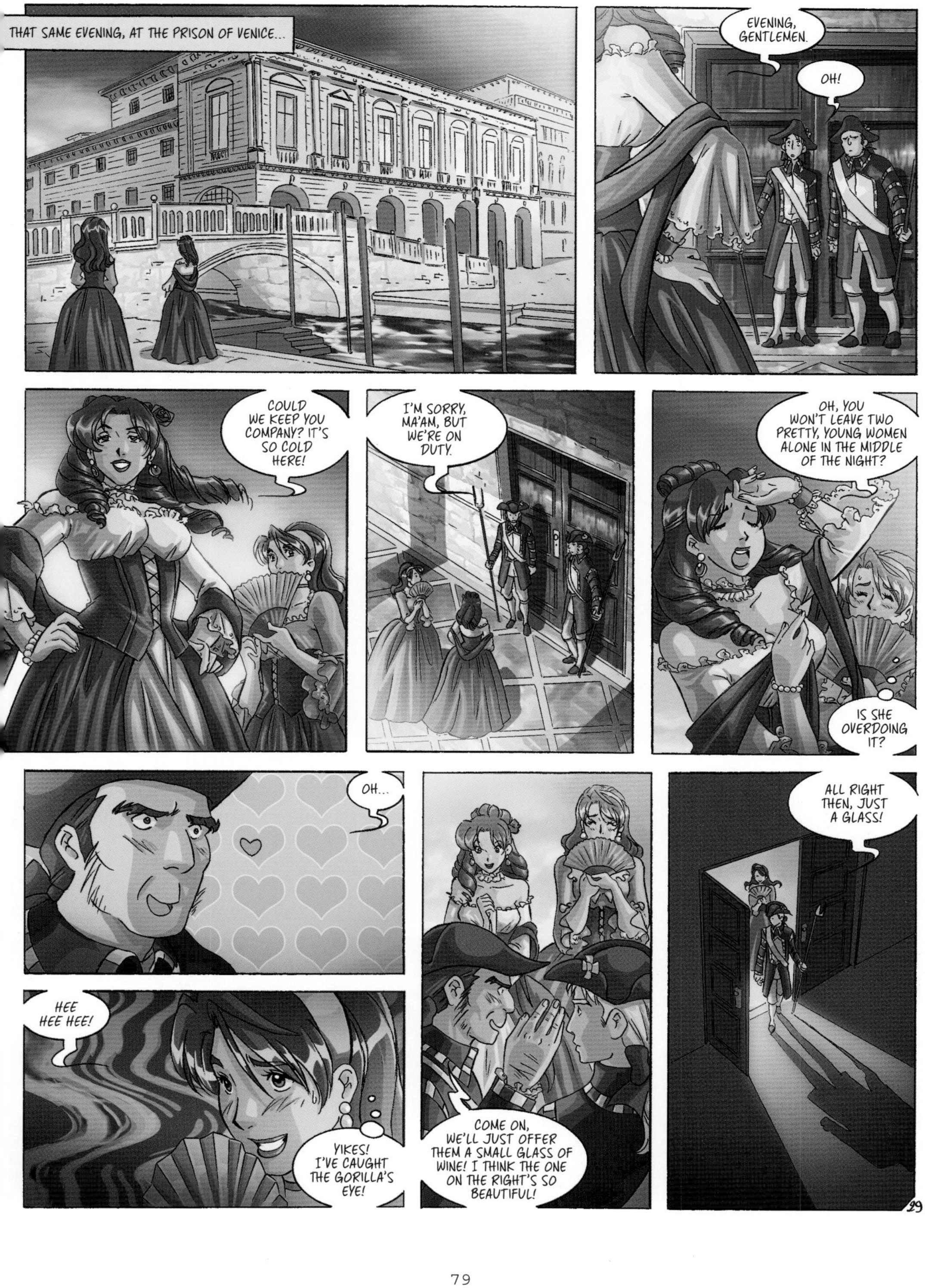
THAT SAME EVENING, AT THE PRISON OF VENICE...
EVENING, GENTLEMEN.
OH!
COULD WE KEEP YOU COMPANY? IT'S SO COLD HERE!
I'M SORRY, MA'AM, BUT WE'RE ON DUTY.
OH, YOU WON'T LEAVE TWO PRETTY, YOUNG WOMEN ALONE IN THE MIDDLE OF THE NIGHT?
IS SHE OVERDOING IT?
OH...
HEE HEE HEE!
YIKES! I'VE CAUGHT THE GORILLA'S EYE!
COME ON, WE'LL JUST OFFER THEM A SMALL GLASS OF WINE! I THINK THE ONE ON THE RIGHT'S SO BEAUTIFUL!
ALL RIGHT THEN, JUST A GLASS!
29

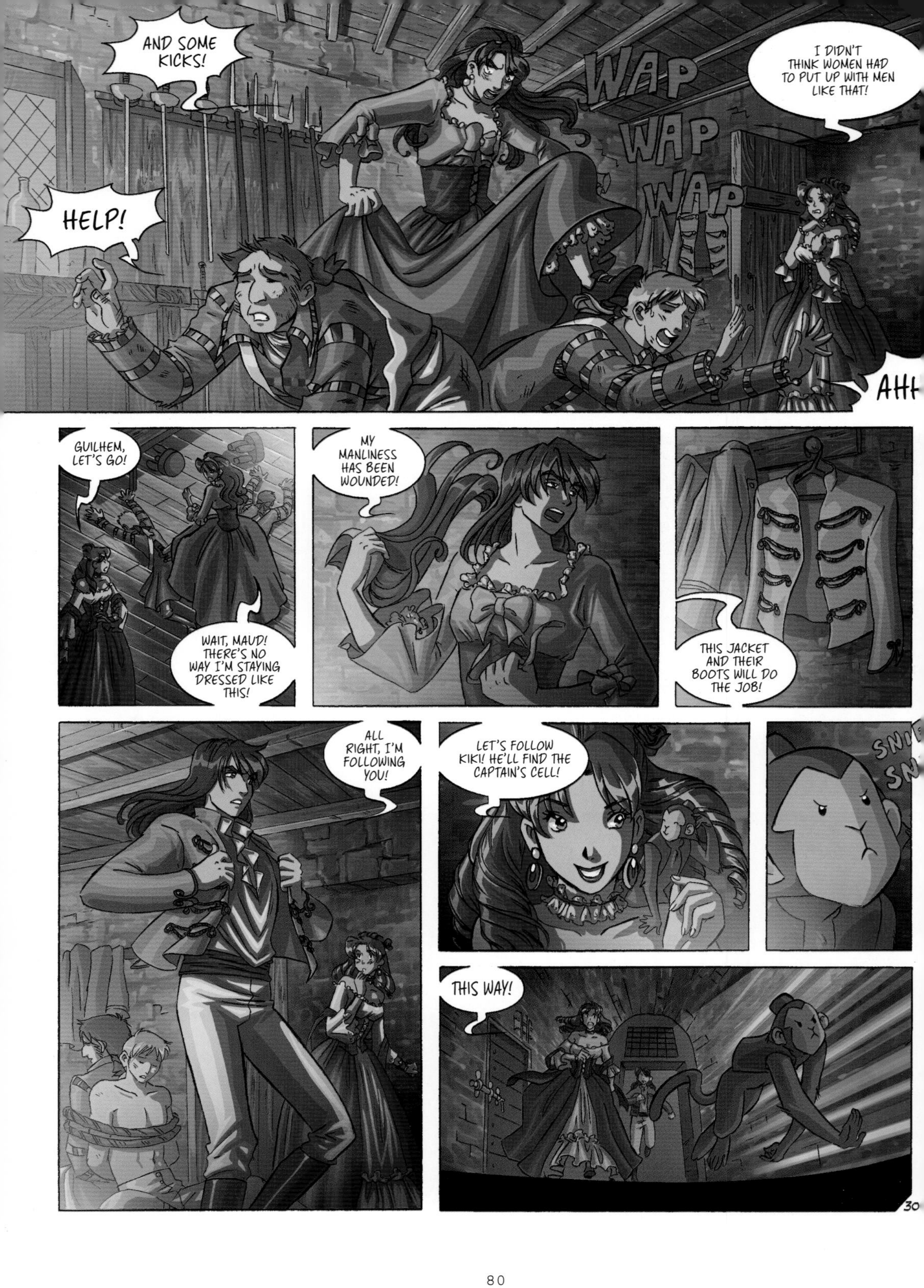
AND SOME KICKS!
HELP!
WAP
WAP
WAP
I DIDN'T THINK WOMEN HAD TO PUT UP WITH MEN LIKE THAT!
AHH
GUILHEM, LET'S GO!
WAIT, MAUD! THERE'S NO WAY I'M STAYING DRESSED LIKE THIS!
MY MANLINESS HAS BEEN WOUNDED!
THIS JACKET AND THEIR BOOTS WILL DO THE JOB!
ALL RIGHT, I'M FOLLOWING YOU!
LET'S FOLLOW KIKI! HE'LL FIND THE CAPTAIN'S CELL!
THIS WAY!
30

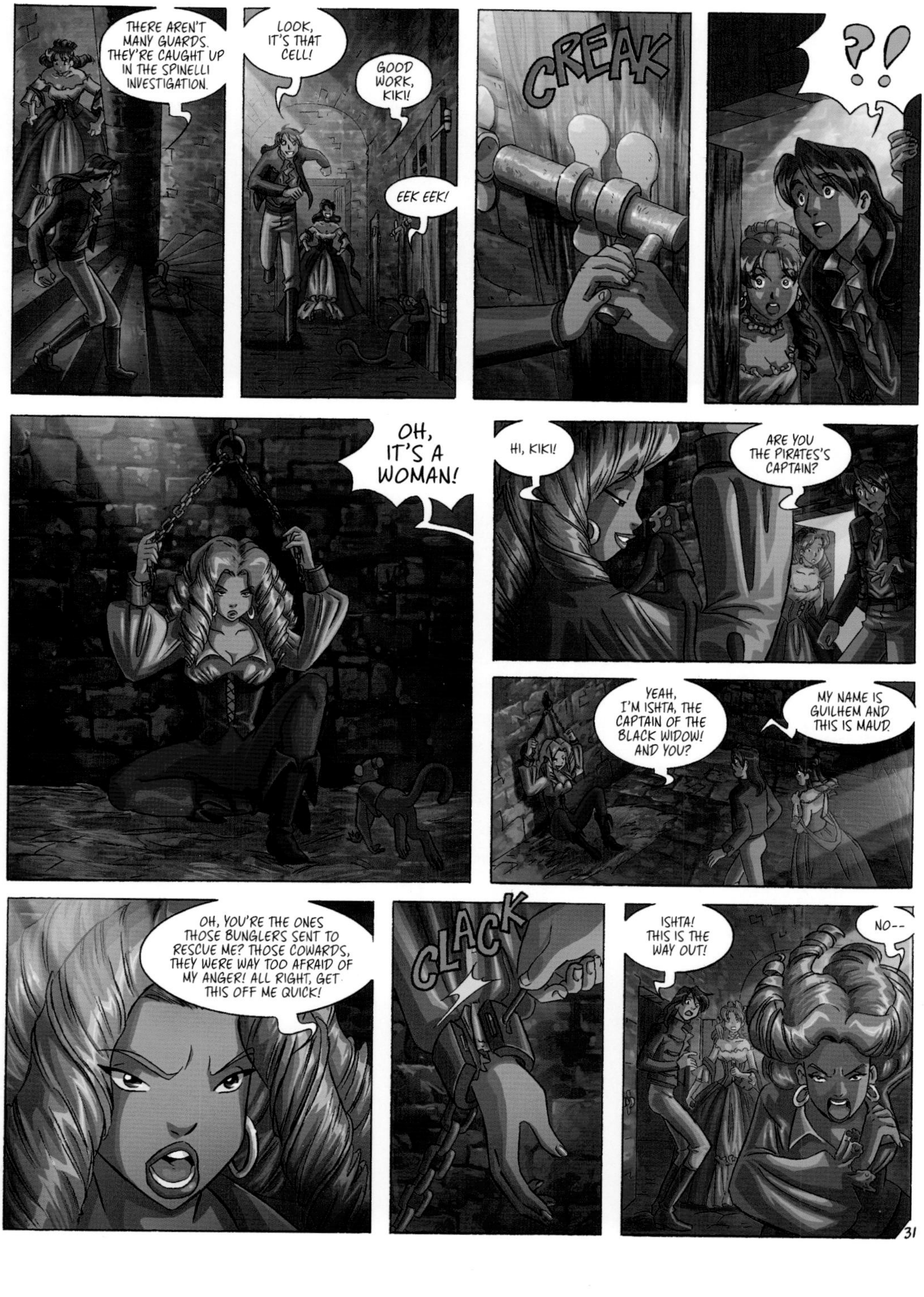

THERE AREN'T MANY GUARDS. THEY'RE CAUGHT UP IN THE SPINELLI INVESTIGATION.
LOOK, IT'S THAT CELL!
GOOD WORK, KIKI!
EEK EEK!
CREAK
?!
OH, IT'S A WOMAN!
HI, KIKI!
ARE YOU THE PIRATES'S CAPTAIN?
YEAH, I'M ISHTA, THE CAPTAIN OF THE BLACK WIDOW! AND YOU?
MY NAME IS GUILHEM AND THIS IS MAUD.
OH, YOU'RE THE ONES THOSE BUNGLERS SENT TO RESCUE ME? THOSE COWARDS, THEY WERE WAY TOO AFRAID OF MY ANGER! ALL RIGHT, GET THIS OFF ME QUICK!
CLACK
ISHTA! THIS IS THE WAY OUT!
NO--
31

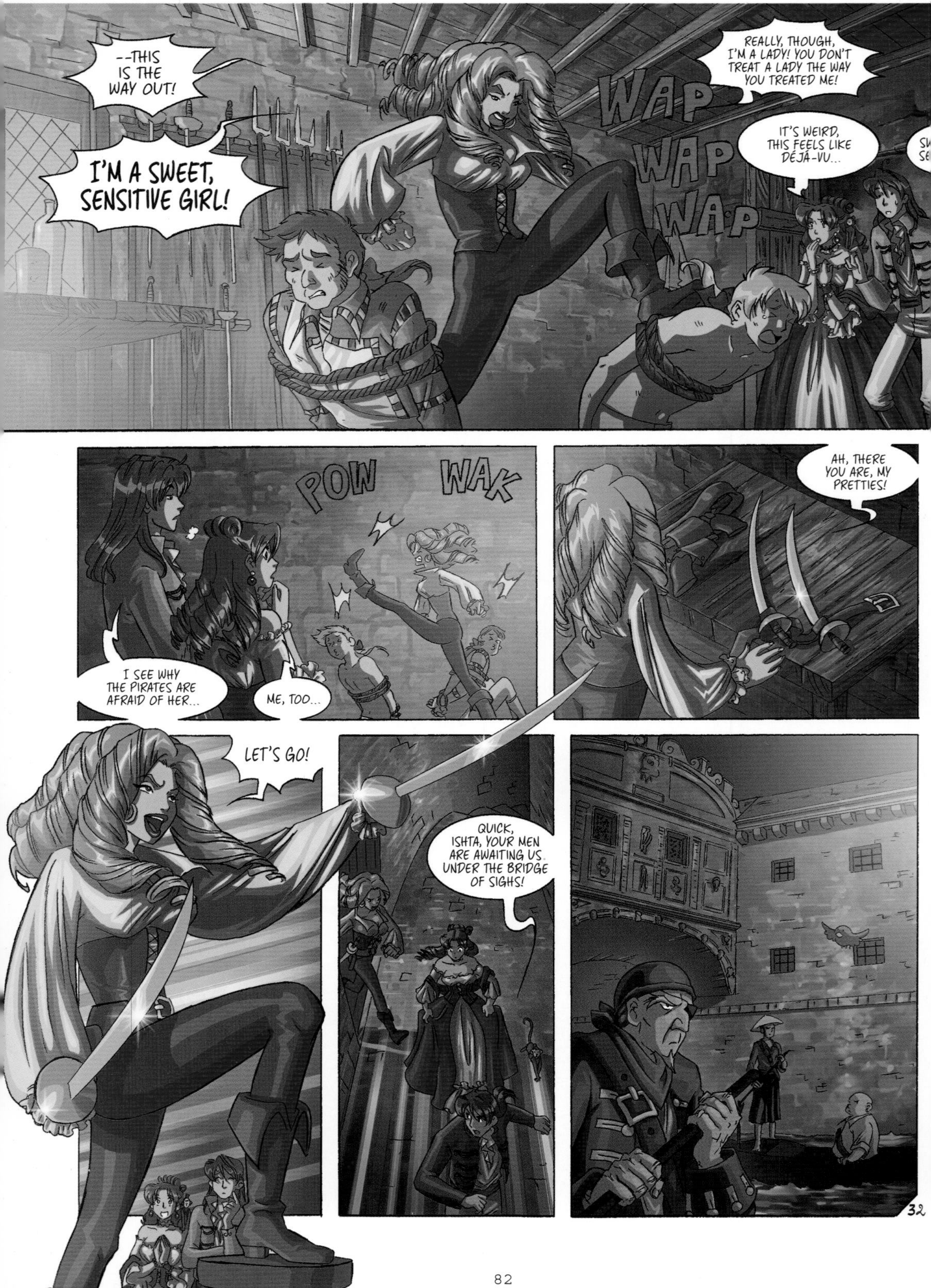
--THIS IS THE WAY OUT!
I'M A SWEET, SENSITIVE GIRL!
WAP
WAP
WAP
REALLY, THOUGH, I'M A LADY! YOU DON'T TREAT A LADY THE WAY YOU TREATED ME!
IT'S WEIRD, THIS FEELS LIKE DÉJÀ-VU...
POW
WAK
I SEE WHY THE PIRATES ARE AFRAID OF HER...
ME, TOO...
AH, THERE YOU ARE, MY PRETTIES!
LET'S GO!
QUICK, ISHTA, YOUR MEN ARE AWAITING US UNDER THE BRIDGE OF SIGHS!
32

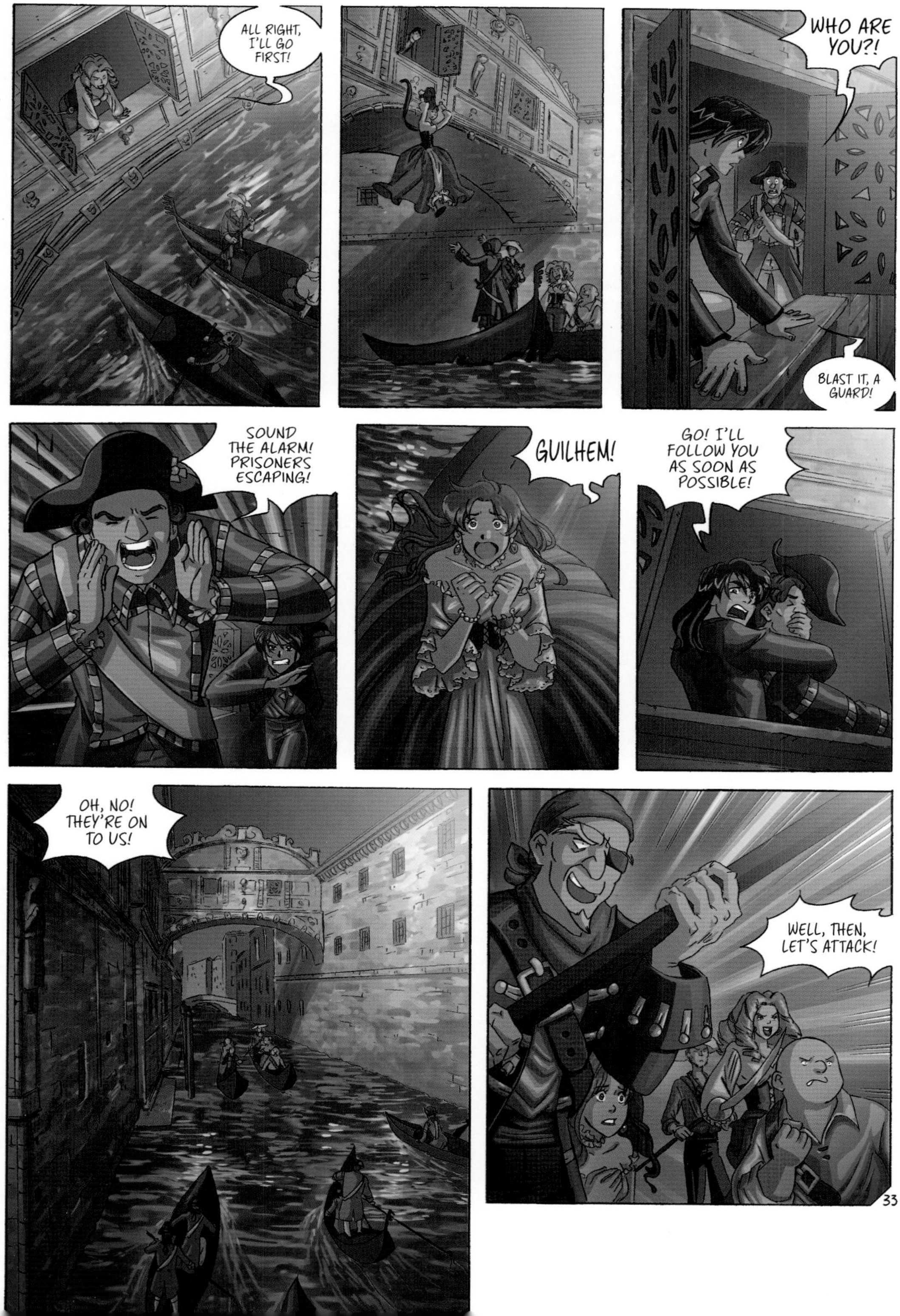
ALL RIGHT, I'LL GO FIRST!
WHO ARE YOU?!
BLAST IT, A GUARD!
SOUND THE ALARM! PRISONERS ESCAPING!
GUILHEM!
GO! I'LL FOLLOW YOU AS SOON AS POSSIBLE!
OH, NO! THEY'RE ON TO US!
WELL, THEN, LET'S ATTACK!

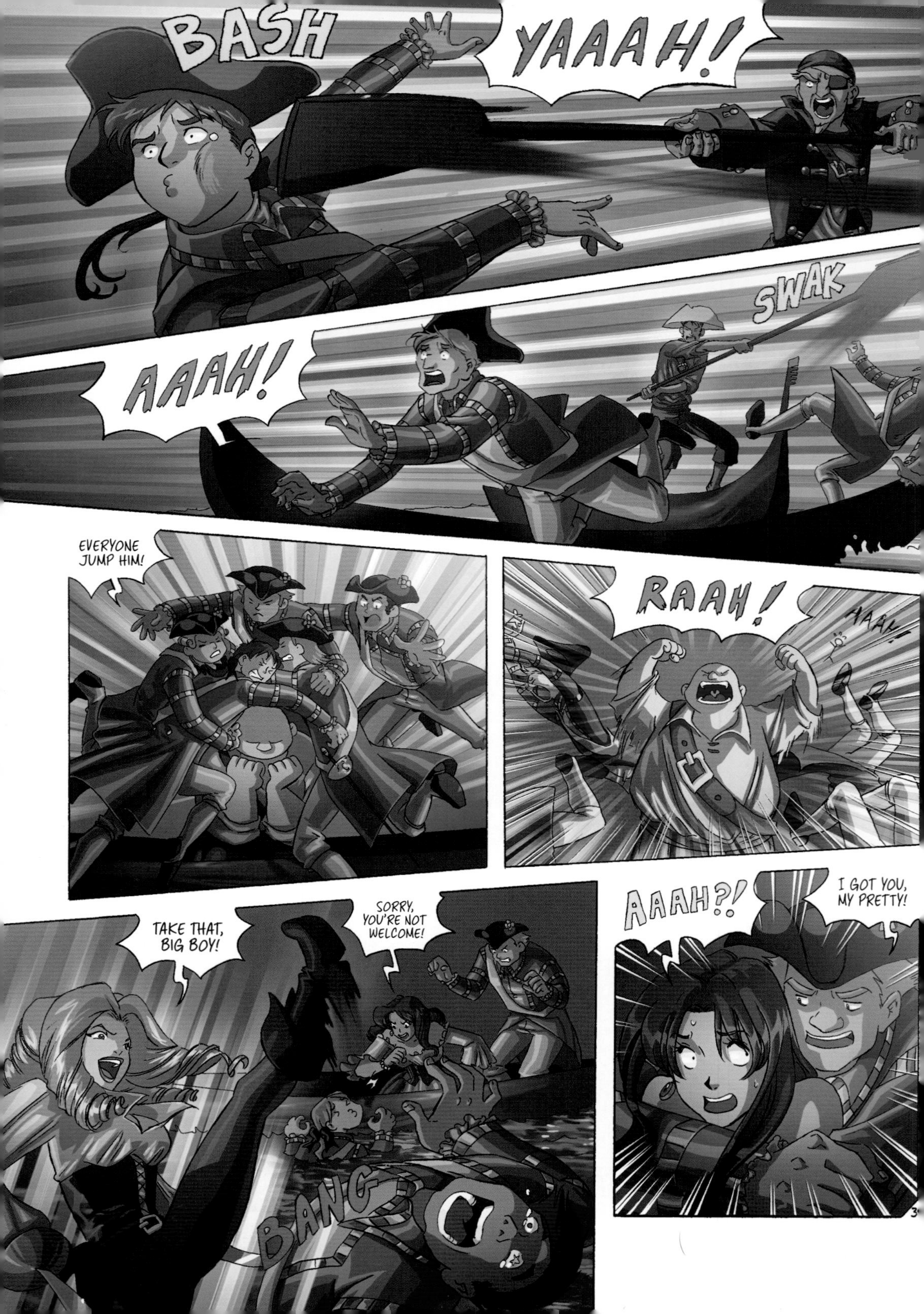
BASH
YAAAH!
SWAK
AAAH!
EVERYONE JUMP HIM!
RAAH!
AAAH!
TAKE THAT, BIG BOY!
SORRY, YOU'RE NOT WELCOME!
BANG
AAAH?!
I GOT YOU, MY PRETTY!

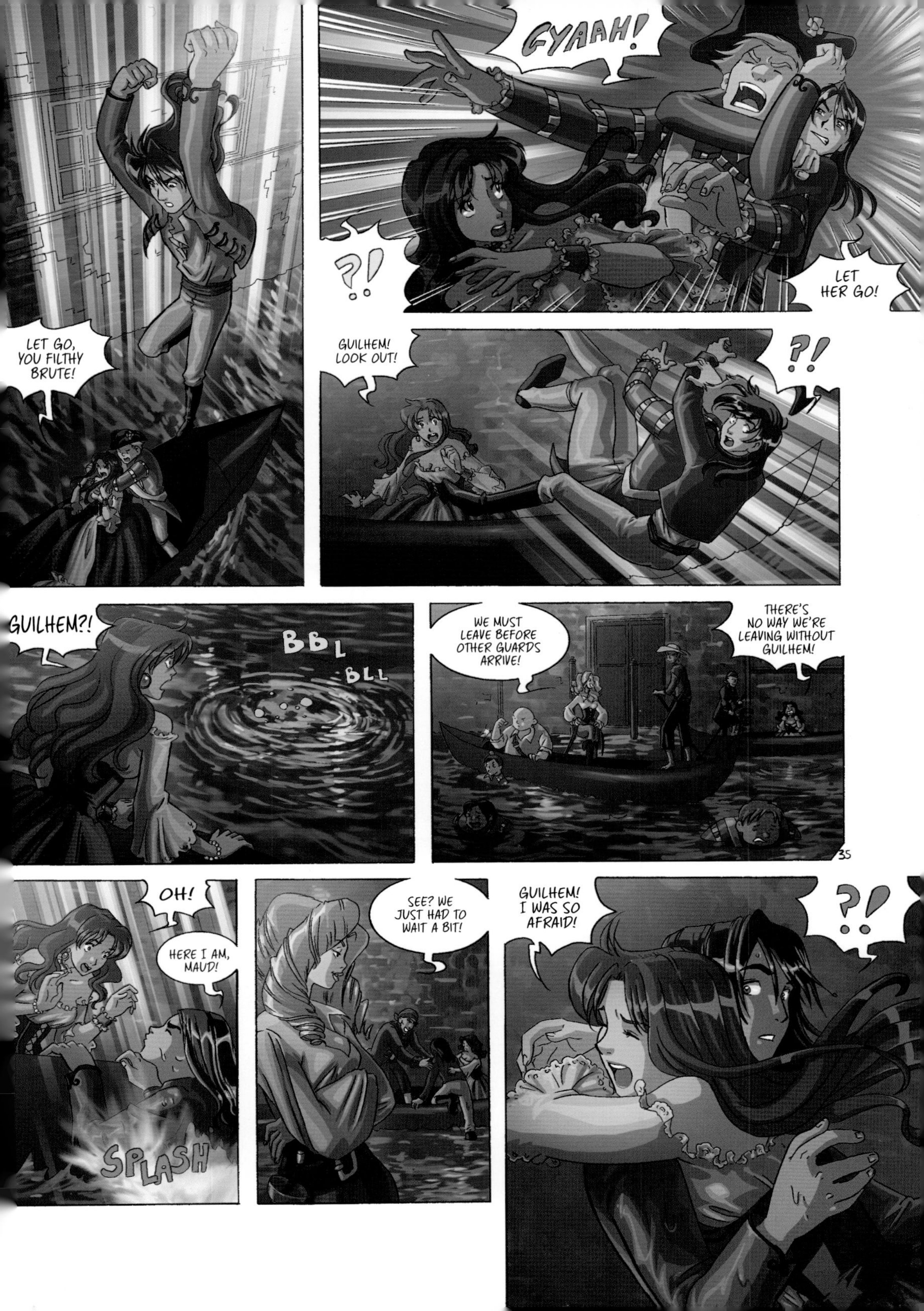
GYAAH!
?!
LET HER GO!
LET GO, YOU FILTHY BRUTE!
GUILHEM! LOOK OUT!
?!
GUILHEM?!
BBL
BLL
WE MUST LEAVE BEFORE OTHER GUARDS ARRIVE!
THERE'S NO WAY WE'RE LEAVING WITHOUT GUILHEM!
OH!
HERE I AM, MAUD!
SPLASH
SEE? WE JUST HAD TO WAIT A BIT!
GUILHEM! I WAS SO AFRAID!
?!

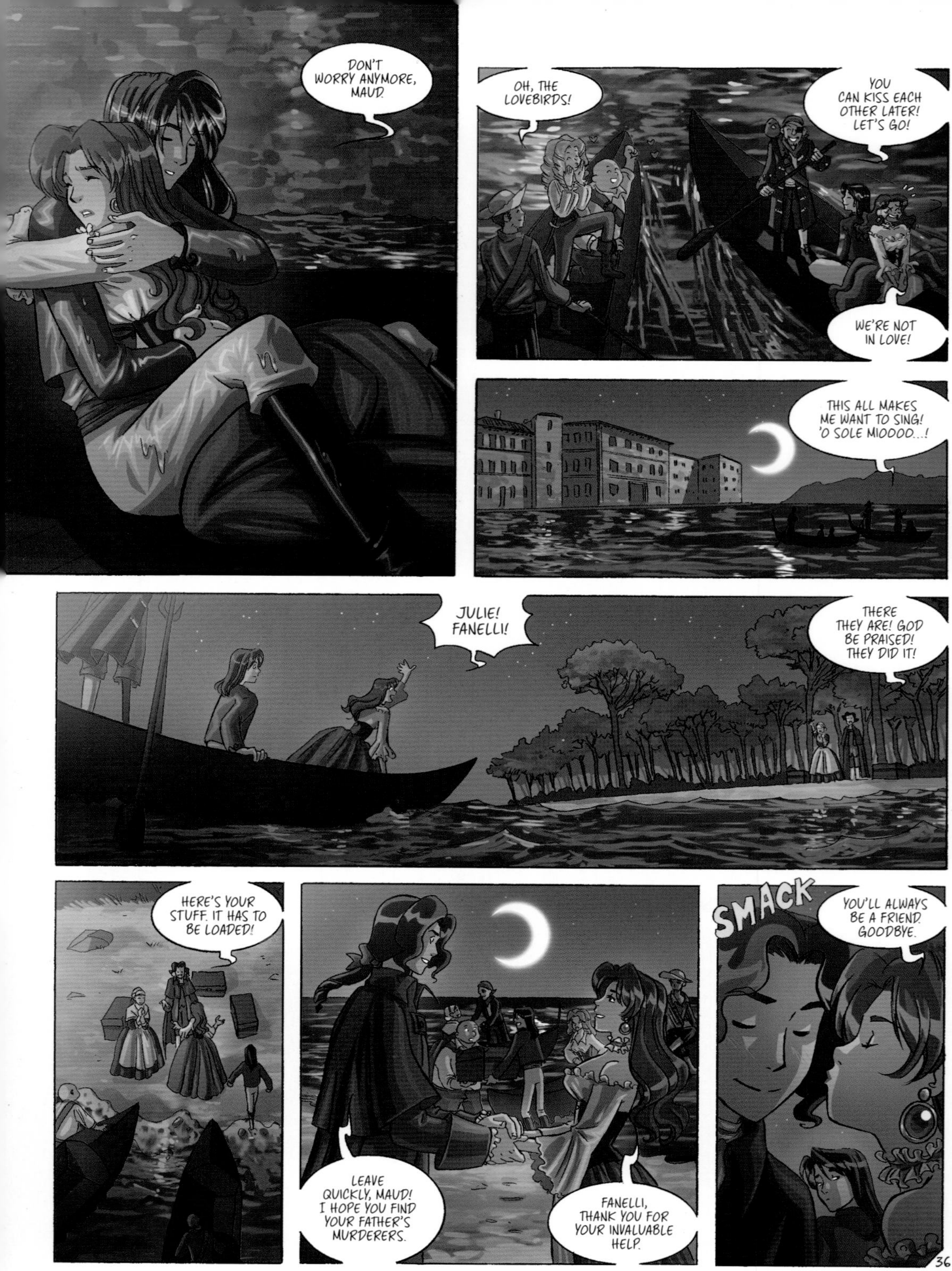

DON'T WORRY ANYMORE, MAUD.
OH, THE LOVEBIRDS!
YOU CAN KISS EACH OTHER LATER! LET'S GO!
WE'RE NOT IN LOVE!
THIS ALL MAKES ME WANT TO SING! 'O SOLE MIOOOO...!
JULIE! FANELLI!
THERE THEY ARE! GOD BE PRAISED! THEY DID IT!
HERE'S YOUR STUFF. IT HAS TO BE LOADED!
LEAVE QUICKLY, MAUD! I HOPE YOU FIND YOUR FATHER'S MURDERERS.
FANELLI, THANK YOU FOR YOUR INVALUABLE HELP.
SMACK
YOU'LL ALWAYS BE A FRIEND. GOODBYE.
36

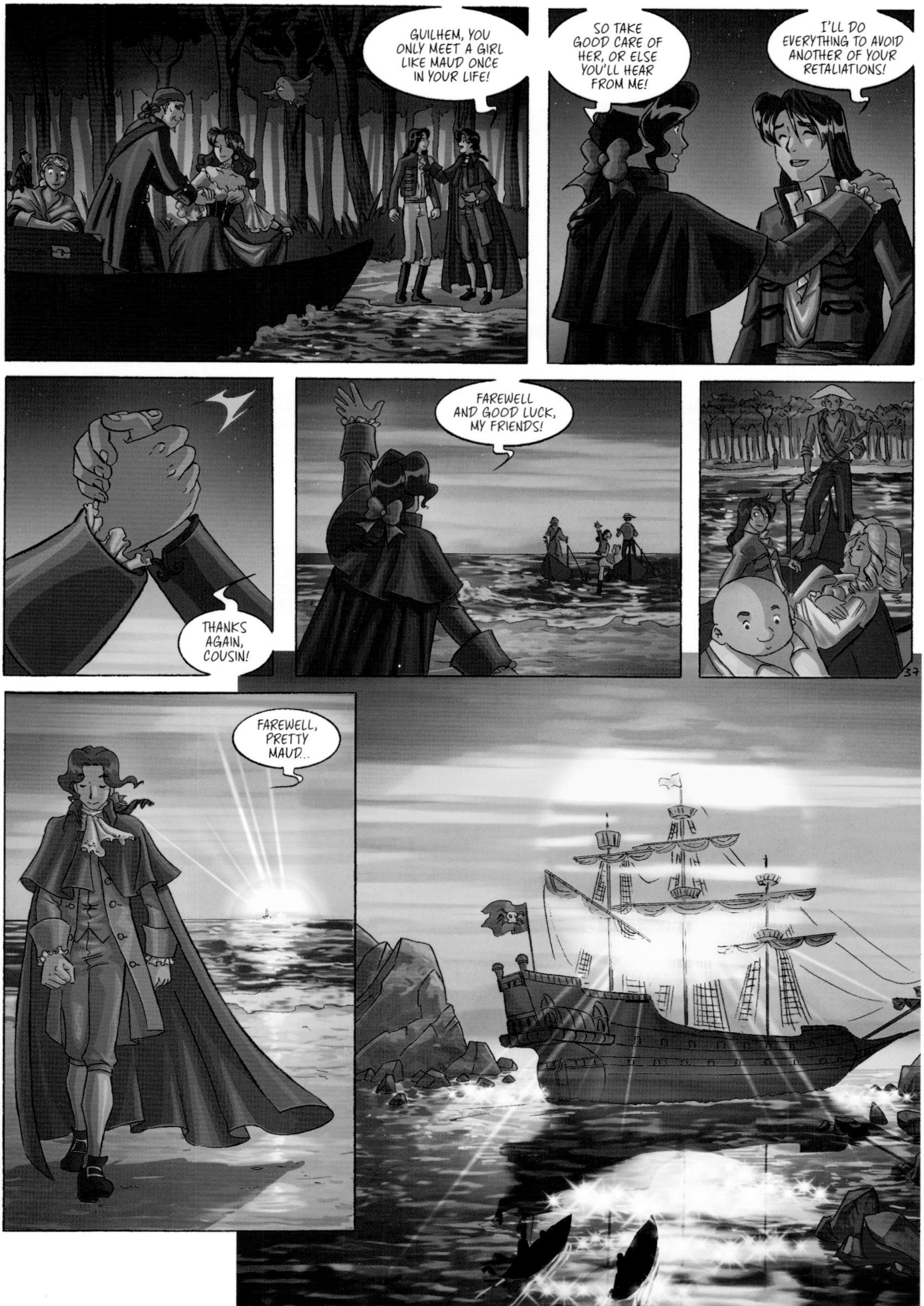
GUILHEM, YOU ONLY MEET A GIRL LIKE MAUD ONCE IN YOUR LIFE!
SO TAKE GOOD CARE OF HER, OR ELSE YOU'LL HEAR FROM ME!
I'LL DO EVERYTHING TO AVOID ANOTHER OF YOUR RETALIATIONS!
THANKS AGAIN, COUSIN!
FAREWELL AND GOOD LUCK, MY FRIENDS!
FAREWELL, PRETTY MAUD...

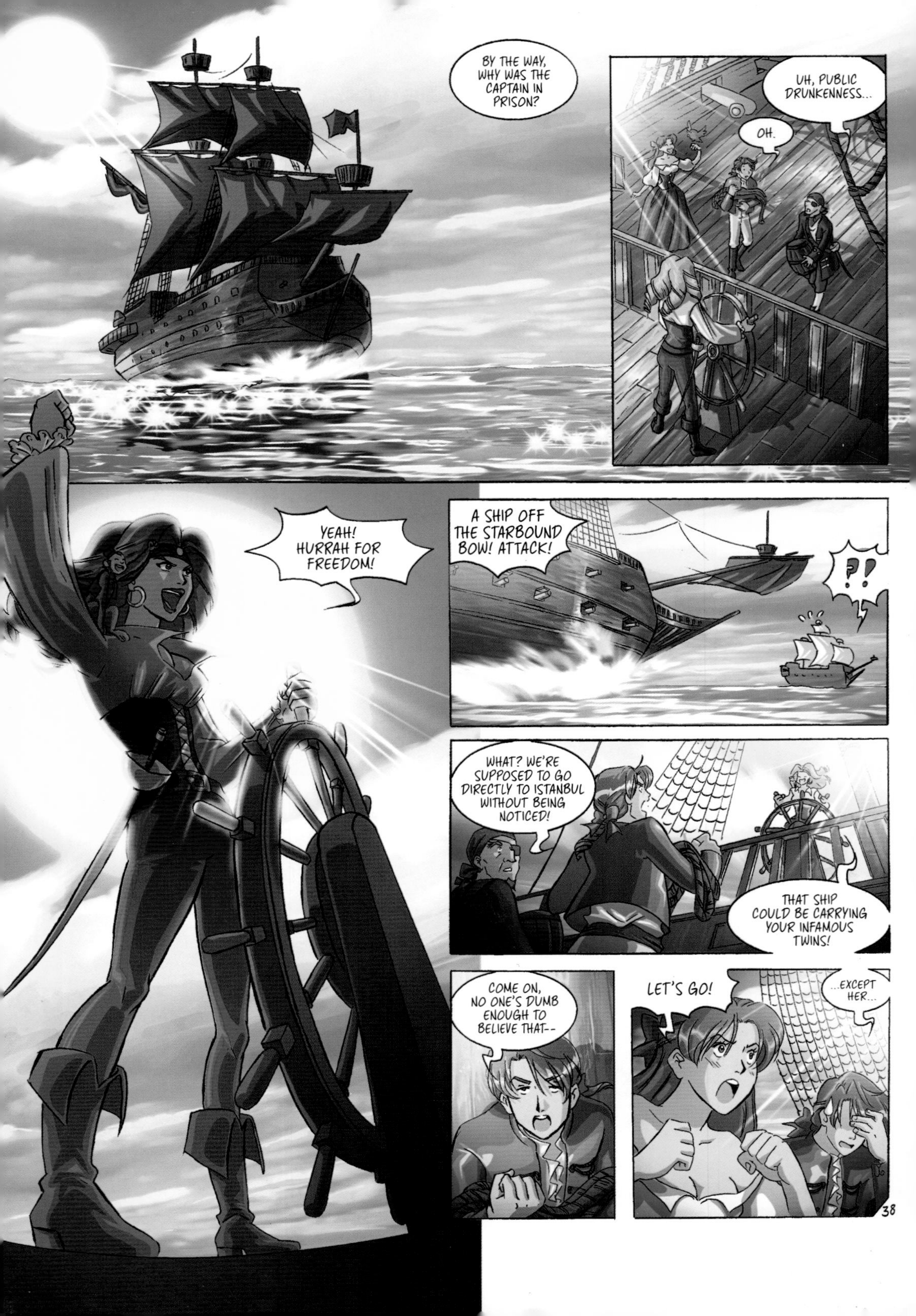
BY THE WAY, WHY WAS THE CAPTAIN IN PRISON?
UH, PUBLIC DRUNKENNESS...
OH.
YEAH! HURRAH FOR FREEDOM!
A SHIP OFF THE STARBOUND BOW! ATTACK!
?!
WHAT? WE'RE SUPPOSED TO GO DIRECTLY TO ISTANBUL WITHOUT BEING NOTICED!
THAT SHIP COULD BE CARRYING YOUR INFAMOUS TWINS!
COME ON, NO ONE'S DUMB ENOUGH TO BELIEVE THAT--
LET'S GO!
...EXCEPT HER...

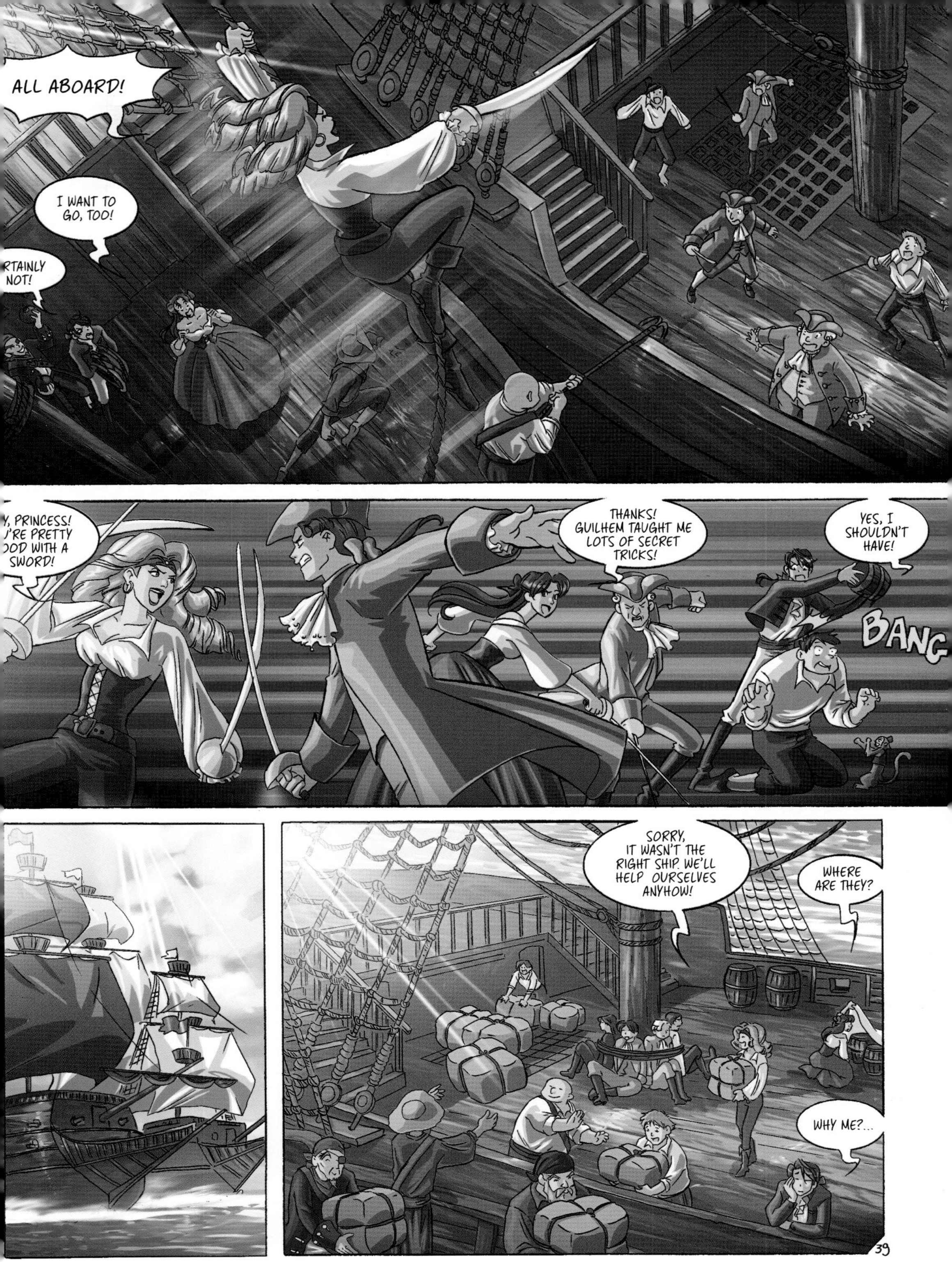
ALL ABOARD!
I WANT TO GO, TOO!
RTAINLY NOT!
Y, PRINCESS! 'RE PRETTY OD WITH A SWORD!
THANKS! GUILHEM TAUGHT ME LOTS OF SECRET TRICKS!
YES, I SHOULDN'T HAVE!
BANG
SORRY, IT WASN'T THE RIGHT SHIP. WE'LL HELP OURSELVES ANYHOW!
WHERE ARE THEY?
WHY ME?...
39

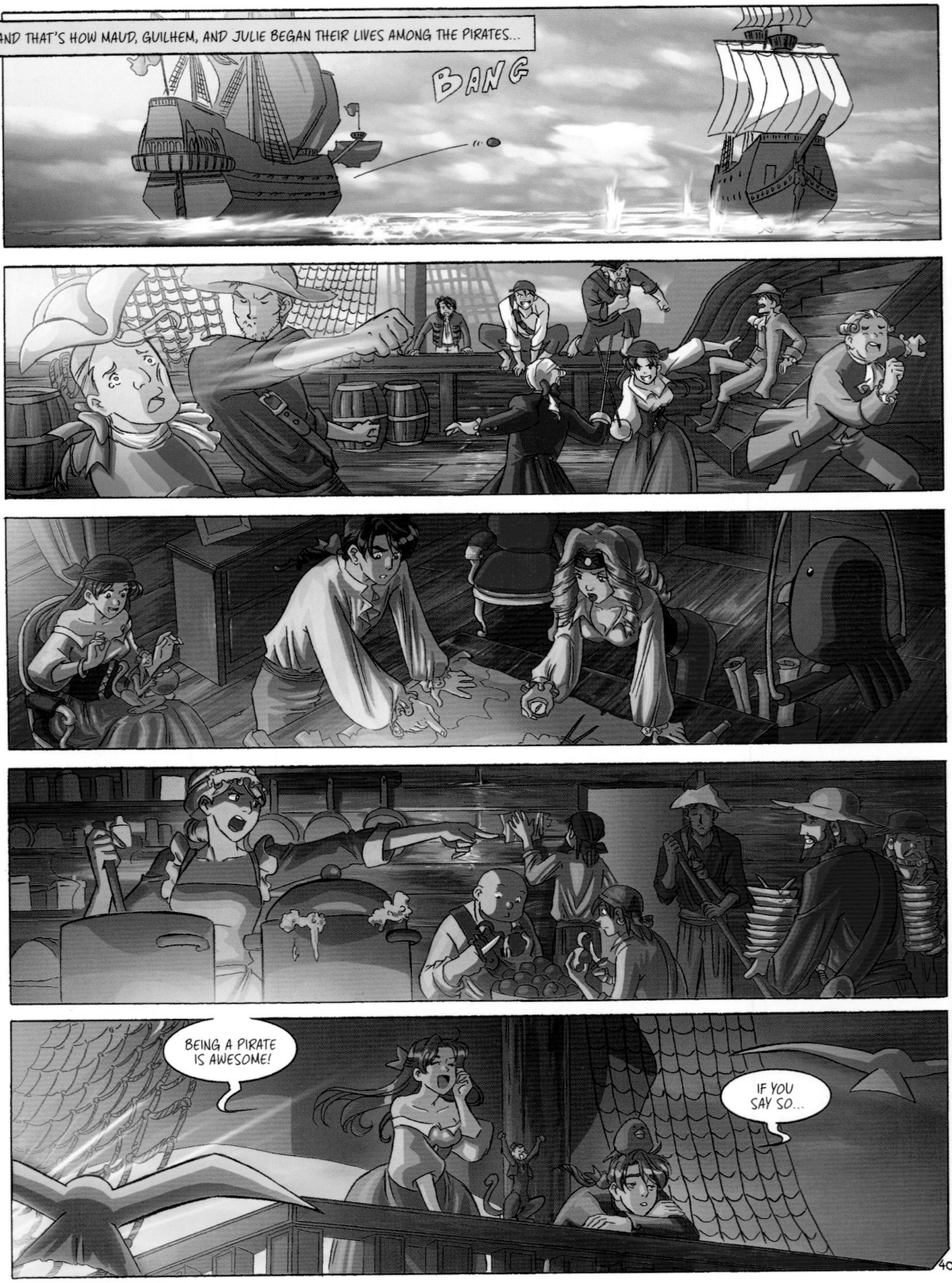
AND THAT'S HOW MAUD, GUILHEM, AND JULIE BEGAN THEIR LIVES AMONG THE PIRATES...
BANG
BEING A PIRATE IS AWESOME!
IF YOU SAY SO...
40

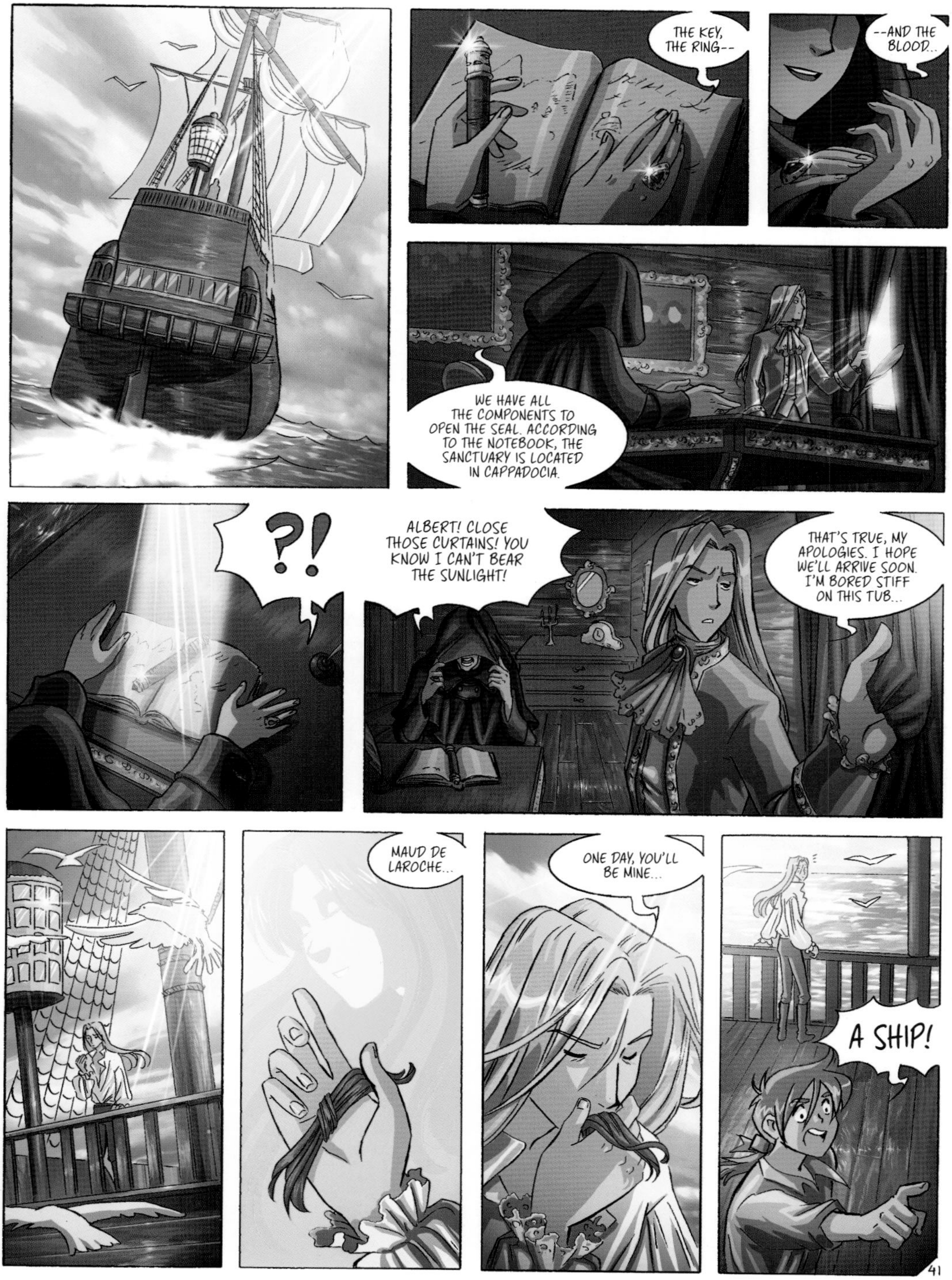
THE KEY, THE RING--
--AND THE BLOOD...
WE HAVE ALL THE COMPONENTS TO OPEN THE SEAL. ACCORDING TO THE NOTEBOOK, THE SANCTUARY IS LOCATED IN CAPPADOCIA.
?!
ALBERT! CLOSE THOSE CURTAINS! YOU KNOW I CAN'T BEAR THE SUNLIGHT!
THAT'S TRUE, MY APOLOGIES. I HOPE WE'LL ARRIVE SOON. I'M BORED STIFF ON THIS TUB...
MAUD DE LAROCHE...
ONE DAY, YOU'LL BE MINE...
A SHIP!
41

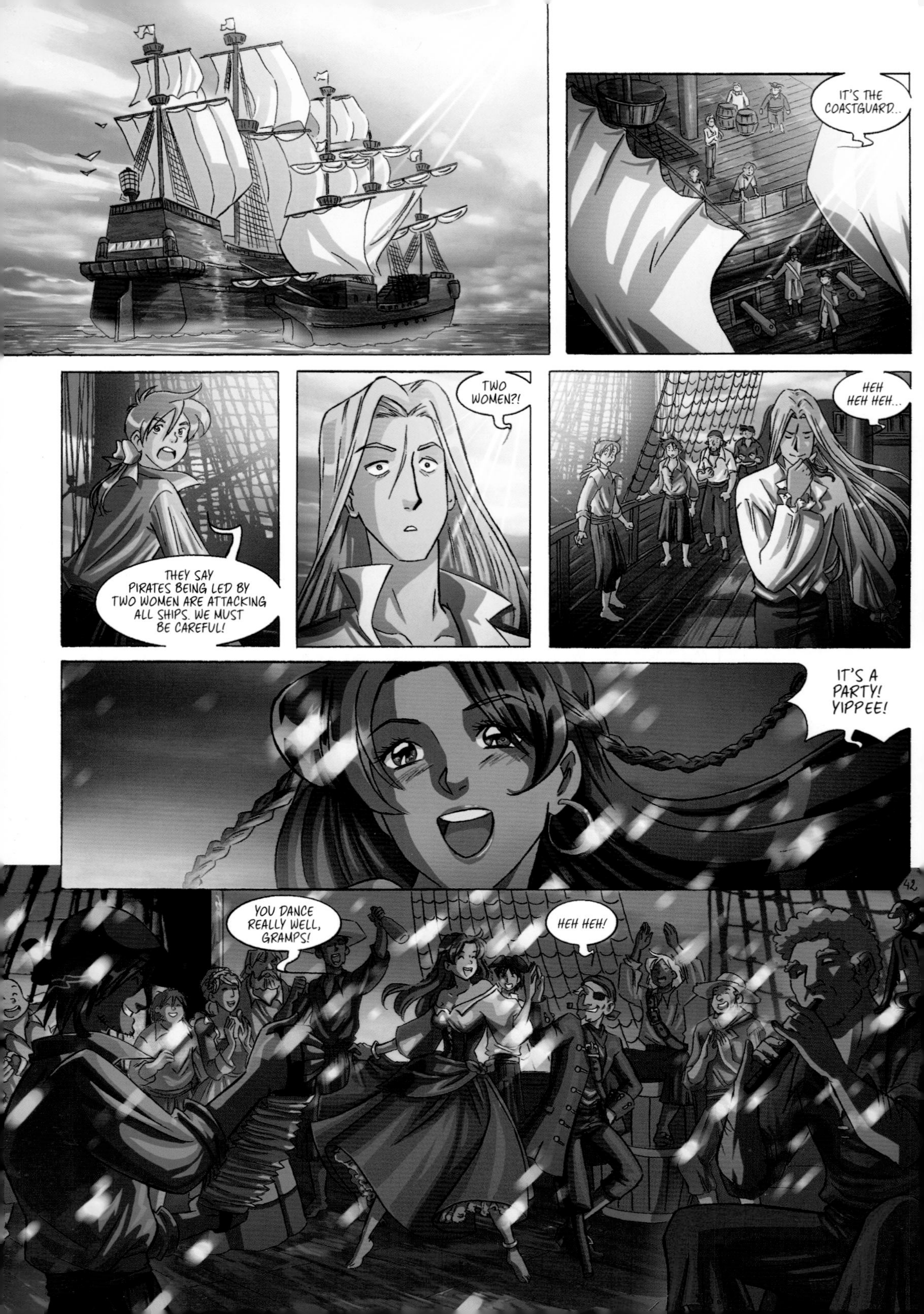
IT'S THE COASTGUARD...
THEY SAY PIRATES BEING LED BY TWO WOMEN ARE ATTACKING ALL SHIPS. WE MUST BE CAREFUL!
TWO WOMEN?!
HEH HEH HEH...
IT'S A PARTY! YIPPEE!
YOU DANCE REALLY WELL, GRAMPS!
HEH HEH!

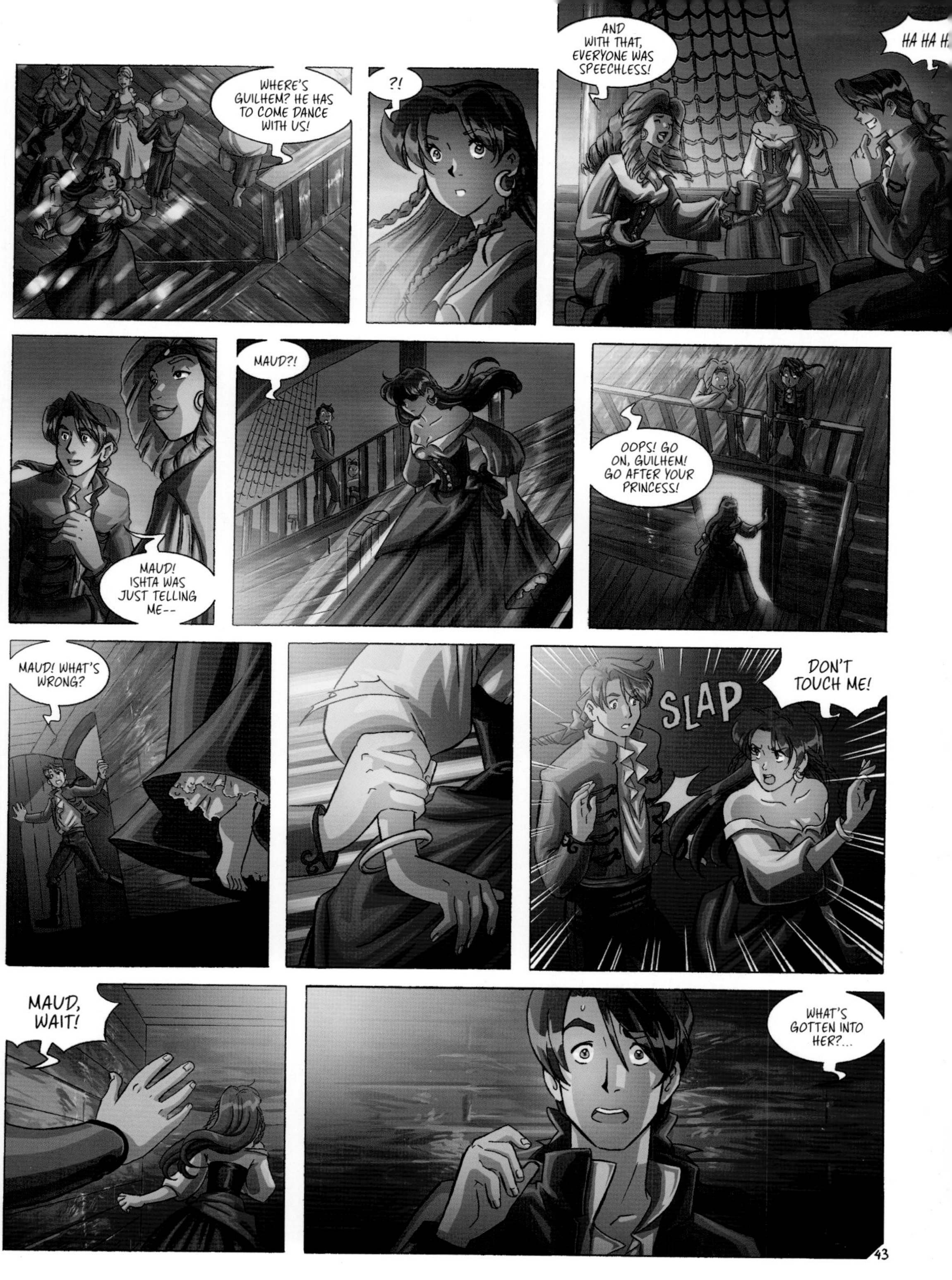
WHERE'S GUILHEM? HE HAS TO COME DANCE WITH US!
?!
AND WITH THAT, EVERYONE WAS SPEECHLESS!
HA HA H
MAUD! ISHTA WAS JUST TELLING ME--
MAUD?!
OOPS! GO ON, GUILHEM! GO AFTER YOUR PRINCESS!
MAUD! WHAT'S WRONG?
SLAP
DON'T TOUCH ME!
MAUD, WAIT!
WHAT'S GOTTEN INTO HER?...
43

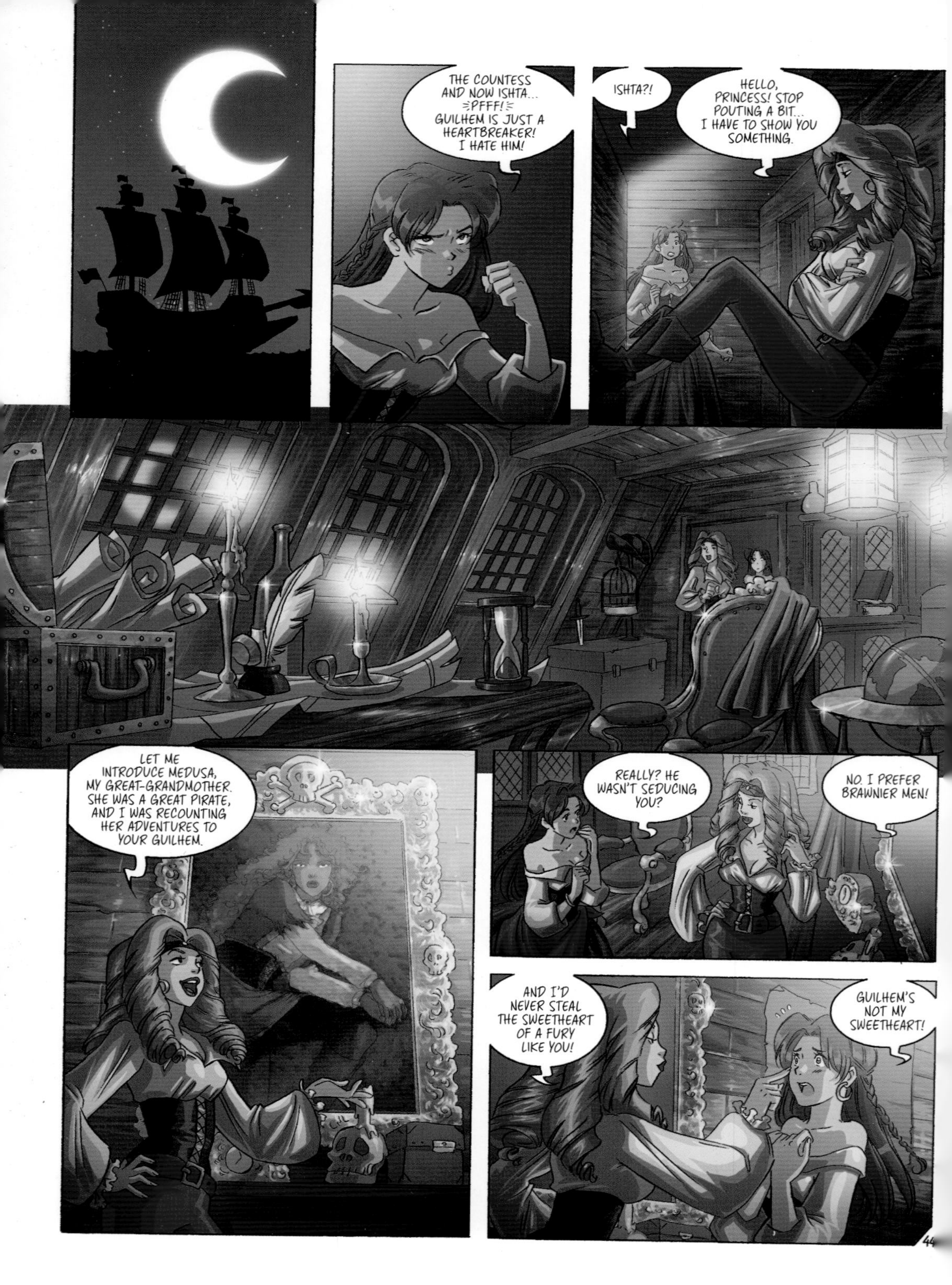
THE COUNTESS AND NOW ISHTA... PFFF! GUILHEM IS JUST A HEARTBREAKER! I HATE HIM!
ISHTA?!
HELLO, PRINCESS! STOP POUTING A BIT... I HAVE TO SHOW YOU SOMETHING.
LET ME INTRODUCE MEDUSA, MY GREAT-GRANDMOTHER. SHE WAS A GREAT PIRATE, AND I WAS RECOUNTING HER ADVENTURES TO YOUR GUILHEM.
REALLY? HE WASN'T SEDUCING YOU?
NO. I PREFER BRAWNIER MEN!
AND I'D NEVER STEAL THE SWEETHEART OF A FURY LIKE YOU!
GUILHEM'S NOT MY SWEETHEART!
44

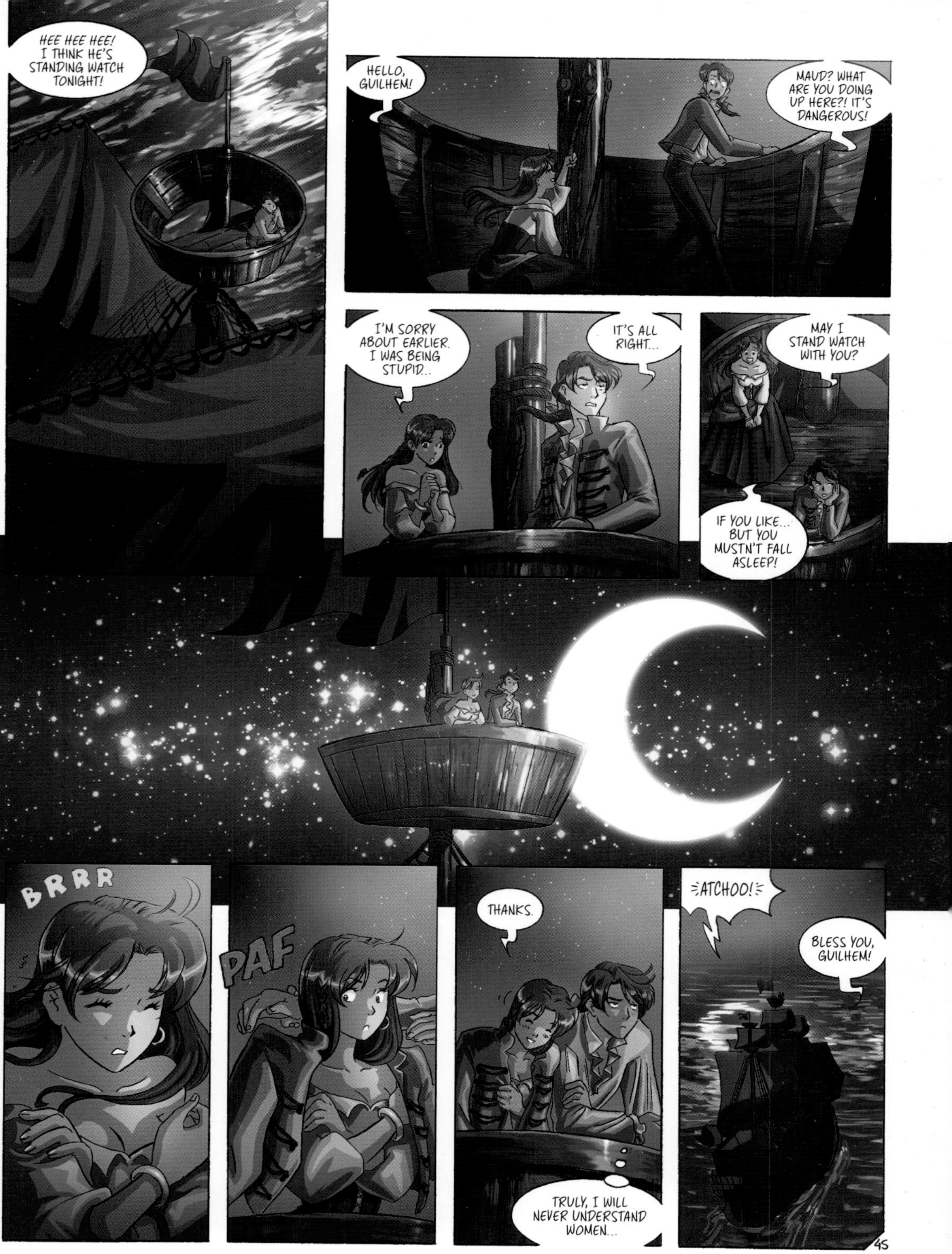
HEE HEE HEE! I THINK HE'S STANDING WATCH TONIGHT!
HELLO, GUILHEM!
MAUD? WHAT ARE YOU DOING UP HERE?! IT'S DANGEROUS!
I'M SORRY ABOUT EARLIER. I WAS BEING STUPID...
IT'S ALL RIGHT...
MAY I STAND WATCH WITH YOU?
IF YOU LIKE... BUT YOU MUSTN'T FALL ASLEEP!
BRRR
PAF
THANKS.
TRULY, I WILL NEVER UNDERSTAND WOMEN...
ATCHOO!
BLESS YOU, GUILHEM!
45

WAKE UP, MAUD!

OH! I FELL ASLEEP, GUILHEM...

GET UP AND ADMIRE THE VIEW!

OH, IT'S MAGNIFICENT!

46

WE'VE ARRIVED!

LYFOUNG-OGAKI MARCH 2008

TO BE CONTINUED...